Saving Mallory
Safe and Secure Book 4
Alyssa Bailey

I0664037

Description

New town. New Job. One new friend who didn't know her name or address. Would anyone ever notice that a madman took her?

Mallory Sasse was lonely and needed a change. She left her hometown to find a new future and maybe a new lover. Determined to make this change successful, she leased a great townhouse and started her new job as the lead pharmacist, then looked for some fun. At a meet and greet in a nearby town, she met him.

He was fit, authoritative, with a gentle smile and greying at his temples. Monroe took her breath away. Her attraction grew over the weeks, fast approaching that relationship commitment line. The day she would take that ultimate step, Mallory found herself in the grip of a madman and all hope for a future seemed lost. But after seeing a dying woman in the cellar with her and realizing her destiny if she quit, survival became Mallory's only option.

Monroe Merton was missing something in his life. Retired Army. Great job. Staring at 45 with no prospects of love ahead. He had been okay with that, but as he watched his friends find love, he wondered. Then he met Mallory. After several meet ups in a group, and hours of phone conversations, Monroe knew he was falling hard for her. When Mallory was as ready as he was to take the next step, he asked her on a date. Alone. Hopefully, alone. Mallory sounded excited the night before, but when the time came, she never showed. The woman ghosted him. She didn't even answer his calls. She had disappeared.

Just when Monroe knew Mallory was in trouble and he was on her trail, the police call. *"Monroe Merton?"*

Love the inside scoop? Sign up for my Newsletter with special offers and bonus content.

https://www.alyssabaileyromance.com

This book is a work of fiction. Names, characters, places, and incidents are products of the author's imagination or used fictitiously. Any resemblance to actual events or locales or persons living or dead is entirely coincidental.

Chapter 1

Mallory smiled to herself as she plugged in her cell phone. She had met the most amazing man who got her as a person. Someone who didn't think her tendency to try new things that some would call kinky was odd. He liked them too. Monroe was kind, sincere, and funny in a dry, droll sort of way and wasn't that nice? He didn't expect her to see things like him, or laugh at his attempts to be funny, or try to lower her self-esteem because she intimidated him.

Men were strange creatures, often mightily threatened by her professional status and education once they saw those letters, Ph.D., after her name. Once she explained their meaning, that is. Sure, plenty of men had good jobs that paid more than hers, but it made her a bitch or cold when a woman did. Mallory had experienced her share of men who tried to overcompensate or present themselves as the type of man they thought a professional, like her, would want. None hit the mark until Monroe Merton. He was the real deal.

And, according to him, he definitely lived the dominant lifestyle when he had a submissive.

Monroe took a breath and admitted, "I haven't had a submissive in a good while."

"Oh, why is that?"

Mallory watched him as he rolled his shoulders in his soft cable-knit sweater in a warm cream color over black cargo pants. He seemed very comfortable, and she could imagine him with a pipe in his mouth in the evenings. The ambiance was there, but he probably didn't smoke because he seemed very healthy. His muscular bulk stretched the sweater in delicious ways. His hair was close-cut like the military, and his graying beard and mustache were immaculate. What would it be like to be his submissive? His girlfriend? His wife?

"Honestly? I was too busy with work and having a good time being single, so topping a beautiful, willing woman was all I had time or desire for until recently."

"What changed?"

"Me. I saw three of my closest buddies find women to settle down with, and they're happy." He shrugged as he turned to look into Mallory's eyes. "I want more than a simple bottom or a Dom/sub relationship now. I'm ready to find the woman I connect with and who is interested in pursuing what could be a permanent relationship."

"I see." She had come for that exact reason, but hearing it vocalized was kinda scary and yet exciting.

"I'm ready to settle down and get a couple of kids before I'm too old to raise them."

He offered her a seat and sat beside her. Close, so close his hard thighs pushed against her too soft ones. She should get in a bit of exercise more often. She could listen to his deep, velvety voice all night. Monroe said he didn't see the dominant/submissive players with a capital "D" little "s" demeaning kind of way, but an empowering, "you are important to me" kind of way.

Monroe had proven to be a good person to explore with. He'd asked if she minded him sticking close to help her understand what she was seeing and hearing. She must have seemed relieved because he slid his hand to the small of her back and took on the job.

They continued to talk for a while longer before Monroe offered to top her or, more accurately, to play out a brief scene. Mallory hesitated. She had enjoyed the leisurely atmosphere of the munch, but do a scene with him? Even a short one might be out of her comfort zone. As though he understood her reticence, Monroe began talking about what he was looking for in a partner.

"I used to think that I would end up with a wild woman who was tame during the day and untamable at night, but I've since come to learn that a woman with a good head on her shoulders that isn't too risky but could take a chance with me by her side is the way to go."

Wise man. He was giving her a way out if she wanted it, but if she was game, he was also saying he thought she might be someone he could explore the forever factor with. He had been clear that was all he was looking for. Bold actions for a man who hadn't been ready until recently. Mallory decided Monroe was a man who didn't jump quickly, but he was all in when he did.

With her heart beating faster, her chest growing heavy with anticipation, Mallory nodded.

"I need to hear you, sweetheart, because I don't want to misinterpret. Besides, until I know you, I want to hear your words, and your sexy, throaty voice gets huskier when you're aroused."

"How did you know?"

He raised his brow and smiled. He was paying attention. "Is that a yes to the scene, Mallory?"

"Yes, please." Her face grew hotter, and her lady parts grew slicker. That telltale tingle and release told her she had grown very slippery.

She'd practically forced herself to go to the first munch or gathering several months ago, had started her on her own journey of exploration, and it was an eye-opening experience. Whatever finally pushed her to try this place tonight appeared to be fortuitous.

Typically, in her experience, munches didn't have more than a brief sample scene, but many didn't even have that. They were for meeting people. They held this meeting in a recently closed bank with offices, so the setup was good. Monroe closed the door after a brief conversation about triggers and a couple of play elements that would be unacceptable for her.

Monroe was not overbearing, and his manner didn't change once they were alone, which Mallory had experienced with others. He worked calmly, with confidence and authority, smoothing her frazzled nerves with his magic fingers kneading her tight muscles in her neck. "Mm, that feels so nice, but usually my top wants more from me than moans of appreciation," Mallory said as she kept her eyes closed to continue enjoying his large, warm hands.

"They missed out on learning what you like firsthand. Submissives sometimes think they know what they enjoy and are often right, but they limit themselves to the familiar. I don't want to miss anything. I can tell when you tense, like right now, that either me playing with your breasts is physically uncomfortable or just new so because I know you've had your breast played with before. Which is it? Painful or uneasy because we are new? This way, I learn by doing so yes, once I know you, I'll want more, but for now, allow me to explore."

"Actually, I'm worried I'll like it too much and...," Mallory shrugged.

"And we won't continue after tonight? Oh, sweetheart, I doubt that would happen. So take a chance. I'm sure neither of us will regret it."

"Okay, I'll try, sir."

"Good girl. We'll play for no longer than thirty minutes this first time. That way, you can know if we do well together or if you aren't interested in going further next time."

"Yes, sir."

"Good, now strip."

Monroe stood back with his arms crossed, his legs braced wide in what she had always thought of as the Genie's Stance. Mallory removed each item of clothing with deliberate actions. Once naked, he led her to a love seat in the room. Monroe kissed her gently, interspersing his easy touches with more daring ones slipping along her thighs. When he touched her belly, Mallory tried to suck it in, and he slapped her inner thigh. She hissed and reached to rub it.

"No, naughty girl. No soothing the sting, that's my job if I think you have earned it."

"Sorry, sir," she whispered.

"That's my sweet girl." He reached down to rub the sting away. "I don't want the Mallory you try to hide behind. I want the real you. I like softness in my women. If being soft bothers you, I'm happy to teach you what to do to strengthen your core muscles, but men should feel hard, be hard. Don't misunderstand me and pull out your feminist card. It's fine for a woman to be the same muscularly hard if she wants to be, but if she's okay with being soft, men love that. *I* love that."

His hand lowered to her muff, and when she stiffened involuntarily, wondering if she had sweated or if her hygiene was up to the standard expected, she felt another sharp slap on her thigh.

"Tsk, tsk. I know when you're worried about something. Your body tells on you. Mallory, sweetheart, you are gorgeous. Your legs are shapely, your lips are kissable, your skin and hair are soft and fragrant, and you fit perfectly against me. I like a woman that I can hold, a woman that is so luscious she's exotic. That's you. And then there is your mind. You're not some follow the leader kind of girl. You think for yourself, and that is damn sexy. So, whatever you're worried or overthinking about, stop."

"Yes, sir." Mallory tried, but she couldn't stop nibbling her lip which he gently disengaged from her teeth.

"We'll figure it out. I think we have just enough time to ensure you're relaxed when you go home." He patted his thigh. "Over you go."

Mallory smiled and nodded, then crawled over his lap. Mallory loved a spanking. It was the go-to activity that the Tops who knew her had gone to when they wanted to make her feel good. For Mallory, bondage and spanking were sure things.

Monroe peppered her bottom with ever-increasing swats covering the whole of her backside, kissing her here and there and interspersing that play with fingering that swept into her channel and teased her clit. More spanks, more rubbing, more clit action. He massaged her tightly ringed back entrance but backed off when she flexed her buttocks hard. Naughty, but it told him plenty about her experience. There would be time to work on all of that but tonight was for introductions. Instead, he zeroed in on her clit.

"Okay, baby, time to fly."

WHEN THEY CALLED IT a night, Mallory tried to refuse Monroe's offer to walk her to her car. She'd gotten off spectacularly by his hand and had agreed to phone calls, exchanging phone numbers. It surprised and relieved her when he had suggested them because Mallory didn't know how to broach the subject herself in case she wasn't what he was looking for as his submissive. Maybe she had been the only one to enjoy the evening.

Self-doubt wormed into her thinking even though self-esteem was never an issue for her normally. Monroe must have sensed that about her. And she wasn't helpless. She walked to her car in the dark after work all the time.

"Mallory, I have to know you're going to be safe. I'm walking you to your car."

She heard his determination, and it was nice to be watched over just a little, so she agreed. "Alright, but I can do it myself."

He kissed her. "Understood. Thank you."

Unfortunately, she had been so nervous when she arrived at this first gathering in a new place, she'd forgotten to lock the car. Monroe roughly pulled her behind him, checking the car and the trunk before turning back to Mallory with a stern expression.

He drew her into his arms and kissed the top of her head. She almost melted into a puddle of goo. "Mallory, baby, I like you. I like you a lot."

Mallory laid her head on his chest. "Me too. I mean, I like you too."

"Good, that's good. I hope you still do after I paddle your bottom for this."

"But you just spanked me." Mallory's voice was high-pitched, shaky. Her nervousness was apparent, and she moved away from Monroe, and he allowed her one back-step.

"Not play this time, discipline. One swat for parking so far from the entrance, even though that deserves a whole spanking all on its own and rest assured if it happens again, you will get one. Two more swats for fighting me about walking you to the car, which won't ever happen again. I put my girl in the vehicle for safety. And a final two for leaving it unlocked. Anyone could have been inside. Which won't happen again either."

"I...um..."

Mallory dropped her forehead back on his chest, but he gently ran his hand around the back of her neck and wove his fingers in her hair, fisting his hand. Carefully pulling her head back up, his lips met hers hard, taking from her what she hadn't freely given.

Mallory stiffened, but after a few seconds, his tongue came out to trace her lips. She softened as he lightened his kiss, ending in a sweet caress of his lips on hers. Mallory melted. She would have done anything for Monroe at that moment. So when he dropped his forehead to hers, still holding her hair fast, she listened.

"You have been alone for too long, Mal. Even if you didn't have a dom, you should have had friends from your last group to look out for you. I have a feeling you didn't. But now you have me, and sweetheart, I am the real deal. I will test you in play and punish you if you don't take care of yourself well enough. I have rules, and you will learn them and follow them if we decide to be together. If you don't follow them, you'll find yourself in this position often."

She tremored at the significance of his words. "Rules? I don't need rules."

"You do if this is normal behavior."

"It isn't. And you're wrong. I had friends at the club, but" she shrugged. "I never found a Dom I wanted exclusively. And even that was six months ago."

He lifted his head. "Well, you have me now, if you want me. But regardless, I'm serious about paddling your ass. Are you going to let me take on that role for you? Do you accept me as your dominant and your boyfriend? I could be just your friend, but I want more from you, from us."

He was serious, and she wanted that with him. Why wasn't she scared or worried to contemplate such a commitment so early, hours into their meet? Her good sense had flown out the proverbial window, and for once, it didn't matter because she wasn't crazy except crazy attracted on many levels. Even after only three hours, she trusted this man, and plenty of others there tonight vouched for him.

"Isn't it unsafe for me to say yes after one meeting and a short play session?".

"It can be, yes. What does your gut tell you?"

His eyes held hers, and the question compelled her to return the stare. She licked her dry lips, and his gaze dropped as a wolf eyeing his prey before devouring her. His breath hitched, and he leaned down to run his tongue over the place she's just had hers. Mallory shivered. He shifted his gaze to meet her eyes again.

"My gut tells me to trust you, and I want to, so badly. The boyfriend part? Let's start as friends."

"Good enough. As your Dom, however, you must take the paddling. It's who I am and what you need."

And dammit, she did need it. Everything the man dished out, she needed.

One quick kiss and he opened the back door of her SUV. Mallory slid into position quickly, but the tight space made it a little awkward. The smoked windows and the dark corner where her car was parked made it unlikely that someone not practicing the lifestyle would see them, but not impossible. That was the mind-fuck that Doms loved.

The sound of Monroe unzipping his bag of toys sent tremors of anticipation through her. She'd just submitted to his spanking less than an hour ago, and the sting had receded considerably. It wouldn't be too bad, she told herself, and it would re-ignite the sting she craved. Mallory assured her churning stomach that he was just making a point.

"These are going to be swift, but they'll sting."

Without further warning, the first swat landed. A paddle! He could have told her he was using a freaking paddle. It seemed okay for a few seconds, then the burn kicked in. Her swift intake of breath told him she felt it. And she was sure the subsequent two squeals told him he was putting enough strength behind those swings. The fourth elicited an apology.

"I'm sorry. I'm so sorry. I was just so nervous I forgot to lock the car. And this was the closest spot to park when I got here. Honest, Monroe."

He stopped to rub her afflicted backside. "Okay, sweetheart, just one more."

The last swat was the worst, eliciting a sniffle, and while she had trained herself not to over-react to the sting, his paddle made it difficult not to kick her legs. "I'm not used to someone being worried about me. I take care of myself."

Monroe rubbed her bottom longer, and then he kissed it, sending shivers of emotional warmth through her. Not for the achy backside, but for the man who dared to show her he cared for her in a way she hadn't had in a long time, if ever, outside of her family. Unconditional affection. How had she lived without it for so long?

"I know, baby, but we're going to change that thinking to include me, aren't we?"

"Yes, sir."

"Yes, we are. Okay, beautiful, discipline is over." He helped her up. And let her slide out of the backseat before him with his help. "Lesson learned."

Monroe hadn't once tried to impress her. Far from it. In fact, as the next couple of weeks progressed, he just talked and shared, encouraging her to do the same, and they bonded. He'd asked Mallory out on an actual in-person date after several meetups with others. She had accepted.

Monroe had been adamant that she needed to be sure of him. No gatherings or parties, but just the two of them. Her belly wiggled in delight and expectation. He was such a confident man, something she wanted in her life. He complemented her personality. No competition or jealousy because they each had substantial jobs. Mallory hoped he didn't live too far from Lexington because the gathering and munches were in another town to save her reputation. Monroe probably did that, too. She couldn't wait for tomorrow night's date.

CRAIG LOOKED AT THE little pharmacist leave with that muscle-bound gorilla again tonight, stopping Craig from grabbing her once again. It was infuriating, but he had learned patience over the years, and the reward for his long-suffering would be the best yet. He would just have to change his plan, but he would do it if she was his prize.

Chapter 2

M onroe stood to leave the briefing, determined to find answers. His life hadn't been so tangled up since he returned from Army Medic training and came back to his off-base apartment stripped of anything of value, including his girlfriend. This was feeling much like that experience, only more perplexing. And if possible, after only two-and-a-half weeks, more painful.

His girlfriend in his early career had no staying power, and he'd known it, but she loved sex and let him run the show in the bedroom without complaints so long as she got off at least twice. He was young and horny then, and if he learned anything from that experience was to be more picky and quit thinking with his dick. He established minimum standards in his life that not every woman who was happy to hop in the sack with him could meet. Soon, his missions started, and he moved back on base, squelching any long-term relationship.

He had a full life, but damn, he missed talking to Mallory. No amount of reasoning or examining their long phone conversations would help him understand why she had ghosted him. He could remember his hand as it warmed her behind at the first munch. She'd gotten off on just that action, but he'd made sure she fired twice. He thought he'd found gold.

She wasn't a newbie, just new to the area and out of practice. He sought partners who knew what they liked and when she had been so turned on after he had heated her ass, he planned a closer alliance. It was a spectacular sight to see and remember.

Monroe had played over the phone with her the following week, and they met the next weekend at a party and one more munch. They agreed to continue the getting to know you dance a little longer before taking it out of the meet and greet environment.

By the middle of week three, they had really hit it off and decided they would go on a very public date and one last meet and greet before they took it from there. Monroe knew they were good together, and he thought she agreed. They might have been made for each other, but right as they were going to the next step, she dropped him without warning. He hadn't even warranted a text. That's why he hesitated to believe Mallory had actually ditched him. His gut told him it wasn't like her.

"Monroe, how're those play sessions going?" asked Sharlee.

Sharlee was the company computer magician, also known as Vapor, in her private underworld life. She'd joined their team several years ago, filling a gap they didn't know they were missing. She'd married Jacquard Reynaud, the CEO of Reynaud, and Associates, less than two years later.

Monroe was invited to buy into the fledgling business, joining Garrett and Jac nearly six years ago, and when he left the service, he became more than an investor. They welcomed him as a member of another family. A family he would give his life for and knew they would do the same. Besides his military career, it had been the best decision of his life.

The security services company took jobs from the alphabet agencies and private citizens who had more money than sense. The diversity was great, but Monroe was ready to raise his own family. He watched his teammates as each found the woman they wanted to spend their life with, and it was time he did as well. Easier said than done.

As a fit man staring at forty-five, he had expectations. He decided to start back at the BDSM gatherings and maybe check out a few parties. He wasn't one to leave finding a woman who was into the same lifestyle as he was to chance encounters. Besides, it wasn't as though he had been looking seriously for long. He liked the single life until recently, and now he wanted more.

There was little doubt that once he found her, he would not be returning to public scening or even parties unless she, whoever 'she' turned out to be, wanted to play in that kind of environment. Monroe would find someone with like-minded kinks, and this was the best way to do it. He didn't share—not in public gatherings or intimate parties, not her preferences nor her body. He was as possessive as fuck and knew instinctively it wouldn't work for him.

Glancing at Sharlee, he answered, "Yeah, not well." He shrugged. "It looked promising, but things changed. I met a cute little thing but mature, carried herself well. She's a handful of years younger than me and has been in the lifestyle for a while but not practicing recently. We got along and played together some. I liked her, and I thought she liked me."

"Thought she liked you?"

"She'd gone to a few of these meet-ups somewhere else before she was with me, and then we met up three times at parties and such. We spent hours on the phone discussing just about everything, and I thought we'd really connected."

Monroe stopped speaking and stared out the office window. "And?" Sharlee prompted.

"Evidently, she changed her mind. Even though we made a date for last weekend and last Thursday night when we talked, it was for at least an hour. She was still excited about going out, and yet, she ghosted me."

"Maybe she just got cold feet. I mean, all of you guys make a statement when you enter a room."

"She had accepted me as her Dom, so even if she had changed her mind about other things, she would have told me. In this lifestyle, at any level, honesty is at the core of the relationship. I called to verify on Friday, but she didn't answer. I thought she'd forgotten, but when she didn't come to the next meet on Saturday, I got worried. My gut grew cold. I called her again, and it went to an automated voicemail. Guess it could have been more me than her, but I can't help thinking something is off."

"What made her so special?"

"You mean besides the fact that she loved my rubber paddle?" He grinned at that.

"Really? Wow, that is something. But, yes, besides that?"

"She's a professional that carries herself that way. She's self-assured, funny, and naïve about silly things like where to park her car for safety. Mallory is the first woman who didn't think that being retired military was all I expected from life. She asked me what I did now that I had retired like I had many lives left to give. That word 'retired' didn't give her visions of a decrepit old man in his last decade of life."

Sharlee laughed and typed on her computer. "What else do you know about her?"

"What I know is something has happened to Mallory. Maybe she's sick or has been in an accident, but I don't know how to find her. She hadn't given me her address or last name yet because I wouldn't let her until Friday. I have her number, but that's it."

Monroe had paced the room as he divulged his deepest concerns that she was hurt or sick and didn't have anyone, him, to take care of her. His frustration at not getting the information he needed to check on her because he thought he was giving her a sense of control, of safety, had boomeranged on him, and it made him nearly go mad with worry. As he verbalized his thoughts, his fears rose.

"That's more than I usually get. Is Mallory her name?" asked Sharlee. "Give me her number."

"It's a cell number."

"Doesn't matter," said Sharlee as she typed in the numbers Monroe recited by memory.

"Mallory, her name is Mallory. The thing is, when you go to these gatherings, it might be your name, or it might not. She told the attendant that she wasn't using a pseudonym."

"Do you use your real name?" asked Sharlee.

Monroe chuckled. "Charlotte, look at me. I scare men and women when I turn on the dominant, so, yes, I use my own name. We never give last names except on the paperwork. The attendant asked if it was the pseudonym Mallory wanted to use because the name was perfect. Mallory denied it was a pseudonym."

"But she could have been lying."

"I told you honesty is an essential building block. Doms, *I*, take a dim view of lying. That's why the community encourages a pseudonym. It would have been the safe thing to do, but since we had just met recently, I would not take over things until after our Friday date, so I resisted the urge to get her full name.

"Now look what going against my gut got me. I didn't listen to my gut on information gathering, but I'm sure as hell going to listen to it now. I think Mallory is her name because there was no hesitation when she responded to my use of it."

Sharlee nodded. "Well, that's a significant observation and a useful clue. Do you know anything else?"

"She's a pharmacist, but I don't know where she works. I assume in town here, but there are plenty of places in and around town that use pharmacists. Since we met in another community, there is no guarantee. And the attendant said she had a great last name for playing. She stopped herself from saying the name, but it started with an "S."

"Let me look to see what I can find. A pharmacist with the perfect "S" name for a play date." Sharlee grinned. "Got it. I don't think I've seen a woman get under your skin the same as this Mallory. I was right. She's special."

Monroe looked out the window and spoke his thoughts. "She is."

"I'm going to find her for you. Give me until tomorrow."

"I'm in the office for a few days, so that will be great. Thanks."

"You bet."

THOSE WHO KNEW MONROE well enough knew he liked things to be organized and to follow the program. It was usually a program he created. When he was still on the Special Ops teams, he always had several contingencies and worked from one to the other, as needed, with a minimum of fuss. That's why he and Carter worked well together. Carter was an incredible strategist and could think on his feet.

Mallory was all he could think of when his mind wasn't on the job. It gave him a punch in the gut feeling when she hadn't answered his calls. At first, his pride took a hit, and he tried to shrug it off, telling himself it was her loss and all that crap people tried to tell themselves when they were deeply disappointed.

Did he get his signals crossed? No, she had given him the green light after he'd called her a few times before asking her out. Over the weeks, they had talked on the phone for hours. Thursday night had been no different, and that was a first for him. He got the impression it had been a first for her as well.

Mallory had been open, disclosing that she never had a bad boyfriend experience; she just didn't have much history at all. And what she did have was less than spectacular. Mostly, she never made it to the exclusivity stage because she liked to date without strings.

"But now," she almost whispered over the phone, "for the first time, I 'm really considering a long-term relationship is a possibility."

Her shy but confident demeanor, even over the phone, brought all his protective instincts to the forefront. It was like the call of the wild. The force of his instincts shocked him because outside of his mother and the women of his friends, he hadn't experienced that strong of an urge to gather anyone under his veil of shelter. That feeling didn't lessen, and the more they talked, the more he wanted to know about her.

She'd been silent for four days now and three long nights and, Monroe's instincts were rampaging, and his brain was on high alert. He could read people, could read Mallory enough to know that now he had worked through his disbelief and hurt, something was wrong, very wrong. Mallory would not have ghosted him. He knew Sharlee could find her, and he would follow up and make sure Mallory was okay. Ask her why she didn't answer his calls. And maybe get out his rubber paddle. She'd respect that.

Even if he wasn't her Dom any longer, any Dom would have worried. Hell, any man worth his salt and the air he breathed would have been concerned. He'd address her lack of insight after he made sure she was safe. His rubber paddle might get more action soon.

He shook his head at himself. And all that was bullshit. He might go Alpha Charlie on her if it turned out she was avoiding him, but since his gut knew she wasn't, he would more likely slay her demons and bind her to his side and then his bed. Literally. Sharlee would find her fast. He had to believe that. Too preoccupied, he went home.

The phone rang just as he climbed out of the shower, and his first thought was Mallory was calling him. Finally. But when he picked up the cell, he clicked to accept Sharlee's call.

"What's up? What did you find?" He knew his voice sounded harsh, raw, but Sharlee was part of their team and married to Jac. No explanations were necessary.

"You owe me a big, fancy coffee for this. I'm sending Mallory Sasse's address to you. Did you know there were people with the last name Sasse? There really are. She has a nice place. One of those exclusive townhouses. I wanted to look at one, but Jac wouldn't let me."

Monroe sighed. "You have a large country estate, woman. Why would you need a townhouse?"

"Oh, before I moved in with Jac, but he wouldn't let me and, well, I did want to share his bed."

Monroe's voice held a hint of reprimand. "Sharlee, hon, I need the rest of your intel."

"Oh right, I'm digressing. Jac hates that. Anyway, Mallory Sasse works at The Apothecary in Lexington as the lead pharmacist. I tried to find out if she was there, but they said she was unavailable the rest of the day. I don't know if that was code for, she's not there today, or she's busy."

Monroe's tone grew glacial. "Anything else."

"Of course. Jac said he sent a car to check to see if anyone was home at the townhouse but no luck. He nearly had to bribe his way onto the property. The car, registered in her name, is still at her work parking lot."

"Meaning she is working," said Monroe in a voice laced with irritation and disappointment.

"Not necessarily. I tapped into the CCTV, and it has been in the same spot since Friday. Jac will send someone in to ask for her like a customer that was told to return. If she's working behind the pharmacy counter, they will know. The next guy, if needed, will ask for the pharmacist on duty. They have her picture and will know if he gets someone else."

"What good will that do?" Monroe asked as he got his pants on, sans briefs.

"Quit being gloomy and think. We will know if Mallory is on the schedule today and if the car's there because she's working and has the habit of parking in the same spot every day or something else is going on. I mean, her car wouldn't be there if she wasn't unless there's a problem."

"Or she found someone to stay overnight with."

"Or her car is broken down."

"I'll go to her house." Monroe put the phone on speaker and began to finish dressing.

"No, don't waste your time. There are no lights on, and curtains are closed like she's gone for the day. Besides, remember the security gate? You won't get in. Wait until closing, and let's see what happens."

"I don't think I can... wait. I've got a call from Lexington police. Hold on."

Monroe clicked over to the incoming call, "This is Merton."

"Monroe Merton?"

"Yes, who is this?"

"I'm Officer Whitley of the Lexington police department."

"Hello, what can I do for you?" Monroe tried to keep his suspicions out of his voice. He didn't have time for some mess with them right now.

"I don't know if you've heard tonight's news, but a woman we believe you know is missing, and we were hoping you could help us. A woman matching the missing woman's description has been located but refuses to speak to us except for asking for Monroe. We think that is you, sir."

"Why would you think that?" His tone was even, but his heart beat a wild tattoo in his chest at the possibility of not only finding Mallory but of her being seriously injured.

"We found your name and a phone number in one phone we located. She tried to reach for it, and we believe it to be her phone."

"One phone?"

"Sorry, on the phone that she identified as hers, so we assumed." Silence lay in the air between them. "I mean, Monroe isn't a common name these days."

"If ever. Now, about Mallory, you found her? Where is she? I'll be right there."

"Sir, I don't think... who is she to you?"

Monroe didn't hesitate to attach a relationship to them. "She's my girlfriend." To Monroe, it wasn't a lie; it was officially true. She just didn't know it yet, so he hoped Mallory didn't out him. "Where is she?"

"Wait, we are contacting her sister."

"She lives too far away and has kids. Where are you?"

That personal information seemed to satisfy the police officers. Once Monroe got the information he needed, he clicked off the call and clicked over to Sharlee. "The police found her. I'm going—" Monroe explained the rest of the conversation.

"Listen. Mallory is on the news, along with others," said Jac over the line.

"Others? I'm on my way to her but get as much as you can from the new story. I'll update as I get more info after I take care of Mallory."

Chapter 3

Mallory couldn't wash the taste of icy terror from her mouth or out of her mind. It was how she imagined chewing on glass would feel like. Being kidnapped had never crossed her mind when she helped the woman pick up her spilled bag of groceries. Mallory saw the woman in the store just at the pharmacy closing time, thirty minutes before the rest of the store closed.

She hadn't seen the woman before, but that meant nothing. She rarely noticed anyone but her own customers when she needed to counsel them on medications. Otherwise, she spent her day verifying and authorizing prescriptions. She didn't think she could go back to that drug store or anywhere public for a long time. Being a self-sufficient woman, it upset her just as much that, for now, that horrible man still held her hostage mentally, if not physically.

Her chaotic and yet frozen emotionally in time, Mallory wondered about the woman who appeared nearly dead on the floor when Mallory had been thrown into that filthy, dank cellar after that fucker couldn't get what he wanted from her. Mallory heard the other woman weakly cry out, but she was sure she'd passed out almost immediately. That was the best thing for the other captive so she wouldn't feel the pain or have memories of their kidnapper's sick, sadistic behavior, but Mallory could not.

Mallory had gotten a glimpse of the items on a wall that memory made her instinctively recoil. The room she had been in first upon being dragged inside had smelled of blood, old blood with some lingering smell of rust, iron, disinfectant, vomit and even a lingering hint of sex which had her gagging. The blood had stiffened places on the sheets that lay in disarray on the bed in the corner of the room. The old iron bedpost had metal handcuffs hanging from it, rough hemp rope lay on the floor in a tangle, and Mallory's own blood ran cold with her fear.

The only time she had felt safe in the last, how long did they say, three days, and this was the fourth night, was when she could concentrate on Monroe. He was so protective of her when they had spoken on the phone and the few times they had been together at the meet and greets. Monroe was the enormous presence in her life that she had grown used to, and she didn't know if she could do without him. He was who she needed. Thank God she wasn't in danger any longer from the man who had kidnapped her. But Mallory couldn't believe that there weren't demons lying in wait for her everywhere.

"Have you found Monroe yet?" she asked the nurse who came in to check on her and take her vitals.

"I'll ask. Is he your boyfriend?"

It was the most natural thing in the world to go with that. "Yes, and don't let him scare you when he gets here. Monroe can be a little intimidating, but he's really a teddy bear." She wasn't sure if Monroe would be happy with that description, but it was how she saw him.

Her mind shifted to the kidnapper, who had left her alone except for when he had brought her to his cellar. He had been out of control for what seemed like hours because the man was almost caught leaving with her. He had blamed Mallory for that and took out his anger on her, physically assaulting her, but not sexually.

Thank God for that, but the pain was still there. Her swollen face was still very tender. Her ribs hurt, breathing was painful, and movement had become excruciating until the hospital gave her medication. Now she rested easier, but she wouldn't rest entirely until Monroe was with her.

Mallory didn't feel safe anywhere now. She'd laughed at Monroe when he had lectured her on how to keep harm at arm's length after she had told him about the guy who tried to hit on her during her lunch break. She'd quickly rebuffed the persistent, amorous attempt and had finished her lunch, only telling Monroe as a laugh, but he hadn't thought it funny at all. And it was cute that he was so protective that he'd overreacted. Mallory had teased him. She wasn't laughing now.

It was irrational, but she wanted Monroe with every fiber of her being. He was her safe place. The police had called her sister in Arizona, but after Mallory assured her she was okay, her sister allowed her to end the call. Candace was sweet, but she had her own career, had gotten married less than a year ago and was pregnant. Candace didn't need to worry about her sister.

As Mallory laid in her hospital bed, she couldn't help but feel on high alert, hypervigilant, waiting for what she had no idea. Even though the police officer assured her they would find her attacker, she couldn't help but believe that madman was still out there, angry she had slipped away.

Mallory did the best she could to describe where she had come from in the hopes that the cops had helped the other woman in the cellar because she could never get away alone. The woman was so ill, she would have to be carried out. That is if she was still alive. The wife or the woman that the kidnapper referred to as his wife never showed her face. The only way Mallory knew she or someone existed besides the kidnapper was when he left in the vehicle, and there was a woman's voice calling a dog.

If he had a wife, didn't she know he had women in his cellar? She had yelled until she was hoarse, her head pounding and her throat raw, but there was no response from anyone. The cellar was likely too insulated by earth and rock.

Mallory had first suspected the wife was the woman who dropped her bag, but she couldn't be sure they were connected. The woman would have had to have a good makeup job because the old lady didn't look his age or even close. The man grabbed Mallory as she was getting into her car, parked away from the front.

Oh, Monroe would have a heyday with that tidbit of information. From what Mallory had figured out with Monroe after that first experience with his red paddle, not parking where others could easily see you was a big no-no. Surely he knew that employee parking lots were often like that. But she had a feeling that would not be a sufficient excuse, so she decided not to even try to make it sound okay.

Mallory wished she could have Monroe now. He would take over, and she would be secure in knowing that he would ensure her safety and woe be the man or woman who got between him and what he had claimed. Once again, she demanded to see him.

THERE WAS A SKIRMISH in the hall, and several male and female voices spoke in that intense, pressured whisper when a person was aggravated but didn't want to make a scene. Had the kidnapper found her? Her breathing ticked up, and she began to frantically look for a place to hide in the sparse room. Then she heard a familiar deep voice, sandpaper rough and yet calming.

As she relaxed and prepared to climb out of bed to meet him, the door to her room flew open and in strode Monroe in all his over six-foot glory. His voice felt like molten honey in her belly. Sizzling sweet but dangerous.

He stopped dead and stared at her for about ten seconds before he spoke. "Don't move from that bed, young lady; you're hurt."

He wore a determined expression as he advanced. His shoulders released their tension, and his militant look of avenging angel softened. Compassion and relief showed on his face as he ignored the chastising nurse and orderly behind him. His arms reached out to engulf her and stopped when he realized she was on an IV.

"Got you trussed up, huh, sweetheart?" He gingerly wrapped his muscular arms around her when Officer Whitley walked into the room. She could feel the tears in her eyes, but this time, they were tears of relief. Monroe would take care of everything.

"Don't let go," she whispered.

"Step away from the woman." Monroe froze in place.

"He's Monroe," said Mallory. "He was hugging me, or he would have if you hadn't stopped him." Her voice was unmistakably chastising. Monroe chuckled.

"Monroe? *The* Monroe you have been asking for?"

"Yes." She nodded.

The cop stalled a moment and then said, "I still need to see him. And is there a reason he is supposed to be your friend, but you don't know his last name?"

Monroe glanced over his shoulder, then straightened to his full height. She could have sworn he broadened his body to create an impressive presence before placing himself squarely between the policeman and Mallory, which appeared to confuse the officer. Monroe was her safe place. She had known it from the moment he had introduced himself to her.

"She knows my last name is Merton but give her some slack. She was likely in shock and scared out of her mind. I would have thought you had some life experience or something to tell you that. I know her last name is Sasse."

He knew her last name? But how? And now she knew his was Merton. Good thinking, Monroe. She knew he could think on his feet, and because she was hypervigilant, she could see he was as well. But that was Monroe. What else had she missed the few times they had been together at public gatherings? His words even told her it rankled that he was being challenged but impatient to be left alone. He was prior military who now worked security or something like that. She could see why.

Mallory hadn't known him long, but the time they had spent together and on the phone encouraged her to leave all this mess in his hands while she pieced things back together. She missed their date, the one she had wanted so much with the added expectation of sex with her guy. Now, even though Mallory had the best reasons to have stood him up, she wanted that date. She wanted that promise of skin-to-skin contact.

She wanted him and was so grateful that she hadn't endured a rape, knowing that would have changed their dynamic, possibly irreparably. She looked up into this man's eyes as he turned around and lowered his head to hers. He kissed her swollen, cracked lips lightly, almost playfully, but it was a serious kiss. There was no mistaking the intensity displayed on his face and the fleeting touch of concern. And the possession.

"I'm okay," she whispered.

"You are, indeed, sweetheart. I'm going to talk to the officer, but I'm not leaving from the front of your door. I'll hear if you call me. And if you need anything, you *will* call out for me."

His eyes told her even more. Mallory nodded. "Yes, sir. Just don't leave me." She knew she was pleading but couldn't care at this point. She'd beg if she needed to.

"Nope. I'm sticking so close to you, you'll be trying to shake me off before you know it."

One more light kiss and, this time, a smile that reached his eyes, showing his relief before he turned to follow the officer out. She kept her ears tuned to Monroe. She could hear their voices, just not what they were saying.

Mallory had recently moved from a little town in Eastern Tennessee. She enjoyed being the hometown pharmacist, but when Chas, her one long-term boyfriend, stepped out of their relationship, she needed a change. She didn't blame him. They had gotten into a rut, so it was almost a relief when he found someone else. It shocked her that he married his new girlfriend in less than two months, though. Mallory decided she could do without men for a while.

The one thing Chas did for her was to bring BDSM into her world because she would never have met Monroe without it. Chas had tried to introduce his version into their sex life. That is when she realized he was a selfish lover. How had she not known that?

They were both new to exploring the lifestyle, but it was a bittersweet reality. The idea excited Mallory, but she'd had little practical introduction except for what Chas had liked. Mallory found she liked a touch of pain, but she hadn't gone further since Chas wasn't into helping her explore that avenue, but Monroe was happy to teach her. He was a great guide. That would have to wait, though, because she was nowhere near ready to do anything but stick close to Monroe and heal.

Mallory touched the raw marks on her wrists. Unfortunately, the binding that she had loved with Monroe brought up frightening memories from the last few days. And the couple of spankings she'd enjoyed at Monroe's hand was still agreeable, along with the edging he had done once, but her mind was the enemy now. When she thought of an open hand, she saw the kidnapper's hand coming towards her face, repeatedly slapping her until she stopped screaming and fighting out of sheer exhaustion. Mallory prayed she would one day get over the fear she now felt.

Monroe would not be into her now that she had these new hang-ups. He had made it abundantly clear that he lived this lifestyle and was looking for something permanent. So had she until the kidnapping. She didn't know how long the fears would last, but in her limited experience, men didn't stick around when things got messy.

Mallory was determined not to be a victim, but there wasn't anything she could do about it for now. Monroe didn't seem concerned, but he didn't know all the details yet. He was so protective she could only imagine what he would do when he found out. She called out to him, and the door immediately opened. She watched her knight in shining armor walk back into the room, concern written all over his face.

"What's the matter, sweetheart?" He checked the room as he waited for her answer.

"I guess I just wanted you close."

"You have me."

His smile reached some of the darker recesses of her mind, and she gave him a sad, paltry attempt at a return smile. He reached out to tuck her hair behind her ear, and she flinched. Monroe shook his head and swore to kill her attacker.

"You're okay, baby. We will need to work on lessening your reaction to touch. My touch, anyway. Yeah?"

She nodded. Sorrow filled her heart. She never wanted to lose this man. He got her and understood what she needed. Now that she was broken, she needed so much more.

"I'm going to hug you again and touch you to reassure me you're no worse than I think. Have you looked in a mirror yet?"

"No, but since I know the stages of bruising, I imagine I won't look for another week or ten days."

"Probably a good idea. I'm going to reach my hand up now." He slowly palmed her cheek and eased down the side of her face. His touch was as light as a feather. "Damn, baby, this has to hurt. What about the rest of you? Where else were you hurt, beautiful? If I ever get my hands on that fucker, he's dead."

Monroe's bluntness startled Mallory, and for a few seconds, she didn't know what to say. She shook her head.

"Words Mal. I need to be sure of all your injuries. I'm already going to have a hard time not storming the jail and ripping the fucker's head off. If I know all your horrors, I'll mentally deal right now and then be able to focus all my attention on getting you well. Did they do x-rays of your face?"

Mallory shook her head again. Monroe had only begun to teach her about the lifestyle as he practiced it, but he had been clear that verbal responses were almost always required when essential questions were asked. She spoke up. "Yes, on the x-ray, well, a CT scan. No, in fact, except for the interaction you see here and the actual kidnapping, he didn't touch me at all."

"I'm going to kiss you again." It was a statement, not a request. It was this Monroe she needed right now. The extra care was sweet, but she needed the man who took care of business.

Her lips were tender, but she wouldn't have stopped him from making that contact with her. She needed Monroe to erase some of the horrors, and his touch, closeness, and protective stance helped. His lips tentatively touched hers again, and when she found herself leaning into him, Monroe took it a little deeper. No plunging, pillaging, and for now, that was how she needed his kisses to be: gentle, careful, present but with a light touch.

Thankfully, Monroe seemed to understand that. As he lifted up, he kissed the tip of her nose, and she wiggled it as she smiled, then grimaced. He laughed, easing the tenuously careful balance that seemed to hang in the air since he had arrived. It helped to ease the tension building and relax Mallory's nagging worry that he was there out of curiosity, or worse, pity.

"Hurt to smile? Sorry, honey. It will heal."

The officer walked in and informed Mallory that her "boyfriend" had checked out and was clear to visit with her."

"Stay with her." Monroe stopped moving the visitor chair closer to her to turn to the officer, pinning him with a hard stare. "You mean you left me alone in here with Mallory, but you weren't sure I was safe?"

Uh oh, the Dom, in protective mode, had emerged again and this time completely without filters. Mallory had heard of what they were like, and she had seen a few in her time, but watching Monroe right now was scary and impressive. She wasn't afraid of him, but she noted his actions and reactions to inform her of possible future behaviors. Safety was big with Monroe. Check.

"We ran a fast check, but the FBI needed something more substantial. I guess they got it because they wondered if you would stay with Mallory, but I guess that was your idea as well. I'll let you discuss that with the Feds." The officer nodded and left the room.

Vindicated, Monroe sat in the chair and laid his hand over hers on the bed, giving it a squeeze. Mallory opened her mouth to speak when Monroe's phone went off. He held up one finger and answered his phone. His hand returned to cover hers.

"Jac, what's going on with this mess?"

Chapter 4

Mallory listened as Monroe's facial expressions combined with his guttural sounds that resembled a threatened animal's response when cornered, then watched his hands as they ran through his short-cut hair in frustration. Those were pretty strong tells that this man was less than happy with what Jac Reynaud, the CEO and one of Monroe's partners in the security firm, was telling him.

Monroe was a strong-minded yet even-tempered man, by what she had gathered thus far, so what Jac had said must have been something serious to disturb him so much. She knew it must have been about her because his relaxed manner of earlier didn't return. She glimpsed his grim expression before he cleared it away.

"Sorry, sweetheart. I didn't think it would take so long to debrief with Jac. He called our contacts at the FBI and vouched for me, or rather, he said he had simply reminded them who I was."

"Um, so you know the FBI agents?"

"A few. We do security, and the government needs plenty of that."

"So you're a bodyguard?"

"Sometimes." He cocked his head to the side and gave her a speculative stare. "Does that bother you?"

"Does hot a bodyguard with grey at his temples bother me? They kidnapped me. I'm not dead." The joke got a frown from Monroe, and she grimaced. "Sorry. Too soon?"

"Years too soon."

She nodded. "But the hot body part isn't." Then she blushed hard, the heat of it rushing up the column of her neck and infusing her face. "Sorry. It's just as rude for me to say things like that to you as you to me."

Monroe grinned and shook his head. "Beautiful, you can crush on me all you want because I sure as hell have been crushing on you since the first time I laid eyes on you. And I have no intention of keeping my thoughts to myself on that score."

"Pfft, there is nothing beautiful about me now." Her teeth bit down on her bottom lip.

"I can see we will have to establish down some rules once you feel better, but a few bumps and bruises just testifies to your inner strength. You could have been super compliant when you were taken. You could have just accepted fate, but you didn't. You fought back even though you were at a great disadvantage. That is beauty,"

Monroe spoke softly, but she knew he meant it. Mallory had done plenty of lifestyle searches since meeting Monroe. Was she ready to try living his way? She'd always wanted to find a Dom who was a real man, not an imitation, and those romances were deceiving, but she didn't know if she could do it. She should answer him, anyway. He deserved at least that.

"Can we go slow right now? I honestly don't know if I have triggers or not. I'm not even processing all of this well yet. Normally, I love myself and my life. I'm just a bit shaky right now."

"I know, and it's to be expected, but I want to tease all of that out with you. And before you respond, the only appropriate answer is Yes, Sir, because I do not intend on allowing you to be alone for quite a while. And that timing will have to be a point of negotiation." He held her gaze, leaving her with no doubt he meant every word. "Do we have an understanding?"

Mallory dropped eye contact. A warm hand gently raised her chin so she could do nothing but look at him or close her eyes. She chose door number two. The wrong choice, evidently.

Monroe's voice rasped over her like fine sandpaper laced with his golden whiskey mellowness and a touch of chastising. "Mallory, eyes open, baby." She raised her head without thinking. "That's my girl. Never leave me to wonder how you feel or think on a subject if it bothers you and even if it doesn't. I can't read your mind, but I try my best to read your cues. It'll take me a while to get those down, so communicate with me honestly. Yeah?"

"Yeah." He raised his eyebrow sharply. "Sir," Mallory added the afterthought word with a swollen face version of an impish grin.

His laugh burst out unexpectantly as he shook his head. "Your name suits you, Ms. Sasse. Let's try this again. I don't trust anyone to keep you safe except my team and me, so that's who's going to do it. Jac spoke with those in the know and the rest of our team. This is what they have so far."

Monroe watched as Mallory tried to suppress a shiver and pulled her, IV and all, closer to him. Holding her might be the best way to tell her the update. He resettled them so that he was sitting on the bed next to her, enveloping her shaking body in his bear hug, her head on his shoulder, his mouth against her temple.

"You did a great job of describing the house and the way you had come from. They found the house and its owner."

"I wasn't sure because we had come in after dark, and there weren't any close houses. Who is he?"

Monroe could hear her voice quiver. Too bad the local PD found him before Monroe had. He would have saved the taxpayers a lot of money.

Mallory whispered. "What about the other woman? Did they find her? Is she alive?"

Monroe rubbed her chilled arm and kissed the top of her head before answering. "They found the lady that fit your description of the one you saw when the door opened. I won't lie. She's in rough shape. She's in a coma, but there's no other information at this time. Her family has been located."

"Do you think she'll be alright?"

"I don't know. It isn't looking good. Search and Rescue dogs are on the property, and they found another woman in a shallow grave in the wooded area just off the property. She was dead. They are bringing in the cadaver dogs for a more thorough search."

"And his wife?"

"Wife? What wife, sweetheart?"

"I heard someone else rummaging around at the doorway, and he referred to a wife several times."

"We will look into it. Anyone else?"

"No."

Both fell silent, just existing in their closeness. It was a gratifying feeling to know you could take care of your woman, and she allowed it. Monroe loved how they fit together so well. He knew they did in other ways as well, but it would take time to prove to Mallory that the only place she needed to be was with him.

Carter and Garrett put their head in, accompanied by Agent Gutierrez. Mallory tried to move out of Monroe's arms, but he wasn't about to let her go yet. She had stopped shivering, but she went back on high alert as the men entered the room. He offered a chin lift to the guys.

"Shh, baby. It's alright. Carter and Garrett are two of the men on my team, and this man is Agent Gutierrez. We've already met."

"We have, Mr. Merton, several years ago. Ms. Sasse, please call me Arturo. I wanted to make sure these men were okay to come in. Will that be acceptable to you?"

He waited for her response, and when Mallory hesitated, he eyed the men.

Mallory nodded. "I'm sure they are here because Monroe requested them so, I'm okay with them staying."

Arturo nodded before addressing Monroe. "I've talked to your boss, and he seems to think his team is the better option to protect Ms. Sasse until we are positive there were no accomplices. We're all out looking for the missing women and, therefore, understaffed. Unless Ms. Sasse disagrees, we have ok'd it."

"Sounds like a plan," said Garrett.

Carter and Monroe replied in unison. "It's not, but it will be."

Carter, without showing a crack in his serious armor, said, "See what happens when you work with the same people for too long in a day. You turn into one melded mind."

Garrett said casually, "I hear they're working on a vaccine to cure that."

Monroe watched Mallory as she glared at the two men, and then Monroe, who couldn't keep his face blank for long, winked at her. The room, even the agent, cracked a brief smile. Monroe laughed out loud with Mallory.

Mallory said, "God, that felt so good. I need more of that. It seems so long... a lifetime ago."

Monroe sobered, as did the others. His team didn't know the entire story yet, but they could appreciate how horror and fear messed with the mind. They'd each been through it and understood the time it would take Mallory to find a new normal. Monroe intended on being there through it all if she let him. Mallory had crawled under his skin, and he wouldn't have had it any other way.

"Ms. Sasse, is this alright with you? One or two of the Reynaud and Associates Security team will be with you 24/7 until we figure out what is happening, and you are no longer in danger. They assure us they have several safe houses and can keep you secured and protected."

Mallory assessed Monroe for a moment, really looking at him, and Monroe held his breath. He didn't want to influence her answer. Even though he wanted to step in and take over all decisions associated with her safety, he knew he couldn't. Mallory had to make this choice. She took a deep breath, nodded, and exhaled.

"I believe that is a wise choice, ma'am," said Agent Gutierrez.

Her inner strength came out in her next question. "Agreed. But I have a question."

The agent looked at her warily. "Okay."

"How will I know I'm safe to resume my life?" Monroe was proud of her question. It meant she intended to take part in her protection.

Gutierrez glanced around and said, "They will know, but practically? When we have the perpetrator in custody, have any accomplices he may have had, and cleared the family. Then you may be confident that you are safe."

"Do you have a timeline?" she asked.

Gutierrez looked at Monroe, who gave a very slight nod of acknowledgment. "Baby, we don't know that for sure, but we'll try to find a new normal as soon as possible."

"Okay. Good enough for now."

The agent left as the nurse came in to bring Mallory medicine, her dinner, and untether her from the IV, removing the bag but not hooking up a new one.

"That's all of that, we hope. We will take it out when we discharge you."

The men moved over to the far corner of the room to discuss things. All conversation stopped when Mallory asked her something.

"When am I going to be released? I'm ready now."

"I'll ask your physician, Doctor Sasse. I guess you would know if you felt well enough to go home."

"I'm a pharmacist, not a family practitioner, but if it helps me get out of here faster, by all means, I'm not too proud to use it."

"When you are discharged, you'll stay with me at Jac's, then my place, until we are sure you're safe. Deal?"

"Deal. Thank you."

"You don't have to thank me. I'm relieved I won't have to sleep on your floor."

"I have a spare room."

"Your floor. The closer I am, the better protector I am."

"What about in my bed?"

"Nope, because neither of us will sleep, and you need to heal."

"Then I suggest you hurry because I feel like I'm still held captive, but differently, so I'm antsy to go. When they offer me the exit, I'm taking it. You all will just have to follow along if you aren't ready."

Monroe leaned closer. "You will go when we are certain of your safety, understood? Sorry, but you can't discharge until we get the plan cinched in. It's for your safety, which I won't compromise on, and my peace of mind. Please, Mal?"

Monroe meant for her to hear him clearly and to know he would enforce any restrictions or penalties necessary to gain her compliance. She had interacted enough with him to be familiar with his different tones. Watching his girl process, he waited. She was intelligent, and it wouldn't be a reach to find that he was right.

"Fine," she huffed, "But hurry."

Now wasn't the time to tell her that topping from the bottom or taking control of a situation he had in hand was not a smart strategy for a submissive of any type, especially his girl. That was a later lesson he would be happy to instruct on. For now, he nodded.

"Thank you, baby. I will."

He repressed a grin and dropped another kiss on her cracked lips. He reached and grabbed her lip balm and gave it to her, knowing hers had to hurt. Hell, everything had to hurt. And his anger began to bubble again. Time to get things moving.

MALLORY LOVED AND HATED what his gravelly "I'm in charge" voice sounded like and what it did to her insides. Still, after all this trauma, it had the same effect on her reactions and responses, and what was worse, Monroe knew it. Damn him. And bless him. For now, she needed to drop the reins, let someone else lead her parade. Knowing he would keep her safe, well, that was priceless.

That she needed that security blanket he was offering her was disheartening. Mallory had run her own life for almost two decades and while she knew being vulnerable was to be expected under the circumstances, she hated it. It had become a source of pride that she had done all the monumental things in her world alone, but she also lived a stark, lonely life. Kind of like that saying, you can be lonely in a crowd of people. That was Mallory.

All the self-talk in the world would not stop her from being sad and rankled at the predicament she was in. Nor was it going to stop the longing she had deep inside her that wanted Monroe. Daily phone calls and a few meetups in a group were all that she and Monroe had spent together, but those times had added up to hours of learning about each other.

They were going to go on a date before all of this, and his conversation and mannerisms said he still wanted her but did her situation now cause him to see her as a job? Did he separate himself from his work, and the growing relationship ended? She wanted him, and he had wanted her before this happened. Depressive thoughts returned, and her fear made itself known again. Mallory wanted to cry.

No, don't be stupid. Monroe has treated you as his since he walked into the room. I didn't make that, and I won't give up without making my thoughts known. He told people I was his girlfriend. That was something I had no trouble accepting, so act like it.

"Mal, I have some things to get ready for your discharge, so Carter is going to stay with you, okay? You should rest, and I'll be back before you notice I'm gone."

Panic rose in her chest. "What? You're leaving? I... I can't... I mean..." Mallory took a deep breath and let it out. Yoga and quiet meditation always helped when she was stressed. However, this was more anxiety than she had felt before because her abject fear encased it.

"Mal? Baby, I promise Carter will protect you with his life. No one will get past him."

Carter nodded. "Mallory, can I call you that?" She nodded. "Mallory, I'm not just big, I'm well trained, and I'm armed. I promise no one will get to you."

She released another deep breath slowly. Mallory opened her eyes, and the panic had lessened.

"You okay?" asked Monroe quietly. She nodded and wiped the stray tear winding its way down her cheek. "I'm sorry. I know you will protect me, and I hate I'm like this now." Anger roughened her voice. "I hate that someone could do this to me." She inhaled, then exhaled again. "I'm good."

"You're more than good. You're perfect for me." His words helped some. His closeness and sincerity helped a lot.

"Go do your thing. I'll be here when you get back."

"They'll probably release you in the morning. Then we'll blow this popsicle stand."

She watched as his head descended to stop just before touching her lips. "Are you really going to be comfortable with me leaving Carter?"

Staring into his eyes, she whispered, "Yes."

"I'll be as quick as I can. Do you want me to bring you back anything?"

"A Dr. Pepper and chocolate."

His lips twitched before he touched hers softly, then he deepened the kiss as though he, like her, was drawing sustenance from the other.

"I seem to have difficulty keeping my hands off you. I'll be back soon."

Her heart kicked up a notch. Her breath followed suit as she watched Monroe and Garrett stalk from the room. Carter pulled up the chair that Monroe had sat in earlier and stationed it so he could see her and the door clearly, keeping his body next to hers.

"I think I'll try to nap. I feel tired all the time."

Carter nodded. "Yeah, all of my Reynaud teammates have dealt with being held hostage or in situations we didn't think we'd get out of alive, so we get what you feel and what you shut down to survive. There are no judgments here. Don't put yourself under a microscope, either. It will take time to get past this. I learned that I don't do well being the victim, so I let go of the horror as soon as I could. You will probably need a counselor to help you through it. I know a good one who is easy to talk to or to sit with. Ivy has used her."

"Thanks. I'll let you know if I need the number."

"Good enough. Now nap woman. I'll be right here when you wake up."

Another thing to be ashamed of. Not being able to take care of her own mental health without help. Didn't that sound pathetic? Her over-active brain, with its rigid ideology on how she should live her life, was at it again. Time to go to sleep.

JAC GOT A PHONE CALL while Monroe talked about the Mallory situation and optional scenarios out with him. Jac placed his hand over the mouthpiece.

"It's Sam Johnson, the FBI liaison. I'm putting it on speaker. Play your cards close."

"Got it."

"Hey, Sam, I have Monroe here. You're on speaker, and my office is soundproof. Go ahead."

"Right, I think you and your group are too close to this, and that is likely to cause a lapse in attention to Doctor Sasse's safety."

Monroe spoke up quickly and fiercely, forgetting all about playing it close. "I won't let anything happen to Mallory. I think you would be too 'business as usual' with her, and I place the value of her life over mine."

"That's what I mean. You'll play the sacrificial lamb before seeing other options, weighing the pros and cons," said Sam.

Jac put his hand up to stop Monroe's words. "I see it differently. Look, Sam. We've pulled your ass out of the proverbial many times, and it has involved some of our own people intimately. We will attach an entire team to protect Mallory. It won't just be Merton. They are just as attached as they were to Ivy or Jessie, or Sharlee. So your excuse doesn't hold water. We have a proven record of taking care of our women."

Sam sighed. "I'm just worried there is someone else still out there. I mean, hell, this guy couldn't have kidnapped so many without someone noticing them missing and connecting the dots. He would have made a mistake at some point. He had them fighting him, surely. The adrenalin alone..."

Jac answered with a sigh. "We both know crazy people do crazy-ass things."

"Exactly why I need to make sure we have eliminated any threat before I say she is safe."

Monroe shook his head at the phone. "I'll protect her. You stick to what you know, figuring out what actually happened and getting those poor women identified and back to their families. I'll stick to what I know, security and that makes me ideal for helping secure Mallory's safety." Monroe lowered his voice when giving a warning and made sure he sounded dead serious. "What good am I if I protect others but not my girl?"

"Okay. I'm signing the order now and will send over a copy. Don't mess this up, Merton."

Monroe grinned at the phone. "Not a chance."

Chapter 5

"Are you ready to go, sweetheart?" Monroe asked Mallory the following morning as Carter stood at the hospital room door.

"More than."

"Okay, we're going to take this nice and easy. I want you to walk nonchalantly outside with us like nothing is out of the ordinary. Garrett will take one side, and I'll be on the other, with Carter taking point. Kaden is in the car."

Carter put his head in. "Change of plans, kiddies. Just got intel that the front is full of reporters. There are two agency vehicles outside, and four men are exiting on their way up. Not sure what they're doing here, but they have drawn the reporters like bees to honey. We need to get out now. Kaden has the maintenance exit covered with a vehicle at the door. Let's move before the party begins."

Her confusion was apparent. "But I don't understand. Why are they here at all?"

Monroe reached for her arm carefully but firmly and scooped up the bag the team's women had brought Mallory because no one could get into Mallory's house yet. The women seemed to need to connect, and this worked for now. He intended there not to be a similar need due to his girl suffering from a trauma a second time.

"Showtime, Mal. Stick with me. We'll be moving quickly." Her nod of agreement was all Monroe needed to follow Carter, who seemed to know where he was going.

Once they cleared the patient floor, Monroe hesitated.

"This elevator takes us to the basement," said Carter as he got into the side elevator.

Monroe would have opted for the stairs to the basement but worried it might be too much for Mallory, and time was of the essence. He hoped they didn't encounter the wrong person, or he would have to go on the defensive. He preferred staying on the offensive, keeping him in charge.

Once in the basement, they rushed through the hot steamy laundry area, then Kaden was in view. The men surrounded Mallory, who at 5'8" might have been difficult to hide well with the men she knew. That was not a problem with these guys. They were easily four or more inches taller, and their combined bulk, especially Carter's, was more than enough to screen her from others' view.

When the men moved toward the SUV, she almost felt like they were carrying her instead of walking with her. In mere seconds, she was in the vehicle and surrounded by four bulky men in a moving SUV.

"Do you guys always do that?"

The man Carter had identified as Kaden turned to look at her from his right and smiled. "Do what? Isn't that how everyone leaves a building and gets into their car? I'm Kaden, by the way. These guys have no manners, so I have to introduce myself."

Mallory smiled. "Nice to meet you. I guess we all technically enter the vehicle that way, but not practically."

The older man driving the car looked back at her through the rearview mirror. "I'm Garrett. I can't remember if we were formally introduced yesterday. Thank God you're safe because Monroe was about to go postal on the world when he discovered you were missing and not just ghosting."

"Shut up, man. We had just pieced it together when I got the call saying she was okay."

"Ah, but when you just thought she had stood you up, it was bad enough. In those few moments of not knowing where she was, once you discovered something had happened to her, tell me you didn't want to head out like Attila the Hun."

Mallory turned and saved Monroe from answering. "You were looking for me? Why? I mean, that's sweet, but . . ."

He shrugged. "You missed our date."

"Sorry about that, but... wow."

"Baby, you have nothing to be sorry about." His arm went around her shoulders as he gently drew her closer. "I'll always come looking for you, and I won't stop until I find you."

"I really wanted to go on that date," she whispered. Monroe squeezed her tighter before loosening his hold.

Carter looked back and said, "Guess we had better brief Mallory on the reception she's going to receive."

"No, I don't think that we should do that until we get there. Jac will want to take the lead on the plan."

"Not that, the intro to our women," laughed Carter. The others joined in. "I'll start. There is Becky or Rebecca, she's my girlfriend. A little quiet until she has something to say, and then you have to work to stop her flow of information.

She is Jac's office manager, and she holds things together with us as a couple and in the office when things get chaotic as they often do."

"Then there's my wife, Ivy," said Kaden. "She's pretty opinionated and can be rather intense when she wants something. Really, Ivy is generous and giving and a loyal friend. She has a martial arts studio and a graphic arts business that she sometimes uses to help the office."

Monroe spoke next. "Then there's Jessie. She's married to Mark, and they are finishing their first trimester of pregnancy. She's beginning to sport a belly. You haven't met Mark yet, but don't let his manner worry you. He is as solid as they come. Jessie is the accountant for the business. She's sweet and always wants to help, too much sometimes, but we all watch out for each other. And Mark is extra vigilant because of the baby."

Garrett said, "Guess we're down to Sharlee." The men made little noises. "Sharlee is our main IT wizard and the ultimate brown noser. She married the boss, Jac. They have a cute toddler named Storm. Sharlee is a force to be reckoned with and more capable than most people. She's a full member of our team. The other women are support personnel. Jac likes his family close."

"You are all related?"

"No," said Monroe, "but all the teams, of which we are one of three, are tight like we were with our teams in the military. We know each other well, life and work like we are in a family business, and the way Jac runs things, we truly are family. There is the security of always having a backup if we need it, personally and professionally. We know how the other members of the team think and will most likely react. It allows us to work seamlessly together and stay safe."

Mallory nodded. "I can see how that would be a good idea."

Monroe added. "And there is Levi on our team. I think he is getting sweet on Storm's nanny, Finley, a prior Marine and one kick-ass Storm watcher. Oh, and Ryker, who handles the attorney kind of stuff in the background."

Mallory laughed. "Sounds like the right nanny for this group."

Monroe nodded. "She is. Now lean back. It will be another half hour before we get to Jac's place."

MALLORY LEANED BACK against Monroe. And it seemed like the most natural thing in the world to trust him, which was not in her usual wheelhouse. Trust was not something she did effortlessly. And Monroe, while gentle, was definitely bossy. She was shaken, and the thought of not finding her normal again scared her. To be honest, everything scared her. Certainly, this team of bigger-than-life men gave her pause, and absolutely the property they had just turned into sent a shiver down her back. This was like a mafia boss place. Be

There was only a glow behind the forest of trees that showed something was back there. An enormous, ornate, wrought-iron gate interrupted the long driveway. Fencing, complete with a guardhouse manned with men and guns no doubt fully loaded, surrounded the property. Garrett pressed the com button and spoke to the gatekeeper, then waited for the gate to swing open. There was another set of similar gate-keepers about a hundred yards down, but the man simply nodded as he opened the barrier.

"Do I have to stay here?" whispered Mallory in Monroe's ear.

"We will both stay. It won't just be you here. Don't worry. Once you get inside, it won't feel as intimidating."

"Wanna bet?"

Monroe dropped a light kiss on her forehead, and while she liked it, Mallory wished it was on her lips that were trembling once again. Intimidating did not even cover her thoughts on this sprawling monstrosity of a house. Actually, mansion would be the right word. Monroe seemed so down to earth it seemed impossible that he could be comfortable in this environment. Mallory had come from an upper-middle-class home, and it was unnerving for her.

She sighed warily, and Monroe leaned down once again to speak low. "Practice your submission and trust, sweet-heart. I won't demand much of you except obedience and honesty, and that comes with trust. Mallory, I would die trying to keep you safe, and so would every team member on this property, inside and outside those gates. I hope you believe that soon."

"I'm trying. It's just recent events that have violated my trust meter. It will take a while to come back online."

Monroe nodded, but the thunder that settled on his face told Mallory that she might not be the only one who had lost some faith in humanity. Mallory nodded without thought and hoped she could feel more in control soon because the floating out to sea look was not a good one for her.

She had always been confident in her abilities, but not in men. Monroe was the only man she had genuine confidence in. She believed in his ability to be what she needed. If she could only extend that feeling to other important areas of her life again, she'd be one content woman.

As they park in the circular drive-in front of Jac's house, Mallory could see they are not the only ones here, not by a long shot. What she wanted to do was run, hide, pretend she was the ostrich that hid its head, but that wasn't who she really was. No, she'd make sure the cars outside belonged to team members before going inside to get the first introductions over. Anyone else was a no-go. She was not an oddity to be put on display.

"Um, this is just your team? Not a lot of other people, right?"

Monroe looked around. "Yep, just us. The women must have driven here themselves because there are a few more vehicles than usual. But I can identify every one of them. You good?"

"I think so."

The overcast skies seemed appropriate for her first day of real freedom since Friday. The sun would come out soon, but it wasn't there yet. The men moved, and while the vehicle was large, Carter had to maneuver his frame out of the door, and the others unfolded and ducked their heads before getting out. Their size confounded her.

And the tremors started again. It's time to rock-and-roll, Mal, she told herself. These people only want to help you. They're Monroe's friends, and Monroe had made it more than clear that she was his. Carter had said it as well. As when leaving the hospital, Garrett, on her left, placed his hand lightly on her arm while Monroe was on the right side with his hand on the small of her back.

One man was guiding and could quickly bring her to the ground to protect her if needed. Monroe was possessive, and his stance allowed him to fall on top of her to shield her. It seemed the others deferred to him when it came to her, which suited Mallory just fine. She knew the male code mandated you never poached your brother's girl. For the first time in her life, that was comforting.

As the car doors shut, she remembered her bag. "Oh, I need to grab—"

"Kaden has it," said Carter brusquely. "And I have your paperwork and the things from the hospital that weren't confiscated by the men in blue or the alphabet agents."

"Thanks. Carter, why is the FBI involved, anyway? Were we taken across state lines?"

"Ahh. We will discuss that with everyone, but the quick answer is that you were not the only person kidnapped. We don't know how many women were taken, but some women were from other states."

"Oh, how horrible." Her trembles increased. The weather was comfortable, so she couldn't even blame it on cool air. She was afraid to be outside.

"Come on, sweetheart. Let's get this over with so you can take a nap."

"But I don't need—" Carter cut the rest of her sentence off as they guided her forward in one movement.

Kaden and Carter stayed at her rear as they walked, flanked by the other two men. The light from the entryway shone through the doorway and lightened some of the gloom of the day. Another man, not as tall as Monroe but with equally defined muscles, stood in the entrance with an air of position and power. This must be Jac.

Next to him was a beautiful but intense woman. She was probably his wife, Sharlee. Next to her was one of the other women.

Carter said behind her, "The dark one is Mark and Jessie, his wife next to him."

Mark leaned down and whispered something in his wife's ear. She gave him such a look of irritation that Mallory half expected her to say something, but Mark laid his hand on her back and slid it down to her backside. Mallory watched the fight seemed to leave Jessie's body. She turned and left from the entrance.

Kaden, from behind her, said in a sotto voce, "She knows better than to put herself at risk right now. Standing in the doorway bold as brass and twice as hard-headed."

Carter rushed his words because they were almost at the top of the steps. "Mark's woman, Mark's job."

"Thank goodness," said Kaden. "Ivy is enough for me." In a louder voice, "Make way, guys."

The entry cleared, and the door closed hard behind them.

So did these men take care of each other's girlfriends and spouses, too? She didn't quite understand the concept here. She'd read the book Forever the Brotherhood and seen enough episodes of those with Military Special Forces, and she had read more than her share of alpha romances, but this was real life. It never dawned on her to ask before now, but were his teammates all like Monroe? It seemed a bit too perfect and a load of surrealism.

"Were you followed?" asked Jac.

"No. And thank God for that," said Garrett as they entered the grand foyer. "It would have been a feeding frenzy if Mal had gone out the front door."

Jac gave a slight nod. "Ms. Sasse, I'm Jac Reynaud, senior partner of the Reynaud and Associates Securities. I'm happy to finally meet you. Monroe speaks highly of you."

"I would assume that's because he doesn't yet know the irritating habits that I have. Nice to meet you as well, and please call me Mallory or, as Monroe calls me, Mal. Is this your lovely wife?"

"Yes, I'm Sharlee. So glad they found you quickly, but sorry it wasn't sooner."

"Thank you for helping Monroe look. I was fortunate to have been able to get out."

The darker man reached out his hand. "I'm Mark, and my more adventuresome half, whom you might have seen briefly, is Jessie. She's in the kitchen pouting that I wouldn't let her stand in the doorway to greet you. It is a matter of precaution, nothing against you. So you'll meet her in a few moments at lunch."

Jac took over the conversation again. "I suggest we go into the den, where we can finish the introductions. Then, after lunch, we can hit the ground running on the plan to keep you safe."

Without waiting for an answer, Jac continued to lead the way into the den. All but Monroe had peeled off into different parts of the room. Carter and Kaden headed for two women who were making room for their men. There was another man in the room, and he must be Levi, the newest member of the team.

The team's inner workings still confused Mallory, but she understood that the men in this room were one team. Jac looked at Monroe, and they exchanged a few head movements, a few facial expressions, and then Monroe gave a final nod before bringing her down with him onto an oversized love seat that was the perfect size for the two of them.

Glancing around, Mallory noticed all the furniture was large that occupied the equally expansive den. There were several spacious lounging and conversation areas, but with the men fitting the room and the furniture, Mallory had a hard time not thinking she had discovered the land of the giants.

"Listen up. This impressive young woman standing with Monroe is Mallory Sasse. Yes, it is her real name." Jac looked down to grin at Mallory before becoming serious again. "We are going to have lunch, then talk about what we'll do to keep our Mallory safe." Jac lifted his head and spoke to the group. "This is Monroe's lady friend, and they are exclusive. She is the focus of a safety issue which we will discuss in detail soon; therefore, one of us will always be with her. And if you see Mallory alone, call Monroe or me. If you can't get him, then stick with her until Monroe returns."

Jac looked at Mallory. "Mallory will do her best to stay in someone's company." Jac didn't appear to need confirmation from her, and all Mallory could do was drop her eyes to her twisting fingers in her lap.

Jac looked at Monroe as he stepped back to yield the floor. Monroe took a step away from Mallory, and the panic welled up. "Until this mess with Mallory has concluded, she is staying here or with me at all times. I haven't told her more than that, but this afternoon, when we discuss things, it will become clear to everyone." He stopped and touched Mallory's cheek before continuing. "Mallory is mine, so I'd appreciate it if you protected her like you do your own women. Thanks. Let's eat."

The group immediately got up to head back in the direction that Mallory had just come. None of them appeared disturbed or annoyed at the sudden change to their schedules and responsibilities. This was an odd group, and yet, Mallory instinctively knew these men were protectors. Defending those who needed it was not only their livelihood but their way of life. On the right, Jac was following a woman she remembered was Sharlee, his wife. Mallory looked around for their son and didn't see him. Sharlee was perceptive.

"He's outside with Finley, his nanny."

"I think Monroe mentioned Finley. She is an ex-marine, right?"

A sandy-haired man, about Mallory's age, with dungaree blue eyes, spoke behind her. She turned and stared into his handsome face. *Another big one*, she thought, but not as bulky as Monroe. "Prior Marine, ma'am. We're still Marines, just not in active service." He extended his hand. "Levi Morrison."

Mallory smiled. "I am learning that is a universal sentiment around here."

"Yep, but a Marine means it." He slapped Monroe on the back and walked off as everyone chuckled.

Having a meal with such a crowd at the same table was overwhelming, yet Mallory could relax and lower her guard a little. She was still jumpy, as evidenced by the shriek of fright when a jar of pickles hit the floor before the seal broke. A combination of shattered glass and an explosion of immediately released pressure created a slight explosion sound.

Monroe immediately drew her into his arms. "Shh, it's okay, baby. It's just a jar of pickles. Nothing scarier than that."

She trembled uncontrollably for a moment while Monroe spoke to her in quiet murmurs. His hands rubbed her arms, and the overreaction receded enough for Mallory to lift her head.

"You okay to finish eating?"

She pushed the plate away. "I'm not hungry."

He pulled the plate back. "You haven't eaten enough to keep a bird alive. You need to try. Two bites of salad, two of fish. If you are still not hungry, you can stop."

Mallory sniffed and wiped the tears from her face, offering him a weak attempt at indignation. "I know when I'm hungry. I'm no child."

"Nope, but you are my lady, and that means I take your health and welfare seriously. Now two of each." He leaned in close. "I was going to make you feel so much better later tonight to help you sleep, but I won't if I don't get some indication, you can follow my direction. Remember, you are practicing your submission when asked to do something. It isn't giving away your power. It's submitting to mine."

He wasn't kidding, and Mallory needed to feel like she was important and special again. Monroe gave her that in spades. And hopefully, it would lead to sex when she quit hurting. She had been dreaming of that eventuality since he asked her out on a date. No, before that.

His voice roughened. "Mallory, you need to answer me."

God, she needed this man. She picked up the fork and stabbed her salad, putting the veggies in her mouth, letting her actions do her talking.

"You are so naughty sometimes, you know that? Next time, I need words. No more getting away with going silent."

Mallory finished chewing and swallowed. She whispered back. "I did what you wanted."

"You want me to spank your ass. But I won't because you want it so much. You are in so much pain. It will be a few days before I give you the spanking you deserve and crave. Don't forget, there are plenty of ways to punish a mouthy sub, sweetheart. Even when she hurts all over." He kissed her temple, causing Mallory to blush hard.

"Shh. Don't let them hear you," she said while looking around furtively for any listeners. No one seemed to have heard him.

"They all spank their women, Mal. And while they might not all be into some of the finer points of bedroom games, I assure you, they all play them privately in some form or another, and when it's important, the women all listen to their men."

"What? That's... wait, are you telling me you are all chauvinist?"

He pointed his fork at her food. She sighed, then took another bite. "No, our women are the most important thing to us and any children we may have. That's protective. I would listen to you in your area of expertise. And while most things are private, it is always consensual because it's not enjoyable otherwise. You should know that. "

"Oh, well... right. I know that's true in my head, but in my heart where all the crazy emotion lives, that's different."

Monroe's kiss was swift and satisfying. "That will change soon. Now eat."

Jac clapped his hands. "Yes, let's finish up, people. We have work to do."

Jac nodded to Mallory. She suspected he heard their conversation or at least enough of it, but Jac didn't indicate he had, and it was more comfortable to pretend he didn't. She ate a little more before sitting back from the table and waiting for the rest. The surrounding conversation was relaxed and animated from some of them and intense and quiet with others.

She hoped she could get her life back soon and feel comfortable with Monroe's friends once she knew them better. They would be the friends she had rarely found in her busy life. The women were familiar, and each had a different but comfortable manner, showing contentment. Mallory wanted that contentment and ease in relationships.

Would she ever be able to relax completely again? She hoped so. She needed a connection like she had before leaving home nearly two decades ago. Wasn't that why she had attended the Munches? To garner a more meaningful connection with a dom that would be husband material? It was time.

"Need the bathroom before we head to the den?" Monroe's hot breath caressed her cheek.

"How did you know? Point the way," said Mallory with a smile.

"I'll take you."

"I can go to the bathroom myself."

"Humor me. I'm still trying to settle my mind about what happened to you. Bear with me while I deal with things. Until further notice, you're with me."

"I'm good with that." Mallory snuggled in as his arm drew her close.

"Besides, you are practicing submission, and I must say, you need practice."

Mallory laughed. "Yes, sir."

"Brat."

She slipped her hand in Monroe's as they found the bathrooms. Jac had two bathrooms off the entryway because he didn't want anyone to wander through his house that he didn't invite to do so. When Mallory entered one room, Monroe went into the other and was outside when she opened her door to leave.

Monroe placed his arm around her waist to bring her close again, then slid it to the small of her back and guided her into the den, where most of the group assembled. A large screen emerged from the ceiling, and Monroe led them to a sofa in the front of where Jac was standing. On the other side of Mallory was Sharlee, who had a laptop on a small stand in front of her. Sharlee smiled as Mallory sat down. She reached over and squeezed Mallory's hand.

Chapter 6

S harlee leaned in closer and said, "These guys are the best at security. I promise they will not only keep you safe, but they will also help fill in the blanks. The guys will, if allowed, figure out the entire story and find closure for the families. They might seem like hard asses, and they can be when necessary, but to their family of which you now belong, there is nothing they won't do. These men, these teams will have your back, always."

Sharlee let go of Mallory's hand and patted it before replacing her own back on the keyboard and typed at amazing speed. She nodded to her husband, and Jac began.

"First off, we got this gig from the FBI, but even if they hadn't wanted us involved, Mallory is one of ours now, so we would have been smack in the middle of this one. It's just nice to get paid for what you were already going to do." Monroe patted her thigh. "Now, Rebecca is passing out an info packet on what we know and what we need to know."

When Rebecca gave one to Monroe, she leaned down, smiled sweetly, and whispered, "I'm Becky, and I date that behemoth over there."

"Carter said you were together. Nice to meet you."

"You too," whispered Becky before she continued to pass out the packets.

Jac waited until they had all received a packet before he continued. "Add to that anything you believe we have missed. I'm sure there are things. Garrett and Monroe, you take it from here. Get us started."

Garrett walked to the front, and Monroe stood to the side, giving the lead to his teammate. "First off, this is what we have from the FBI. Our contact there is a man named Arturo Gutierrez." They showed a picture of the agent on screen. "This is the local police officer, officer Whitley. This is our lovely Mallory." The next slide appeared. "This is Craig Romaine, our suspect." Mallory made a strangled noise.

"Shit." Monroe had her plastered against his side in two seconds, hiding her face against his shoulder.

Garrett continued past the disturbing photo and came to several photos of identified women buried on Romaine's property. Monroe kept Mallory tucked against him until the slideshow was over. "They have found three, but, likely, there are more, as the cadaver dogs are still getting excited. They must mark the spots and then continue. As the forensic team is able, they will uncover the bodies one by one."

Carter spoke up. "What about the woman Mallory had with her?"

"Yes, she is still alive, but it will be a long, painful recovery, both physically and mentally. She isn't out of critical condition yet. The family, which they found before we left today, told me it would be months. But they expressed their appreciation that Mallory had gotten help when she did because she saved their daughter."

"I hope she can recover emotionally because otherwise, the pain won't ever go away," said Jessie.

Ivy said, "It won't ever go away completely, but hopefully, she will get someone to talk to about her fears. It helps."

Jessie got up to leave the room. Mark stood to follow her. "Pregnancy hormones make emotions hard to control," he explained as he followed his wife out of the room. There were murmurs of sympathy, but none moved to follow them.

Jac stood up. "That brings up a good point. Unless you are an integral part of the process, it isn't necessary to be here just because your other half is on the team. So, Ivy, you and Jessie are welcome to leave, and unless Mark or Kaden think you should be here, I'll let them fill you in on what we decide on things with Mallory. I had thought that since you will spend time together, it might help to know what we're doing. Jessie's response reminded me it isn't necessary."

There were several more slides of the property site and the first place he lived, presumably alone. "This is where the FBI will start their investigation after processing the present location."

"Are you okay, or do you need a break?" Monroe studied her face as he waited for her answer.

"I'm okay." Mallory took a deep breath. "I'll be fine. It was just a shock to see his face again."

He studied her a little longer before nodding. Mallory noticed Mark and Jessie slip back in and sit down. Monroe moved to take Garrett's place at the front. Garrett sat next to Mallory and patted her knee in platonic comfort. He really was a nice guy.

"Right, well, we need a game plan. Mallory and I will stay here for a few days until the press calms down over this story. Then, we can go to my house or a safe house. Not sure what would be the best option, so we'll have to reassess then."

Mallory leaned over to Garrett and whispered. He spoke aloud to Monroe. "Mallory has something to say." All eyes were on Mallory, and she grimaced at Garrett and then Monroe.

"Just say it, honey," said no-help Monroe.

"Um, well, I need to get some of my things. My clothes and everyday stuff."

Monroe shook his head. "Not happening. The girls can go into your place and grab what you need, but under no circumstances are you going anywhere that others can identify you. Not for a while."

"I don't see why not. I can do it myself. It will be so much easier than trying to describe things to others. I will remember things I need as I walk through the house. Besides, I have plants that are likely dead by now."

"I saved your plants. I grabbed them yesterday," said Ivy. "I took them home. When you're ready for them, I'll deliver them."

"Oh, that was kind of you. Thanks."

Kaden grabbed his wife's hand. "You what?"

"I grabbed her plants. I didn't know what to grab for her, but when I saw the poor babies wilting, and I knew it might be a while before Mallory returned, I grabbed them. A person was waiting in their car for someone, and he stared at me like I had done something wrong. I told him I bought them from my sister's friend when he asked. But when the man asked the friend's name, I gave him a disgusted look and said he didn't act like he lived there. I said I should probably call security. He left the parking lot."

Monroe asked, "How did you get in past the gate?"

"Um, I drove through it because the lock wasn't engaged."

Jessie added, "It wasn't the first time either." Becky nodded her agreement.

Mallory added, "That's true more times than management will admit."

Kaden was not happy, and it was the first time Mallory had seen him even come close to getting upset. "What the hell, Ivy? Have you learned nothing from your recent adventures?"

"I learned not to take anyone with me and to do it myself. That way, no one is in danger."

"Besides my wife, you mean?"

Ivy seemed a little lost, and Mallory watched as Kaden stood and walked out of the room, shuffling Ivy along with him. There were a few heated words, then five flat-handed swats on a jeans-covered ass were easily discernable, then a few more words. No one seemed disturbed.

"I thought you said it was a private thing," whispered Mallory to Monroe, who had moved closer.

Monroe grinned. "Except spanking. It can be public among us. That happens wherever it needs to."

"Oh. I'm not so sure about that. I have a reputation that public chastisement won't be good for."

"And you won't lose it. They will come back and be fine. Watch. No one will mention it."

When the couple returned from their meeting in the other room, Ivy seemed a little pouty, but none the worse for the swats. Kaden seemed relaxed and not irritated at all. They sat down again, and Kaden drew Ivy close, kissing the top of her head and pulling her back into him.

"Now, where was I?" asked Monroe. "Oh yes. Mallory, you will not go to your place, especially if it isn't secure at all times. In fact, we are going to have to discuss that issue later."

Jac stood. "And that goes for all of you, ladies. Understood?" He made eye contact with every woman in the room and waited until they all agreed before he sat down again.

Monroe nodded. "Now, moving on."

"But you never answered my question," said Mallory.

"Make me a list of what you need, and I'll take one of the guys."

"I'll figure it out," said Mallory.

"I'll go with the guys, so there is a woman there. I'll take my phone, and we'll video chat as I walk through your place so you can see what I see, and if you remember something not on the list, I can grab it."

Mallory smiled her relief. "Thank you, but won't you get in trouble?"

"Pfft. I'm a team member, and I can go. Right, Jac?" she said a bit louder.

"With escort." Sharlee winked at Mallory and turned back to her computer.

Garrett and Jac resumed the briefing, which lasted for another fifteen minutes, covering the lost and found victims and those still missing that they hoped to find. Mallory had explained again about the impression there was a wife, but she hadn't seen her. Mallory also described why she believed the kidnapper was going to go and later, when exactly she didn't know, return, remove the other woman and make Mallory his primary focus. She sobbed the last sentence and shuddered at the memory. Monroe shocked Mallory by pulling her into his lap.

"Monroe," Mallory whispered frantically as she tried to scramble out of his lap.

His arms tightened, and he gruffly whispered back. "Stop. We comfort our women around here, and I don't care if this makes you feel uneasy or worried about other's thoughts on the subject. You'll get used to it. I won't embarrass you with your own colleagues or anything, but I don't want you to think I won't do what I have to for you. Always. Right now, you need me wrapped around you while you go through these memories." With that, he pulled her close and laid her head on his shoulder. "Just accept that I care enough to give you what you need."

Her sigh of acceptance signaled her submission, if not her complete understanding. She nodded as she took a deep, cleansing breath and then let it out before resuming the conversation. Monroe nodded with affection shining in his eyes. It was way too early to think it might be love. Way too early.

Jac continued. "Did you get a read on his thinking?"

Mallory sat up. "It was as though Romaine," she paused after saying his name for the first time, then continued. "It was like he could only deal with one captive at a time. Like he'd taken me before he was ready. He said something like, 'she'll be gone soon. We just have to be patient.'"

Monroe's strength shone through his tenderness. "Easy, honey. Take your time."

She took a shaky breath and leaned into Monroe. When she spoke again, her voice was more assertive, more detached. "Romaine said she was taking longer to die than he had thought, and he actually apologized that his attentions were divided."

Mark asked, "You were in a cellar, right?"

"Yes. A dark, damp, chilly cellar. Not a basement because there weren't footsteps above us as you would expect in a basement. Also, the floor was dirt, the stairs were wooden."

Mark was thinking. "And how many times did he come down to check on you two?"

"That's the odd thing. He didn't come back. I mean, someone threw down a burlap bag of potatoes and carrots and a jug of water, but that was it. The other woman never spoke to me nor regained full consciousness, but she was alive."

Levi asked, "How did you know?" The room was silent, as though everyone was letting him process his own question. "Oh, right, a pharmacist is a doctor."

"Besides, you don't have to be a doctor to know if someone is breathing or not," said Sharlee.

"I guess my real question was how did you know she was not awake and just staying quiet because of the fear. No offense, but she'd gone through a lot in the time she had been there, and we don't even know how long that was."

"Actually," said Jac, "we do. If what Mallory said is true for all the women, he didn't concentrate on a new one until the old one had died, which means we check the known dates of abduction and work backward to when each woman likely died."

"Did he say what he did for a living?" asked Carter.

"No, honestly, after he finished slapping me around because I wouldn't quit fighting him or yelling, he told me about what I already told you and that he'd never played with a pharmacist before. He said nothing else to anyone that I heard."

"Wait," said Monroe, "Were those his words? 'I've never played with a pharmacist before?'"

"Yes, why?"

Garrett looked at Monroe, and that non-verbal thing they did happened again. "Well, tell me," she demanded impatiently.

"Listen to those words, 'played with a pharmacist.' What does that make you think of?"

"I don't..." Mallory's eyes grew large. "You don't think..."

Monroe nodded. "I do. I mean, it's a possibility we have to explore. It could mean something totally different, like a cat-and-mouse thing, but we need to check everything out."

"Wait," said Sharlee, "It could have meant that he chose her because she had a different profession than the others. We should look at what the others did for a living. Once we identify them."

"You mean I wasn't random. It was all set up so that man could grab me specifically."

"Possibly." Sharlee's fingers flew over the keys.

"Then maybe the woman who dropped her groceries at just the right time *was* his wife," continued Mallory. "I thought she was older, but maybe not."

Monroe shifted in his seat, moving Mallory with him. She tried to get up, but he gave her a warning look. She settled back down.

"Okay, so the easiest is to start with what we know. How many groups did you attend before meeting me?"

"Three."

Monroe nodded. "At the same place?"

"No, I tried three different ones and only repeated a group with you."

"Okay, we start with those four places to see if he knew you before he snagged you."

"Monroe, I would have recognized him."

"Not necessarily. Unless the groups were so small, it would have been inevitable that you saw or spoke to everyone. I know the one we met at had thirty or forty people. I know we didn't meet them all."

"I have been operating on the assumption that he didn't know me, but he knew I was a pharmacist. I never disclose more than my first name with customers, nor when I go to munches or clubs. Everything else private is off-limits, and those attending the munches, or parties, didn't even know I was a pharmacist. No one even knew I wasn't from their town or close. The other three I did in different towns, away from Lexington."

"Well, we have to start somewhere. It could be someone who had tried and was denied entrance because of his inappropriateness for that environment. He could have been outside waiting. We have to explore it."

"And my pharmacy?"

"Yes," said Jac. "Everywhere they might have run into you routinely. So, Monroe, you and Garrett work on Mallory's routine and isolate those places he could have seen her or where she frequents often. Then check those out."

"I go only a few places routinely. Wouldn't this guy have to work?"

Mark nodded. "Good point. Jac, you need to get everything the Feds have on Romaine, including his full name and occupation. Family members would be a good place too, but Sharlee will have to work on that because they will be off-limits to us."

Garrett nodded, and Jac stood. "Agreed. Let's divide up the assignments and make the bodyguard schedule. Get Mallory's things, without Mallory going," the look Jacquard gave to the newest member of his "family" was impossible to misunderstand. "Am I understood?"

"Yes. I've agreed already."

"Good. Now let's get this done. I'll call Arturo and find out what new info he has and let you know what we find out."

"Wait, what am I going to do?" asked Mallory as Monroe stood her up in front of him before he followed suit. "I will not be a victim in all this. I was proactive and got away. Now I want to help with the rest."

"Take a nap. Read a book. Stay inside," said Monroe.

"But I'll go stir crazy. You aren't listening to me."

Monroe moved her to a corner of the room. He crossed his arms, making him seem huge. Mallory didn't care.

"I hear you loud and clear, but you aren't listening to me. You are high profile, in danger, and hurt right now. So the answer is anything you want but stay inside."

"I'm not a child."

"Then you had better stop acting like one who isn't getting a treat. I will bring you in on things when I can. However, I refuse to risk your life, and if you thought hard from my point of view, you'd see someone could still be out there looking to kill you, with or without torture. Do. You. Get. Me? You are in danger."

"But whoever they are, they can't win. I won't be able to handle that."

Monroe drew her into his arms and kissed the top of her head. "I know. I promise we will finish this. Now, please, practice your submission and stay inside."

"You won't leave me out of the loop?"

"Promise if you follow what I say you have to do." He raised his brows ominously.

"Fine."

He kissed her lips. "Good, now answer me properly."

"Yes, sir." Her pout was uncontainable.

"Mallory, we can go for a swim," offered Ivy from the doorway. Mallory turned her attention to Ivy.

"Really, that would be great, only I don't have a suit, and Mr. Rules here says I can't go outside." Mallory graced Monroe with a sour face.

Monroe raised his eyebrows. "Keep it up, woman. I would remember what I do for entertainment, baby."

"Monroe," she hissed.

Mallory melted at this part of Monroe, but it embarrassed her when he openly referred to it. His way of kink floated her boat, so to speak. She was wired the same way he was, and by the sound of it, the same way these people were. And acceptance was apparent. How refreshing it was not to have to hide her inner desires from others, even if it was an intimate group of Monroe's colleagues.

Jessie laughed as she came to stand next to Ivy. "We all know he has a rubber paddle in the glove box of his car."

Mallory's eyes widened. "You do?"

Sharlee laughed. "It's Monroe's standard threat if we don't do what they think we should. These men. Honestly."

Jessie added. "And we crave it. Well, unless they are having a session on our ass because we didn't do what they wanted. These men have a hang-up about safety and health. I mean, most men do for their women, but these guys..."

Ivy wiggled her eyebrows. "Even that can turn into sexy times."

Carter shooed Ivy and Mallory toward the door to the pool, but before they left the room, Jac sent Sharlee to take a break, then head to the office. Becky went with Sharlee. As Becky passed Carter, she gave him a wink. He swatted her backside playfully. Mallory marveled at the ease with which this group of people felt with each other. It was a little awkward, but it was more invigorating.

Mark sent Jessie home to take a nap.

"I'm not an invalid, Mark. I'm pregnant. My job isn't taxing." Jessie's hands landed on her hips.

"Physically, I agree. If it were, we would be having a different discussion. It is mentally exhausting. We've been at the debriefing for over an hour, and you worked this morning."

"Mark, it's my job."

His hand reached up and smoothed her hair. Jessie didn't flinch. In fact, she leaned into his hand. The longing in Mallory's belly to be able to do that without recoiling burned. "Please, just take an hour. If you feel like working after that, I won't complain."

"Okay. Just an hour." Mark drew Jessie into his arms and kissed her. "Thank you."

Mallory watched the interaction with interest. Here, Mark started with a demand and a face to match. Mallory wouldn't have been able to answer him back without cringing. Jessie had no trouble disagreeing without breaking a sweat. Mark softened after their dance and clash of wills, and Jessie yielded with a hook. It was a dance and one she could believe they often did.

Monroe leaned into Mallory. "Hey."

"Hey. I'm going swimming."

"I know. Ivy is waiting for you at the door." He nodded in the direction of Mark and Jessie. "Learn anything?"

She turned to him. "How did you know?"

He chuckled deviously. "I told you I watch everything about you. I'll be working in Jac's office while you swim." He kissed her, turning her in the direction of the doorway. "Now, go." He swatted her butt, and before today, doing that in public with anyone in the room would have set her off. Now she glowed warmly inside.

She needed to shake off the residual effects of the afternoon's debriefing, so she followed Jessie to the pool, and they both borrowed suits to swim in.

"You can bring one to leave here if you like. Becky doesn't like to share suits, and Sharlee wears black and navy suits only. But Ivy and I don't have any problem sharing. I mean, we all were tested soon after becoming exclusive with our men, so there aren't any issues there, and the guys have to be tested after they change girlfriends, or monthly, so everyone is squeaky clean."

"Oh, I don't think I've ever been tested for STDs."

"No? Not even this time in the hospital? Well, I have twice. Once when I got with Kaden, and then the second time when we got back together."

"Oh, you mean you broke up and then got back together?"

"Yes. I'll tell you my story since I already know yours. Well, this last week and all. Fair is fair. It will also help you know why Kaden and I are getting married next month."

THE EVENING MEAL WAS quiet. Mallory had gone back and swam a second time after Ivy had gone home. She had done some laps as Sharlee sat in the water with Storm and let her son play around her. After playtime, Finley, the toddler's nanny, came to take him out. Sharlee then turned to Mallory.

"How are you holding up with all the changes in the last few days?"

Mallory wasn't easily impressed or intimidated. She liked the confidence of Sharlee, but she had to admit that there was a minor concern about whether or not the other woman would take to her. She knew that Sharlee, being married to the boss and being a force of nature in her own right, Mallory needed to connect to what was essentially the Alpha female of this group.

"It's a challenge, but Monroe is helping me handle it, and of course, all of you."

Sharlee leaned back against the side of the pool and kicked her legs. "So, Monroe said you had a lot in common."

"We do. It surprised me because most of the guys I have met in the last few years have been immature or weren't a good match. I mean, by this time in one's life, you would expect guys to be more put together. More in tune with themselves and the world around them. I have found that is not the norm."

"Monroe is older than you, so I imagine he does seem more secure and confident."

Mallory scrunched up her face. "It's more than that. My job or my doctorate did not intimidate Monroe."

Sharlee nodded. "He was impressed with you, taken with you, actually, which is why we started looking for you. He didn't want to let you go without knowing why."

"I'm glad he didn't just walk away. Even though I was out of immediate danger, his presence stopped me from losing my mind in fear and panic when everyone descended on me. They wanted me to talk immediately about what happened, and I could hardly believe I was safe. Actually, I didn't believe it until he showed up."

Sharlee was quiet for a few moments. When she did speak, it was in appreciation for Mallory seeing the good in her friend. "Monroe is such a nice guy, and honestly, he has been one that didn't see any reason to do more than play and go home. He likes the more regimented lifestyle of being a professed dominant, but I think he just had found no one he connected with on a deeper level than play. Then he found you."

Mallory stopped treading water and floated on her back against the wall next to Sharlee. "Monroe settles me, and how could you not fall for a man that is present when he is with you? We love mysteries, going for long drives, quirky wine, and late-night dinners and board games. We haven't been able to do any of that together, but we can now."

Sharlee smiled. "I think you are as smitten with him as he is with you."

"Smitten?" Mallory laughed. "Yes, you're probably right. The things we connect on aren't anything fancy or different from the things others connect on, but it's huge for me. He doesn't compete with my job, and I'm okay with him not disclosing about his."

"I can see why Monroe is so taken with you. You're his dream come to life. Granted, Monroe and Garrett are both men to keep their secrets to themselves, and Monroe had kept your budding relationship secret until he couldn't. I'm so glad he found you. You're going to fit in perfectly with our group."

"I hope so because I know Monroe loves you all. I just want to be a part of his life. But..."

"But?"

Mallory shook her head and gave a depreciating laugh. "Nothing. Thank you for letting me stay here for a few days. I know that it put you out."

"Are you kidding? We have more house than we will ever use, so it's great to share when we can. And some of the others have used it for this very reason on previous occasions, but I'm not letting you off the hook. What were you going to say?" Sharlee could be as demanding as her husband with the same air of compliance expectation.

"Just that if Monroe decides he doesn't want to be long-term with me, I'll be devastated."

Sharlee nodded. "I get it, but don't worry. I've watched him with you. He's in it for the long haul."

"What are you ladies chatting about?" asked Jac.

"Us? Nothing." Sharlee's shrug and grin said the opposite. Mallory looked down as she tried to busy her hands by rearranging her suit.

Jac and Monroe walked to the side of the pool. Jac helped Sharlee and Monroe put out his hand for Mallory. The metal sheet came down outside to cover the large window to the side yard that the pool looked out over during the day.

"This place reminds me of Fort Knox," said Mallory.

Jac nodded as he dried Sharlee's hair. "Good, then you will know how protected you are. You might get a decent night's sleep."

"Only if I don't dream."

"If you still have disruptive dreams in another few days, I'll get my physician out here to prescribe something to help."

Mallory shook her head. "I'll assess my need when I get home. I imagine I'll have dreams for a while. But thank you for the offer."

Jac nodded and then gave Monroe a look. Monroe answered the nonverbal communication. "She's the pharmacist, but I'll keep a close eye." And that didn't offend Mallory in the slightest.

Chapter 7

That was the second dream tonight, and Monroe couldn't stand that his girl was so terrified in her sleep. He padded into her room and pushed her over in the bed.

"It's Monroe, baby. Move over."

"Monroe?" she asked. She was still breathing hard, and her arm was clammy.

"Move over. I'm sleeping with you, and maybe you'll feel safe enough to sleep."

"I don't know if I can go back to sleep."

"Come, lay on me." She scooted closer. "Keep going. Lay on me."

She hesitated and seemed to peer into the half-light of the room at him longingly. "There is plenty of room over here."

"But what about you sleeping?"

"I'm sleeping with you. I'm perfectly content."

Mallory giggled. "I guess they made these beds for your team because they are huge."

"Probably, or when we have something warm and cuddly to sleep with." He brought Mallory up against his side with her head on his chest for a pillow.

"You are kind of hard to snuggle up to. Not much soft-ness."

He laughed. "That's your job, to bring the cushion. You don't want your man to be soft. Anywhere."

He pressed his erection against her belly and groaned when her fingers grazed over the soft spongy top, spreading his pre-cum around his manhood and sliding her hand down his shaft.

"Don't start something you can't finish, woman." His rough, gravel-toned words making her shiver and leak her own arousal fluids.

"And before you answer that, you are still very sore and hurt, and we don't have a handle on what your triggers are."

"Oh, I can finish, but you're right, I do hurt. That and I haven't done any of this in a while. I'm no virgin, but I'm out of practice." She continued to slide her hand up and down his stiffness as he moaned his enjoyment.

"I like the sound of that because if what I'm experiencing is your lack of practice, I'll die happy when I've had my wicked way with you a few times."

Monroe's hand slid up her belly to her ample breasts and played whisper softly. He weighted each mound, then squeezed them tenderly, then more purposefully. Mallory arched into his hands and moaned. He followed that up by teasing her nipples, rubbing, and stretching them carefully. Next, he pinched them, which brought on a squeal, then another moan. He removed himself from her grasp.

"So responsive, you make me want to play with you for a long time."

Finally, when he thought she was getting too aroused for continued play, he stopped to her immediate whine.

"Hush baby, I'm not stopping; I'm changing things up." His hand came down her tummy to her curls between her thighs. "So soft."

He worked his fingers down into her panties, and the wetness that already painted her inner thighs and muff now coated his fingers. Kissing her lips, he shifted to the bottom of the bed. Positioning himself between her legs, he spread them further apart. Fingers and a palm slid down to cover her womanly attributes, and Monroe slapped her hand.

"Oh," she said as she jerked it back.

"Never cover yourself from me. Not in daily life, and not when we play. I love looking at you. If you want to use your safe word, that's fine, but don't try to stop me otherwise because there are consequences for telling your Dom no."

Monroe looked into Mallory's eyes and could see her relaxing and submitting. After what had happened to her, he wondered if it was going to be too much for her. They had never had sex. That was not what one did at a meet and greet. It was to explore, but nothing more than a spanking or getting your partner off and possibly a demo. Monroe had done those things with Mallory, but now she had nothing but a nightshirt on.

Now, she would have no panties, and if he could work it, no shirt either by the time they were done. "Mallory? What's your color, baby? Are you hurting, scared?"

"What? No, no, I'm okay."

"Did you understand me about covering?"

"Yes, I understand. Sorry, sir."

"Good girl. Now, if there is anything that I ever do that upsets you, I had better hear that word. Or once we work through the problem, your ass is going to be a red mess when I get done with it. This is all just sexy fun, but being your Dom means more than that. It extends past the bedroom doors and into our everyday lives. I'm not over the top, but I'm certainly not docile about it."

"Okay, sir, I understand, but you don't have to, you know..."

"Taste you?" She gave him a slight nod. "You're right. I don't have to, but why would I deny my own pleasure while giving you yours? I can't wait to taste you. So, are you ready for my remedy to sleep soundly?"

She wiggled in anticipation. "Yes, sir."

He opened her channel with his tongue. He held her open with his fingers and set about charging into her molten area of need. Licking and sucking on her, stabbing her deep, hot entrance with his tongue as he played with her breasts, his sounds of enjoyment seemed to excite her. He could feel his own cock stiffening more, and the tweak of pain surrounding that hardness was incredible.

She wiggled and then cried out as he bounced his hand off her outer thigh. "No moving, sweetness."

"But..."

He spanked her other thigh. "Do I need to stop and give you a spanking so you will do as you're told?"

"But... what if I can't?" her concern made him smile.

His reply was matter of fact. "You can, or there will be consequences, baby."

Going back to his teasing and tasting, his sweetheart kept as still as he knew she was able. She strained to hold back her gratification, but it was time for her to go back to sleep. Monroe rubbed the side of her clit, and then, just as she arched and stiffened, he pinched it and watched her explode in blazing glory.

Monroe observed her closely as he kept steady pressure on her clit and two fingers in her depths, drifting along the walls as they, like Mallory, undulated, writhing in ecstasy. He'd never seen anything so beautiful in his life and certainly never in his bed to sleep. As she released the final vestiges of her climax, he rubbed his face on her sheet, drew her close, and listened to her soft snore a few minutes later.

Mine was all Monroe could think of. Mallory was all his, and he would slay all her dragons and annihilate all her enemies to wipe away all her fears. He breathed in her slight floral scent and her muskiness still on his face and smiled. Time to take care of business, starting with finding out all about the man that dared take his woman and find any of his accomplices.

JEANNE LOOKED AT THE place she had called home for over fifteen years. She had been the first woman that Master had ever brought home. She had learned a lot about him over the years, and while she had hated him at first for stealing her away from all she loved, she had learned to love him in an odd, desperate way. Even more, she learned to crave him and his way with women.

He demanded that Jeanne call him Master, but when he had tried to join a group of others he said were like-minded, he was almost immediately ousted because of his enthusiasm. He said they were all just amateurs and not really masters like he was, so he had left. At first, she had her doubts, especially in the beginning, when she didn't long for his cruel touch. That was a long time ago, but it marked the time when her master changed.

Three years after Jeanne's abduction, another woman showed up. Master had laughed when she had begged him to let her go. Margo was her name. But he'd said he needed more than just Jeanne. Then when Margo had mysteriously disappeared, another woman immediately took her place, and so it had gone on until last week when he brought home the pharmacist, Mallory.

He had been so happy and would have had her to play with, but his job called him away for the week. The captive had run when someone drove into the driveway after she tossed down more water for Mallory. She'd assumed the other woman had died by now. Master had been very clear that Jeanne must ensure that Mallory was alive when he arrived home on Friday evening.

Jeanne could see that the car had stopped at the wrong place and watched it back out of the drive. Good. She went back into the house and didn't recheck the cellar until the following day. When she called out, she didn't get an answer from anyone. She hadn't gotten one the other two times, but this was odd, and she hadn't locked the door. No one had escaped before, and she felt positive this Mallory's fear would stop her from trying as well.

But she had been wrong, and now, the police had torn up her house, taken her master, and found women buried on her property. All because of Mallory. Her master would never return. He would rot in jail forever, leaving her alone with no one to take care of her. Her life was ruined, all because of that pharmacist, Mallory. She would find her and make that demon woman pay for destroying her life.

Chapter 8

Mallory woke refreshed as the sun streamed into the bedroom window. During the night, she woke twice with two horrible dreams where her kidnapper had stolen her out from under Monroe's protection. Still, after the second nightmare, Monroe had made her relaxed and tired with his incredible fingers and tongue. She'd been like a limp rag and had slept in his arms until he left the bed sometime this morning.

She showered and walked into the kitchen to coffee and the man she had glimpsed last night in the kitchen, now making a scrumptious scramble for breakfast. Monroe and Jac looked up as she grabbed a cup and poured coffee.

"Hello, sweetheart. Did you get enough sleep?" Monroe stood and dropped a kiss on her lips. That he did it in front of Jac didn't bother her. Monroe was changing her already.

"I did, thank you. How about you?"

"I watched you sleep for a few minutes, then I was out like a light."

Jac reached for the plate the chef was handing him. "Sex will do that to you."

"You should know," said Sharlee as she waltzed in, holding Storm with Finley right behind her.

"I should indeed." He held his hands out for his son, and Sharlee leaned in closer so Jac could lift their son from her arms.

"Mmm, breakfast smells wonderful, Robert. Thank you," Sharlee said as he poured coffee for her.

After taking a sip of her sweet, creamy coffee, Sharlee leaned back in the chair and sighed. "I have to go into the office today, so I can go dumpster diving with Kaden, but what is today's goal?"

Monroe, who was always the keeper of the plans, explained what they would work on and what they needed from Sharlee and Kaden.

"And what about me?" asked Mallory.

"Nothing. You are to be a woman of leisure until we have eradicated the threat." Monroe took another bite of his cooling breakfast.

Mallory replaced her fork on her plate and pushed her plate away. "I can't do that. I've not had a list of tasks to complete since the ninth grade. That was when I learned if I worked hard, my grades would equal college money."

Monroe took his last bite of toast. "Well, then you can put together a list of places you have been in the last two weeks prior to your abduction, highlighting any routine or multiple stops. Then I need a list of the employees at your work, adding any strange occurrences or strange people you have encountered, not just customers."

"Then what?" asked Mallory.

"Then you show it to me. We'll work on those lists to see if there's anyone that might have been connected to this guy or you." Monroe turned to Jac. "Did you get verification on the perp's name and demographics?"

Jac paused in his play with his son. "I did. Craig Romaine is correct. I'll send you the rest. Does that name ring a bell, Mallory?"

She thought for a moment and then shook her head. "I don't think so. I will always remember his face, though, and it seems like I should know him, but I just don't. Do we have a picture of his wife?"

Jac shook his head. "No wife. He has never married, it seems. Guess your thoughts that he had a wife were off, or he has a significant other, and they haven't married."

Monroe leaned back in his chair. "Could she have been the woman who dropped her groceries, like you wondered?"

"I don't know, do I. The name seems familiar, but it isn't, and yet his face haunts me. He said there was a wife, but I can't verify enough to prove it. Someone could be out there looking for me because I got away, and I have nowhere to look. We don't know if Romaine has an accomplice, and I can only sleep when I'm with you. Now, how worse can my life get?"

"Mal..."

"Don't Mal me. It's not your life that's been turned upside down. Not you who's afraid of your own shadow unless someone is close by. My life is in ruins, I need to set it to rights, and I can't see a way to fix t."

Sharlee reached out her hand and lightly touched her thigh. "I think I get it. My experience is like yours. It takes time to figure things out, and I'm not telling you anything you don't already know. What you aren't accepting is that you aren't Superwoman. It isn't something you did or said to make you a target, and just because you have head knowledge doesn't mean you can accept it."

"I'm a broken mess. I can't even go to work the job I love. I don't even want to go back to The Apothecary, maybe never."

Monroe placed his hand over hers on the table. "You will as soon as we're sure you're safe. But until then, I'm not taking any chances, so it isn't you can't go because you are incapable, but because I won't let you, not yet."

She yanked her hand back. "You don't understand. I can't see people I don't know for fear someone else tries to steal me off the street. It's illogical, I know, but I still feel it. My chest hurts just thinking about it." Mallory's voice cracked in the fierceness of her emotion.

"Maybe not intimately, but I do," said Sharlee. "I understand the terror at the thought that it might happen again and how you measure every interaction, every step to see if it opens you up, makes you more vulnerable to being taken again. You analyze every move you made before the abduction to see where you misstepped. What judgment call caused you to be kidnapped. It's worse when you find there is none because that means that you don't have the power to prevent it from ever happening again." Sharlee paused. "How close am I?"

The sobbing that suddenly erupted answered her question. Monroe's arms surrounded Mallory, and he automatically drew her into his lap. The dining chairs were generous because of the men that frequently sat in them, and Monroe was never more thankful than right now. He had a fleeting thought that he needed to ensure they had generously sized seating in their place.

Mallory had not broken down like this since he saw her in the hospital, and he figured it was about time. Everyone else left the room as Monroe held his girl tight and let her mourn the loss of her safety, the fear of her continued protection, and her lack of control. While Mallory had never mentioned it, she was mourning her loss of power in her life.

Not only when she was kidnapped here, but now after the event was over, she still didn't choose where she went, what she did, or where her thoughts and fears took her. Romaine may not have violated her sexually, but he violated every other part of her mind and body. Monroe's fury was erupting in him. It was a rage that he could do nothing about until they knew everything about this Romaine guy and who the accomplice was because Monroe believed Mallory when she said there was someone else. It was a matter of discovering who that person was and apprehending them.

Having his capable woman fall apart was good in that he could build her up from here on, but bad because it wounded him that he wasn't able to protect her then and, in some ways, now. The outside world wasn't a problem, but her inner demons had to be demolished as well. That would take more than him to kill them off. It would take her hard work, coupled with his and her new friends' support.

"Mallory, baby, are you feeling better?"

Her laugh was wobbly. "In some ways, but not in others. I was a blubbering idiot. I'm sorry. You have to be so embarrassed."

"Stop it. Look, sweetheart. There is nothing to be ashamed of, and I'm so proud you allowed me to comfort you. Our relationship started off different in that we played a little before we ever went on a date. Our first meaningful discussion was to negotiate our limits in play."

"Are you saying we did this backward?"

"Not at all. But it was only after playing some that we talked about more personal things for hours on the phone. I still haven't taken you on a proper date. When I had planned on wining and dining you, life changed in a flash. I have you back now, but some pieces are cracked, and I am trying to help you glue things back together."

"It's too much to ask you to do. You wanted a whole person. I can't offer you that."

"Fuck, baby, I want *you*. I want every fractured and splinter piece. It doesn't matter if you are put together perfectly or find some of your bits don't fit quite right anymore. I want you, the real you and not one I couldn't be comfortable with. We all have cracks and crevices we didn't have before, but it makes us who we are. I want who you are. If you can take me as I am, then I say, we make a go of this connection we have. Let's not waste it."

Monroe cuddled her back in his arms and gently rocked Mallory as she digested one of the longest speeches he had ever made to a woman. This one mattered. He hadn't known how much until she verbally spewed her tainted way of seeing herself, and his reaction to that imperfect being had been visceral.

Monroe knew with absolute certainty that if she allowed him, he would claim her forever. She was likely not ready for a lifelong commitment, but he was sure she wanted it. There just needed to be more chipping away at her archaic ideas of how a man expected his woman. Wasn't that supposed to be his line? His perfect woman would learn his standards were more reachable than the ones she imagined.

Mallory sat up slowly, stretched out her legs, and stood. "How do you feel?"

"Good. Much better than earlier. I'll get on those lists."

Monroe decided now was the best time to teach his girl what he expected and how he expected it. He grabbed onto her hand and kissed the palm before standing.

"New rule."

Mallory gave him a spunky look, and he grinned. "Oh, a new rule, huh? I might disagree."

"Oh, I have a feeling you will be all for this new rule."

He drew her closer to himself and leaned down. His lips were a hair's breadth from hers, and his tongue came out to trace her lips, wetting them for her. She bit the bottom one, and he could imagine her biting his lip. The direct heat from that thought shot through his gut into his stiffening member. Concentrate, Merton.

"Open your mouth, baby, and let me in. You can't leave me to do anything else until you kiss me. A real, heart-pumping kiss."

"I can't do that everywhere, Monroe. It's an impractical rule."

"Nonetheless, you will do it until further notice. Now kiss me."

"But..."

"I can pull rank on you and make you suck me off before you leave, naked after I paddle your ass rosy-red with my rubber paddle. I just thought that while I would love that, you might have something to say about it in the common areas. Now, doesn't a kiss sound much less harmless?"

"Nothing is harmless with you, Sir, but I will kiss you to avoid the more socially unacceptable things."

His slow grin spread across his face. "Then stop talking."

His head descended, and Monroe kissed deeply, drawing sustenance from her lips, his chest pushing against her pert nipples that hardened in her arousal. The kiss was eternal, and Monroe was sure they would end up on the tabletop if he didn't rein it in. One of the hardest things he'd ever done was pull away from Mallory. His forehead landed on hers, and he kissed her nose and calmed his breathing. His cock was going to be standing at attention for a while. He could see Mal was affected as well. Good.

She wanted more, and this was not the time. "Later, baby."

"What was it about not starting what you can't finish?"

"Brat. I can finish, but the parameters stay the same. You are hurting, and I don't think Robert wants to clean off a table we have had a little morning wake-up on. Besides, we have work to do, and you have some lists to make. Come find me when you want to discuss what you have."

"What about if I want to discuss this right here?"

"That happens after work. Tonight I expect you in my bed."

"Isn't that chauvinistic? What about my bed, my sore body?" She was cute when she tried to pout. She didn't know how to brat, and that was fun all by itself.

"I have all the toys in my room." He raised his eyebrow and watched her. Her whimper and roaming hands told him he was in for the ride of his life.

"Oh, okay, you win for now." She turned and shook her backside enticingly. He swatted it hard. The sting would stick with her for a few minutes at least. His hand was certainly tingling.

"Oh." Her hand flew back to soothe her butt.

"No rubbing."

She rubbed anyway, and Monroe shook his head. Her genuine personality was showing, and she was a sassy one. He liked it. He liked it a lot.

Monroe was a firm but careful Dom and an attentive lover. He never forced, but often encouraged, his play partner to push her boundaries. He suspected that pushing her boundaries would not be the issue. It was trying to rein in her explorations that would be the greater challenge. She had already shown that if she saw a need, she rushed in, head-first, into the troubled waters without considering her own immediate safety.

While she would never have helped the woman pick up her groceries if she had even an inkling that the act would put Mallory in danger, helping was in her nature. He didn't want to discourage that, just the way she went about it. He walked into Sharlee's computer room and got to work.

Chapter 9

It was near the end of the day, and Monroe was restless and disheartened. They had tried to locate where Craig Romaine worked, but he didn't seem to have worked anywhere. Monroe told Sharlee to look at the social security or tax records, but Jac put his foot down at her breaking into the federal databases.

"I have my contact for that kind of information. Arturo has asked for another interview with Mallory. I have requested he do it here. He is going to see if he can get authorization for that. However, I clarified that she was to do it with us in attendance and her attorney or not at all."

Kaden walked in the door and said, "Hell yeah, they have to do it here. Didn't we learn from law enforcement's less than kind tactics with Ivy? Have you put in a call to Ryker?"

"I've called him, and he agreed to be here whenever anyone wants to talk to her. He wants to meet her and read the reports. Since she doesn't work for me, Ryker needs Mallory to pay him a dollar to officially retain his services."

"I don't want her to do it at all," said Monroe. "But if she does, you're right about the circumstances."

"I want to help, Monroe."

Monroe looked up to see Mallory in the doorway, her arms crossed. His girl was feisty, but there were some things she would have to know he wouldn't give in on and keeping her safe was one of them.

"If they come here, then we can monitor the interview with Ryker, and I'll be fine with that."

Mallory took a step into the room and leaned against the wall; arms still folded. "I interviewed without you the first time, and they were not pushy at all."

"Because you were in the hospital and had just been found. They would have had their asses handed to them by the hospital staff and, later, me if they were anything but careful. They knew Jac was attached to this case the minute you asked for me."

"Then why did Jac have to vouch for you?"

Jac answered. "It's a game with the Feds. I make them verify their people, and they reciprocate. The difference is I vet my people and theirs... well, let's say things can change. I checked Gutierrez's record from his first case. They vouched, and I vetted. That is the only reason he can come here at all."

"Who is Ryker?"

Jac lifted his head. "He's our attorney. He has a small firm and is U.S. Army, retired. After he graduated college, he went to law school and then military law. When his wife died in a home invasion while living in post housing, he had to change the direction of his life. It was another soldier that murdered his wife, and his office had to defend the man."

"Oh, no. How devastating for the poor man. Did they convict?"

Jac nodded. "They did, but it was little comfort, as I'm sure you can understand. He finished his time, retired, and came here when I asked him to be our legal counsel. He has been with me from the beginning and has done everything from criminal to civil to corporate law. You'll like him."

"I'm sure I will." Mallory sat on the sofa and laid her head on her palms. "I just want to do whatever it takes to get this over and done with, and if that means another interview, then so be it."

Monroe spoke with conviction. "I'm good with that if it's well attended." He walked to the desk to grab a sheet of paper. "New subject. The lists are hard to go through because, in the groups, we only have first names. I don't know if they aren't pseudonyms. If the Fed's want to get the full names with a court order, then so be it, but I understand the need for some anonymity. Sharlee and Kaden will tell us how they think they can make this work better."

Kaden nodded. "Right, I'm going to go through and tap into the surveillance cameras that are around each location of the groups. Mallory can look at them and connect the faces to the names and then Sharlee will run it through her recognition program and try to find last names or real names."

Mallory spoke up. "Then what? Are you going to call them up? I'm not good with that. It will take away their security when going to these events."

Sharlee smiled. "Nope. I don't have to with the recognition program. I can do all sorts of background checks with a name and a face, even telling you where most of them were when you were taken. And I can probably tell you if you have crossed paths."

"But," said Jac, "all that takes time, and we are short on that. We have to figure out if there is an accomplice, so using old-fashioned groundwork will go a long way in finding that out. And networking. So if you are up to another interview, then we might get more information."

"But I don't understand." Mallory pulled her feet under her crisscrossed legs on the sofa. "If the FBI and the local cops don't have certain information, then how can you expect to get it?"

Mark walked in and leaned against the same wall Mallory had earlier. "We do things differently."

"What do you mean, differently?"

Monroe leaned over the sofa back. "Our methods are more goal-oriented because we don't have the same protocols that we must follow to get the job done. If we find tidbits of information, we just follow it instead of talking about it and getting approval. We have a primary target and a plan to get there."

"I don't want anyone arrested because of me," Mallory said decisively, drawing a smile from Monroe.

Carter strolled in and dropped some papers on Sharlee's computer desk. "Nope, Jac would beat our asses. I like to be the one doing the beating."

Monroe laughed and agreed. "Baby, we know what we're doing, and we are careful. Jac, when do you expect to get the information on Romaine back?"

"I imagine they will hold their information for when they get Mallory's interview, a kind of quid pro quo. I'd like to have the information that Mallory will give them before they get it if you know what I mean."

"But if they do all the work, then you don't have to," said Mallory.

"No, they miss things, and we would still have to do the work, but then we'd be behind them." Jac sat next to Sharlee. "If we can show them that we are steps ahead of them, their director will hire us to do part of the job. That will mean they will pay us for what we intend to do anyway, keep you safe, and make sure you only had one maniac after you. I expect a contract in the queue tomorrow morning."

Sharlee spoke up. "Jac, you better see this."

"What's going on?" Jac leaned over to read the intel. "Damn."

Monroe pulled Mallory over into his lap, and she didn't protest. "What is it?"

Jac said, "Looks like our suspicions were correct. That asshole Romaine said that he had an accomplice."

Monroe tightened his hold on Mallory. "That's messed up as fuck. Now we have someone else to find. We have to have those CCTV recordings."

"I'll get to it in the morning. Right now, I'm tired and hungry. I have the recognition program running on certain people we have identified from the party you both attended together and the employees and the office personnel at the townhouse."

"Thank you for doing all of this, Sharlee. I know it's a lot to ask," said Mallory.

"This isn't hard. It just takes time and patience. One of which we have a finite amount of and the other, Monroe has not a trace of in this case," said Sharlee.

Mallory joined Sharlee, laughing at Monroe's expense. "Hey now, I have shown incredible restraint and superhuman patience because you don't know what I've had to do to maintain instead of going into battle mode over this mess with you," he said. The skin around his eyes crinkled in merriment.

Mallory continued to laugh as she stood. Monroe swatted her ass once, hard. She gave him a mock look of offense and a sexy grin before leaving the room. Everyone agreed to leave the work until morning. After a subdued dinner, Monroe stood to follow Mallory upstairs. Jac stopped Monroe before he left.

"This means Mallory can't go home or even to your house. One of the safe houses is an option, but this is the best choice right now."

"Agreed. I'll break it to her. If you hear a ruckus, just ignore it. I have a feeling I'll get some push back."

"She may surprise you."

"She may indeed. Goodnight, Jac."

MONROE WATCHED MALLORY as she stood in front of his bedroom door. "Problem, baby?"

She sighed. "I'm not sure I'm ready for a full-on relationship. I want it, but..."

"I hate to burst your control bubble, but you are already all-in with me, and just because we aren't having intercourse yet, doesn't mean we aren't in a completely committed relationship. Unless you need me to convince you further." He wiggled his eyebrows, and she ignored him.

"Are you sure? I'm more broken than when you met me, and I don't know when I'll be mended enough to give you everything you deserve." Her eyes beseeched him to reassure her, and yet her deflated stance told him she had already answered her own question, but not with the answer he would give.

His arm wrapped around her, and his finger lifted her chin. "You are mine. You are everything I want in a woman and a life partner. When you're ready, I'm going to ask you to be my wife." Mallory shook her head. "When you're ready. Until then, I'm going to plug and spank your ass, kiss you breathless, taste your sweetness and bring you off so many times it will hurt to think about it. I'm going to bind you to my bed, then fuck your mouth, your sweet valley entrance, and your tight backside hole. I will deposit my essence in every place I can. And do you know why? Because you are mine. Questions?"

"One. Can I go to the bathroom first?"

Monroe smiled and shook his head in disbelief. "Good girl." He turned her towards her bedroom. "Get your things and bring them in here. You are officially moving in."

When Mallory had returned with her duffle full of clothes and items Becky and Ivy had gotten for her, she said, "I'm only staying here a few days. I intend to go home after that."

Monroe grabbed her bag and stood it next to him. Then he sat and patted a spot beside him on the bed. When she had taken her place next to him, he grabbed her hands in his.

"Because we have found out there is an accomplice, you won't be able to go home as soon as we would have hoped."

Mallory jerked her hands out from under his, but his big hand clamped down on her thigh, not hurting her but keeping her stationary. "That is unacceptable. I have to do the best I can to put my life back together."

"Baby, it's been a couple of days, that's all."

"I need to go back to work," she said with a type of desperation in her voice.

He cocked his eyebrow. "No, you don't, and I know as well as you do that you are on leave of absence with no definite return date. You had a meltdown over this exact thing this morning, so I know you are stalling. I have told you we are in a relationship. You know the lifestyle I live and the one you want to live with me. There is only room for honesty in that type of trust bond. So, I'll give you another chance to tell me what's going on."

"Or what, you'll spank me?" Her belligerence was a good smokescreen that a less experienced dom might have missed, but Monroe knew how to cut through the crap.

"Yes." Mallory's eyes grew large, and once again, she tried to get up. Monroe wasn't sure he was doing the right thing but felt it was a now or never situation. His chest vibrated with his tone. "Mal, look at me." When she purposely refused to comply, he sighed. "I guess the old saying, 'begin as you mean to go' is what we will do here. I had thought you would see I'm trying to keep you safe, and that is my highest priority, even over your happiness."

"I think I should be able to decide if I go home."

"Actually, if you were honest, you would say you don't want to be vulnerable and going home would put you in an untenable position should the accomplice find you. This was a sick man, and he would have an equally ill cohort."

"But I can't hide forever." He watched her as she half-heartedly tried to plead her erroneous position.

"And no one expects you to, but you are always going to be my highest priority, and right now, that means safety and staying away from your place. Do you intend on being honest about how you really feel, or do we take this a step further?"

"I don't consent."

"Are you safe-wording?" Monroe was calm but persistent, and he hoped it worked.

"I... we don't have a contract."

"Mallory, are you saying we need one to be together now? Because when we spoke on the phone, you and I laid out the entire limits lists, discussed it all, and you said you agreed to the list. Are you trying to stall?"

"I'm satisfied."

He nodded. "Then you are stalling and being dishonest with yourself and me. That won't do, sweetheart. You need to lie over my lap and let's get this over with. I think you just might need this spanking." She opened her mouth, and he put his finger over her lips. "No more talking. I've spanked you when we played. You like it."

"But it was play. When you spanked me in the car, that wasn't play."

"Honey, it's all play to a point. Yes, I'm disappointed that you won't open up to me more, but that will come. Now, lay across my lap. I need to feel your ass under my hand."

MALLORY NEEDED THIS in her own way, as much as Monroe. She needed to feel his connection with her and the amount he cared for her shown physically. She craved spanking, and Monroe was so good at it. It was her biggest kink. She'd experienced three previous spankings at his hand, and one included a taste of leather, one included his rubber paddle. She adored it. Although he didn't play around when he spanked, it impressed her with the skill level and care he took.

On the limits sheet she had filled out, next to spanking, she had written, 'yes, please,' but this was punishment. She didn't ask questions and try to clarify things. She didn't disclose how afraid she was to remain a victim and yet terrified of being alone. Instead, she'd said she needed to return to work. Monroe had countered that, and here they were. She was placing herself over his lap because of her inability to address the issue honestly.

Besides all that, they had agreed to this lifestyle. Mallory knew Monroe would be a careful, dominant, and loving partner. She gave herself to him, took his comfort and more last night, all because she knew he was the real deal. No subterfuge in his actions or words. She wanted that. So, by default, this was part of the package.

"I'm starting over your leggings to warm you up, but you know the rest will be on a bare bottom."

"I know." She wanted the whole thing, but the anticipation nearly sabotaged her enjoyment.

He applied three hard smacks to her butt. "How do you answer me when we are here, and you are being punished?"

"Yes, sir, but sir, am I really being punished?"

"In part. You keep too much in and argue when you should ask. Besides, you need it, and so do I. It's a two-fer baby. When I'm done, I'll get you off in spectacular fashion."

There were no more words as a half dozen swats turned into a dozen and then two dozen. Mallory's breath became shallow quicker. "You okay, sweetheart?"

"Yes, sir," came her husky reply. She felt the warming effects of the spanking.

"Good. Lift your bottom."

She whimpered but did as he requested. Monroe pulled her leggings down to her calves and rubbed her ass with his oversized rough hand. The coarseness heightened her sensations. He patted her bottom again, sharply, with increasing intensity. He stopped to rub the sting away, but it wasn't enough to conquer the burn. Now his palm landed heavily as he increased the tempo and the force with which he bounced his palm off her rear. The sting was increasing.

Mallory was acutely aware of the intensity of the fire he had lit on her backside and the precise way he had of delivering her spanks. The heat was suffusing throughout her core, and the fluid was slippery as it slid from her core to pool near her clit. It was almost ticklish. The rushing of arousal juices increased, making his pants under her center wet and slippery as well.

It took a little pain to reach her peak. She needed more and rubbed her fleshy bits over his thigh. He gave two more swats but allowed his fingers to land on her slit, the bite stinging horribly, but it raised her passion higher. That was the masochist part of her.

By now, she couldn't stop from rocking over his thigh in an animalistic rhythm to achieve climax. The cadence was deep inside her, taking over her very thoughts as she swayed.

"Are you ready, sweetheart? You are sopping wet and such a good girl to get excited. Lay still so I can take over, love."

"Please, Monroe, please?" her cry of anguish made Monroe chuckle, but Mallory needed him to get her off. She was an inferno of emotional need, and it would soon consume her.

"You asked so nicely. How could I refuse? Now be still so I can do it right. I'll have to stop if you don't settle down."

His voice was gentle and dominant at the same time, and Mallory didn't know how long she would last. As he swirled his finger and thumb in her channel and over her clit, that was made fully accessible by her sprawled position, partly on the bed, partly over his lap. He smeared her copious arousal over her clit and her back entrance. Mallory tensed.

"Ever played here, baby?"

"No, sir." Her voice sounded raspy and frantic even to her.

"You get wound up with spanking. I know you will enjoy some backdoor play. I'll work on that later, but right now,

I'll just introduce a finger or two to get you oriented to the feel." He immediately slipped in one finger, then another, giving her the experience of incredible tingling and sting. More arousal gushed.

"Hmm, you like that, don't you, baby?" When she didn't answer, he squeezed her still throbbing backside. She cried out. The sensations were too much.

"Please, sir, I need to come so badly."

"Then you should answer me when I ask a question." He leaned down and kissed her bottom cheek. "Okay, I'll finish it. Then I want inside you."

"I want that too."

Her wish was his command. Without another word, Monroe rubbed the side of her clit, just the way she liked it and then over the tip while he finger-fucked her back entrance. The cry of completion was a mixture of a moan and a whimper in higher volume in a voice she couldn't identify. His cock was steel and jabbing hard against her leg. This woman lit his body on fire.

Monroe removed his fingers from her ass. Laying her on the bed, with her feet on the floor and his finger still massaging her clit, he unzipped and yanked down briefs and pants at the same time. Mallory had long since rid herself of her leggings and panties. Spanking her a few times to reheat her cheeks, he slammed into her channel and sunk deep into her depths.

He would not last long, and because he wasn't a young buck, it would be at least an hour before he could get this type of hardness again. He needed to make sure Mallory got off one more time before he shot his load.

She was on the pill, so he didn't worry about an unplanned pregnancy, but he did plan to get her pregnant as soon as she was ready. Something so monumental as this had to be a mutual decision on the timing. Tonight, he had little finesse. While he slammed into her over and over, he also made himself slow down and give her a respite, rubbing the right areas for her to feel him and the gathering climax in both of them. Mallory obviously thought he was going to stop, and she tried to impale herself with his cock. Well, okay, message received.

The fire he tried to stave off would only delay for a few angst-filled moments. The need to release his sperm nearly cramped his back muscles. Mallory was pounding into him, meeting his thrust with her push back. Their pelvises hit hard at the point of impact, over and over. The sweat rolled down his face, his body slapping against hers. All thought left him as he felt the heat roll through his core as she screamed her climax.

Damn, she was hot, and he was falling in love. Hell, he was probably already there. He grunted and groaned as the white light of the orgasm overtook him, and he pumped a few more times, emptying his essence into her depths.

As he lay down next to Mallory, he pulled her close. She wiggled and changed position so many times, he knew there was only one way to get her to go to sleep.

"Hands over your head and legs spread wide. No comments or I'll spend the next hour denying your next orgasm," His sex-harshened voice commanded her.

She whimpered. He chuckled. "Lay nice and still and no talking. I don't want to pull out my belt this late at night, but

I will if you don't mind me. Too bad my paddle is in the glove box."

Monroe watched as she grabbed the spindles in the headboard. He went straight for her clit, and his mouth latched onto her plump breast and sucked hard. He teased her clit without mercy, and in minutes, she was writhing in the throes of her passion. Monroe did it again and a third time before he sensed she was exhausted.

He licked his finger and heard her moan at the realization that he savored her taste. He then leaned over slowly and kissed her lips before drawing her close to him. "Now sleep, woman." She chuckled at his grumble, but he didn't hear a word from her until morning.

Chapter 10

Agent Arturo Gutierrez arrived promptly at ten the following day to re-interview Mallory. If it surprised him that three men and another woman now surrounded her, he didn't show it. He chatted informally with Jac and Monroe, was introduced to Ryker, accepted coffee before he got serious, and settled down to the business he came to conduct.

"Ms. Sasse..."

"Please call me Mallory. I'll feel better about being under a microscope."

"Alright then, Mallory. Please don't let the title intimidate you. I'm just an investigator trying to find all the clues I can so you can get on with your life, and we can capture and keep perpetrators like Romaine and his cohort off the streets for good."

"I appreciate that. Now, what do you think I can tell you that I haven't already?"

"Right, well, in cases of trauma, sometimes you can remember things better after the initial shock has left."

Mallory nodded, and the FBI agent began. Monroe stood nearby, looking like he was ready to pounce. It was unnecessary, but she nearly cooed with appreciation that he ensured his presence and priority were declared to the agent.

It helped her breathe easier. And made her wiggle a little because, dammit, she had gushed again.

Ryker was leaning back casually on the sofa next to her. The agreement was he would intercede only if necessary.

"Did he use words such as master, follower, helper, apprentice or anything like that?"

Mallory seemed shocked at the question for a few seconds and cast her concerned expression toward Monroe. He knew what she was thinking. They had already discussed this possibility, and it looked like they weren't wrong. She sat for a few moments, and it was evident to Monroe that she was trying to remember what she, on a conscious level, had tried to remove from her memory banks.

Ryker sat up quickly. "I think that is a leading question." He turned to Mallory. "Mallory, did Romaine refer to himself in any way?"

"No. He mentioned his wife but no name."

Arturo asked, "Need I remind you that she is a victim giving me her eyewitness statement? Now Mallory, what can you tell me about his wife?"

"I don't know who it was, nor did I see her face or even hear her voice. I know I was told by the local police that there was no one at the house and no wife, but he didn't have to be married to her legally for him to call her that."

"That's true. When Romaine spoke of his wife, what did he say about her?"

"He said she would be watching if I tried to escape. He said he gave his wife a shotgun in case she needed to use it for protection, and if I tried to escape, that would be grounds for needing to protect his property. That's it."

"And you took that to mean she was on the premises even when Romaine wasn't, that she knew you were there, and that she would use the gun to shoot you if you tried to escape."

"Yes."

"Did that cause you to fear for your life?"

Mallory gave Arturo a look of disbelief. "Did you honestly ask that question?"

"I need to establish your emotional state and your mental thought processes while on Romaine's property. Well, his mother's property. She is in a nursing home for early-onset dementia."

"No surprise there," Sharlee whispered under her breath, and Mallory quickly squelched the little giggle that broke through her stoic stance.

Arturo looked down at his shoes, but Mallory knew he was trying to stop his own smile. The moment passed, and the agent looked at Mallory again.

"Yes, I was fearful from the moment that monster pushed me into his car to the moment Monroe walked into my hospital room."

Monroe squeezed her hand, and she turned her palm up to thread her fingers in his.

"Romaine has shown that he was the master because he was the smarter one, and his little helper just did what Romaine instructed, but he has never indicated a particular gender for this 'helper.' Maybe he doesn't see the helper as a human. Many sociopaths don't. The forensic evidence is plenty, as though the monster didn't expect to be caught."

Jac joined in. "Except if he said he had a wife, it is likely a woman because he was kidnapping women for entertainment. He clearly had a preference."

"The women don't appear to have any similar hobbies or jobs, and they aren't physically similar. I mean, three were blonde, but Mallory isn't, and neither is the victim in the hospital. We believe there are more on the property, and he lived elsewhere before moving into his mother's place after she went to the nursing home. He seems to be interested in sex with his captives because he has plenty of implements to decide the direction of that interaction."

"Okay, so his wife is a woman, he has sex toys and likes women of all types. That covers more than half of the male population. We need more. Do you have any hints on the names we gave you?" Jac asked.

"The employees and apartment residents? Sure, some, but nothing even remotely similar to what we're looking at. The connection is not showing itself, and Romaine isn't giving us anything else to go on."

"Okay," said Mallory, "let's think about this. He is obviously narcissistic and wants everyone to be impressed with what he had done. If you want him to give you more information, then you need to make him think you aren't as impressed as he expects you to be."

"Good thinking. Arturo, can you speak to him about other serial killers or kidnappers that have more deaths to their record than 3? And 5 kidnapped, but two were rescued doesn't even rate. That will make him stew. He will tell you about other victims to up his body count and make him seem better than the rest."

Arturo nodded. "It's a strategy worth pursuing."

Sharlee spoke up. "If Romaine calls himself the master, either he has a slave or is into some psychological brain game. He could be fantasizing that if there really is an accomplice in the duo, he, Romaine, is the brilliant one. He must control his environment."

Gutierrez shook his head. "Possibly, but not all people who want control are psychos."

Jac and Monroe spoke simultaneously. "Of course not."

Sharlee rolled her eyes, and Monroe felt his hand itch. He had to remind himself that Sharlee was Jac's now, so no one else could make any attitude adjustments. Monroe looked at Mallory as she sat so straight in the seat, wound tighter than an eight-day clock. She rolled her shoulders, and he reached to massage them but stopped, knowing she wouldn't appreciate that gesture right now. She needed to retain her power.

Mallory spoke. "Or he is the puppet, and now that we separated him from the puppeteer, he believes he's the master instead of the peon. No matter how this actually plays out, he is the one who kidnapped me, and I don't want anyone to lose sight of that fact. Slave or master, he is a kidnapper, first and foremost and a murder. A serial killer. I want him to never hear my name or lay eyes on me ever again."

Arturo sighed. "Mallory. You'll have to testify."

"What if I don't? I mean, no one can make me face that monster again. He didn't keep me long enough to have any major damage except to my psyche. Eventually, I'll push through that, but all semblance of safety will dissolve if I have to be in his presence again. I just don't know if I can do it."

The agent leaned forward in what Monroe could only assume was an effort to connect with Mallory, but she wasn't having it. She leaned back and crossed her arms. If she had done that with him, Monroe would have addressed her show of disrespect, but he was not inclined to redirect her attitude in this situation. Arturo had overstepped his bounds, and he knew it.

"It is likely going to be almost a year before we go to trial. We are still investigating. Don't decide now. Just relax and get back to your life. I'm going to bank on the longer it is, the more likely you won't feel threatened when it's time to actually make that decision."

Monroe could see his girl had shut down, her manner cold, but he was proud that she was willing to finish. "Anything else you need from me?"

"Yes, I have a few more things to tease out." Arturo continued asking his questions, and Mallory appeared exhausted by the time the FBI agent stood.

Monroe closed the door behind Gutierrez, and the weight of his tightly held body and concern over how Mallory would fair, lifted, leaving him stiff and achy but relaxed. Monroe walked back into the den and stood behind the sofa where Mallory sat and rubbed her shoulders.

"I'm more sure than ever that we should focus our efforts on the little parties and munches that Mallory attended prior to the incident."

"Agreed." Jac turned to Mallory. "Now tell me the places again, and let's go over the list of places to see if we can find

CCTV for those particular nights. It's possible we can locate Romaine there and if there was anyone with him."

Sharlee nodded. "I'll keep up what I'm doing for name searches and facial recognition but do that in the background. I'll focus my energy on the cameras and then sit with Mallory to identify some players."

Monroe, Ryker, and Jac joined Sharlee when Mallory went to the bathroom. "How do you think your girl is holding up?" asked Jac.

"Pretty good, but the signs are there that this is taking a big toll on her. I'd rather take her to the safe house in town if it's possible."

They discussed the possibility for a few moments. Monroe still advocated hard to get Mallory in a safe place. While they would have cameras strategically located, he needed to get her alone. Start to build a new normal she could live with for now.

Jac stopped to think for another moment. "Yeah. So this is my thinking. Let's keep surveillance on her house while we move the things she will need out of there and any valuables. Just in case." Monroe understood, but Mallory came in on the last part and seemed confused.

"Just in case, what?"

"Mal, Jac is worried that if there is an accomplice, they will get into your house and make away with your valuables, important papers, and the like."

It was at that moment Monroe knew he had to protect her. "My house? Do you think someone might go into my house? Might know where I live, maybe even have watched me?" She was shaking, and her voice was unsteady when she spoke. "How will I ever be comfortable living there again?"

"You might not be, baby, but it's better if you take control and not let this jackass or his asshole helper, if there is one, keep you in fear, controlling you, enjoying your pain. We will get him, but we have to be smart about this."

Sharlee piped up. "Or her. Don't forget it is likely a woman."

Jac sat on the other side of Mallory on the sofa. Monroe had her hand in his. "If we are proactive, then we won't need to worry about being caught off guard because we won't be. We'll be prepared for any eventuality. So Monroe wants to take you to the safe house, and I agree."

Sharlee added, "Your name hasn't gone out yet, but I will lay you odds that any moment that will not be the case. Your name will be plastered all over the news, and if you are in a safe place, one that has a safe room in case of an emergency and is in the middle of an older neighborhood, I would say you are well protected."

Monroe nodded. "Yes, I'll be there, and we will have one other person and the outside cameras keeping the place watched. Nothing will happen without us knowing so we can slip into the room safely."

"I'll have to think about it."

"Mallory, what other choice do you have right now?" asked Monroe. "Your house will be swarming with every reporter trying to make a name for themselves, every person fascinated with the whole thing, and every crazy wanting the same experience will follow this story and how it plays out for their own future terror. I can't allow you to be where you will be a target for anyone. Don't ask me to."

"I just need to think." Mallory allowed Monroe to pull her back against his chest, and after a few moments, Jac went to the office, and Sharlee put the CCTV videos on the wall so Mallory could stay deep in Monroe's arms. Ryker went in search of Finley.

"I'll watch so I can cue them up for you. Hang tight. It might take a bit of watching." said Sharlee. Monroe smiled. She was picking up lingo from her hubby and the rest of the team.

Monroe spoke softly to his girl. "Mallory, we need to talk about this while Sharlee is looking for the right dates and times." He pulled her close and kissed the top of her head. "I know this is surreal because I deal with things like this all the time. Thankfully, you don't. The biggest hurdle for me, of course, is that I am determined to keep you safe. That being said, I want to be what you need me to be for you right now."

"But I don't know what I need. I'm so tangled up in knots, I have seconds when I feel panic returning as though I'm still trying to escape, but this time, I get shot trying to get out." Monroe hugged her tighter.

"This is such a FUBAR that even if I wanted to fix it all for you, I couldn't. And I don't. I want you to be happy, carefree even, and that won't happen until we finish this."

"I don't want to deal with anything. I just want to go to sleep and wake up when it's all over. Monroe, I don't think I can do this alone."

"Alone? What the fuck, baby? You aren't alone. You won't ever be truly alone again. Even if you are the only one in the house, you won't be the only one in your life. You have everyone on my team backing you up. They have your back, and I have all of you."

"I love that I feel so sheltered with you, and I freaking hate that I'm not the keeper of my life right now. I hate that. In all honesty, I don't want to go home, go to work, or even buy my own groceries. I want a new life where none of this happened. I know I'll have to work this out eventually, but I just don't want to do that yet."

"No," Monroe's tone darkened. "We have to work this out. Your more than capable man and his team, who are now your friends, are going to be right beside you. I suggest you ask Ivy, Sharlee, and Jessie just what happened in their lives when they had to call on their men and the team for help. The load was easier, and we solved the problem."

She shook her head. "I don't ask for help often or easily."

Monroe put his knuckle under her chin and lifted. "Then it's about time you learned. And it's about time you understand that I am always going to be there for you. I'll stand between you and any danger. Trust me on that."

"I do. Will you take over and run my life? Just until I can do it myself again?"

"I'd do that in a heartbeat if you really want that."

"Just until every little decision doesn't feel like a life-changing event."

"Are you serious?"

His finger was still under her chin, and he gazed deeply into her eyes. Mallory's eyes showed her vulnerability, her pleading. She nodded, then shrugged.

"Yes?"

The lilt at the end of that one word made him ask again.

"Mallory, do you want me to take over all the decisions concerning this mess and all the things that seem so important until you can do it again?"

"Yes." This time she said it in hushed tones while nodding her head, then snuggling back into his arms, leaning on his chest.

"Okay, then that's how it will go until you don't need it."

Her body almost went limp in her giving over. She was such a transparent submissive, but that wasn't really what was going on here. She wasn't asking Monroe to take over in the bedroom because that was already in place. Mallory wanted someone to take the reins on the big stuff and the stuff that felt too large to handle. She was overwhelmed, and he could help with that.

Monroe was like Mallory in that he didn't want that kind of lifestyle forever. He admired that she was typically confident in her everyday world. Dr. Mallory Sasse was a kickass pharmacist that cared about the people she filled prescriptions for.

He smiled at that last name and decided that when they got married, because he was determined they would, he would insist Mallory keep her maiden name because a last name of Sasse-Merton tickled his fancy... a lot.

Sharlee was still watching the feed she'd tapped into, and Mallory completely relaxed in his arms, her breaths coming evenly. She'd gone to sleep, and it sounded like a good plan. He closed his own eyes and made himself comfortable.

His baby hadn't been able to sleep for more than a few hours at a time. Mallory thought he didn't notice because he didn't let her know, but he watched her as she lay awake several times each night, chasing her sleep. She seemed to rest best in his arms, and he fucking loved that. The team would neutralize the immediate threat. The rest would take time.

Monroe woke to his cell phone ringing. "Hello?"

"Mr. Merton?"

"Yes?" Mallory was awake now, watching him and running her hand slowly down his shirt and back up. "Who is this?"

His hand covered Mallory's when she ran her fingers down a bit too far for his phone conversation to continue unimpeded.

"This is Agent Gutierrez."

"Yes, could you hold just a moment?" He placed the call on mute and grasped Mallory's chin, lifting her face up to see his. "If I have to stop this hopefully important call with Gutierrez because you are naughty, I'll spank your ass right here in this room, and whoever observes or hears does. Get me?"

Mallory's eyes grew large as she sighed dramatically and nodded before snuggling back into his chest. His arm came back up to hold her close. Usually, Monroe would have been all in for the teasing and spanking session, then followed it up with a good session of lovemaking, but he needed to hear what the agent had to say first.

"Sorry about that. What's up?" He placed the phone on speaker.

"We have a development, and I'm not sure if it's good or bad, really. Romaine took the bait on how he was less successful than others that had gone on before him, and he gave up a name of an accomplice."

Monroe rubbed Mallory's arm. "That's good news."

"Well, it could be, but it's uncertain whether he is really a cohort in these crimes or if he was just a random choice. The man worked with Mallory. Ty Ranger. He's rather young."

Mallory jumped up and clipped Monroe's chin. He tightened his grip on her arm, and when she looked into his eyes, he shook his head. She shook her head back.

"Are you sure? Mallory doesn't think that sounds right. Let me have her tell you what she's thinking."

Mallory leaned in to speak but grabbed the phone instead. "Okay, listen, Ty is a stocker for the Apothecary. He's in college on the Dean's list and the College soccer team. He also coaches a city league team and stocks part-time. I'm telling you, between college, soccer practice and coaching along with his part-time job, there is no way that kid has any time at all to do more than catch a few hours of sleep here and there."

"That's what we were afraid of."

Mallory continued, warming up to her subject. "Besides, on the day he kidnapped me, he was out of town at a tournament, and it lasted all weekend. He left Thursday morning and should have returned Monday afternoon. Check it out. You'll see you have the wrong guy."

"Thank you. We have to check out Mr. Ranger's alibi, but it helps to know what to check before bringing him in. I'll call back if we have any new information."

Mallory handed Monroe his phone back and turned to walk away. His arm wrapped around her waist tighter, pulling her in closer. She scrunched her face in a question.

"There are going to be some changes, now that I'm in charge, baby."

Chapter 11

"Changes?"

"Yep."

"I don't know what you mean?"

"I mean that if you have given me the reins, then you need to allow me to hold them, not grab them back when you want to."

"You mean the phone call? It was just easier if I held the phone."

"No, not the call itself, but I want you to keep out of the investigation as much as possible."

"What? I don't think I can do that. Besides, you put it on speaker."

"An error in judgment. Now listen. There are plenty of good people with mounds of experience and access to information necessary to find things. We are going to work on getting back to some semblance of normalcy or rather create one between us."

Monroe shifted to a standing position and clasped her hand in his. He led her into the dining room.

"I didn't mean you would take over everything. I still have a mind that works perfectly well in some areas."

Monroe stopped, and it looked as though he would say something but changed his mind. "Okay, just what area did you consider off-limits?"

"Well, I don't know, exactly. I mean, I can pick my clothes and stuff."

"Thank God because I wouldn't have a clue. You'd be in sweats and pajamas every day."

"That would be fine, but not for work. Something I should get back to."

"After a few days? No, you aren't going unless you're ready, which you are not. It hasn't been long enough. Besides, we haven't found the second person, so talk to me after that happens."

"You don't get to dictate things surrounding my career."

"I'm not, but if I am to be in charge, take the burden off you for now, then that is a big stressor, and I am saying no work for right now."

Mallory tried to take her hand from his again. This time, he let it go to her chagrin. "I think we need to negotiate this over lunch."

"I think that sounds like a good idea. Soup and sandwiches, okay?"

Over lunch, Mallory fought hard for her idea of what giving Monroe the lead meant, but she won little ground. "Why do I feel like I've been overruled or outmaneuvered on all the big things, and you've given in on a few small things to make me feel like I won something?"

"It's military strategy, sweetheart, and it might go better for you in the future if you didn't challenge everything I said before I explained myself."

She huffed and crossed her arms. "I should have safe worded."

Monroe laughed out loud. "You can't safe word when we are negotiating."

"I don't see why not, especially since I wasn't winning much in the way of concessions."

"Mal, look, you are under a lot of stress right now, and you want me to take as much as I can off your shoulders. I agreed. In fact, I was relieved when you asked. But with that added responsibility, I am also awarded extra control."

Mallory answered in a frustrated tone as she conceded defeat. "Fine, I know. You already made your point. When are we going to review the CCTV?"

"Now, if you're ready," said Sharlee as she walked into the dining room and handed Storm to Finley. "I saw Ryker visited yesterday."

"He did, and don't try to put any clandestine meaning to the visit. We're friends. In fact, he and Levi and I are going out on Friday. There's a sci-fi marathon starting at seven."

"Oh, that sounds like fun, except for the sci-fi part," said Mallory with a laugh.

"You don't know what you're missing. Okay, little mister, it's time for our nap."

Mallory watched Finley take Storm to the back of the house and acknowledged she wanted that. She wondered if she could ask Monroe for a child. Maybe only one, no, one was too lonely, so two children. Two would be perfect. She was younger than Monroe by about seven years, and if she wanted two, she'd need to get started soon.

While Monroe was precisely what the women working at the pharmacy would call a 'daddy,' she didn't need a daddy in the lifestyle way, but a man who took control when she wanted it and sometimes when she didn't. That was definitely Monroe.

They spent the afternoon identifying by first name those she could as she watched them come in and out of the munches. Mallory had hoped that they would find Romaine outside the venues and waiting in a car or on the street corner, something, but no luck. It encouraged Sharlee that she had something to further identify possible suspects in the kidnapping. Searching for full names and backgrounds was fun for Sharlee. She was in her element, but all this was discouraging to Mallory.

Mallory went upstairs to take a nap, exhausted by the flashes of memories of the people and events that may have led up to her being kidnapped. Finally, she fell asleep only to dream of the recent past when she had the world in her hand. She was excited about the next stage of her life. When she woke up, it was with a new determination. She got up and started throwing her things in the duffle bag the women had grabbed for her earlier today. All packed, Mallory turned to carry the bag down the stairs, only to meet Monroe coming in.

"And just what the hell are you doing, and where do you think you're going? Your answer had better be a good one, sweetheart."

The best defense was a good offense, so she took the more aggressive stance, putting him on the defensive. She hoped her strategy would get results. "Don't take that tone with me. I'm sure you can see what I'm doing. Now move out of my way, please."

He raised his eyebrows, then seemed to measure his words. "No, I can see you have packed and are attempting to leave. What I don't know is where you think you're going. What I also don't understand is that we negotiated all of this. We discussed who made the big decisions when we disagree."

"It's too difficult to give in to you and worry about another crazy out there."

"It's why you need my help, why you asked me to step in. I am trying to keep your stress down, and when your input is not mandatory, I would take the lead and handle things. This right here, little girl, is not following even the spirit of the agreement. It also is not how you behave with me on any day. Now, I ask you again, where, and why are you going? Mind how you go."

Dammit. Monroe's tone made her weak in the knees. He was such a good man. It hurt her heart to go against him, especially since he was doing exactly as they had agreed. She could safe word, yell "red," but that isn't how she was feeling. She was restless, antsy, confused.

"I'm tired of the way I can't settle my mind. I think that if I were at my own home, I could do that."

"And what about the protection detail we promised to give you? Or that all hell would break loose if you tried to leave the property? Or that the FBI would take over, leaving you with fewer choices than you think?"

She stood straighter. "I don't honestly know. I'll take my chances, I guess. Something has to give."

"If you leave, we have to call the FBI. They will pick you up, and for the foreseeable future, they would take you a good distance from here with no access to your friends, your old life, or me."

Mallory could hear her own voice tremble in fear at the thought of being alone. At the thought of leaving Monroe. This was such a mess, but what else could she do. The last place she had any control was when she was in her home. That is what she wanted, to transport back in time before the kidnapping, and that is what she would do.

"No."

Mallory scrunched up her face in confusion. "What do you mean, no?"

His arms crossed over his chest the best he could, given his muscle mass, and he reminded her of that hulky man on the cleaner bottle. Except Monroe had thick hair cut in a military style.

"I mean, no, you are not going anywhere unprotected. No, you aren't returning home to be a target for reporters, and crazy people, to be hounded and harassed. No, I'm not sending one of our security guys to guard your place. No, you aren't making the decisions right now because that's my job. No, you aren't leaving me to stay alone and exposed. No, I am not re-negotiating anything, and no, if we go somewhere, it is a safe house that I choose, and we will do it under cover of darkness and with a diversion."

She dropped the duffle bag with a thud and flopped down on the bed heavily, but the softness of the bed and comforter muffled her movements. "Then what can we do? I need to leave, get out of here. Everyone is great, and I appreciate their hospitality and willingness to help me, but I honestly feel like I'm in a tailspin with the ground rushing at me and no way to pull out of it. Being around all of this work on the case makes it hard for me to forget why I'm here and why my life is upside down. I won't ever get back to anything resembling normal until I can separate myself from this mess, and I can't do it here."

She watched as Monroe walked further into the room, scooped her in his arms, and sat on the bed with her. "I know. Let me work on a few things. I thought we would go to the safe house today, but they released your name to the press this morning."

Mallory groaned, prompting Monroe to kiss her forehead and rock slightly. She melted. He didn't get mad in the way she thought he would. He didn't yell, storm off or any of the myriads of ways he could have reacted. Monroe spoke quietly and reasonably, even though he told her 'No' a lot. Even while her insides were jumpy, she could let him figure this out.

"All that means is we have to be more careful. I'm wondering if we should take the house that is in the country. Less chance of being found."

She leaned into Monroe. His scent lingered like an evergreen forest after a summer rain. "But if I *am* found, I have less chance of protecting myself out of the city where there are people and police close by."

"You haven't seen our safe houses. They're cool. You won't be alone because I will be there. This comes down to trust. I have to trust that you won't take off on a whim because you're unsettled, and you have to trust me enough to keep you safe, so you don't want to strike out on your own."

"I hate that 'trust me' sap. I don't trust most people after the abduction, and I can't say how much I trust myself or anyone else right now, no matter how much I want to. If you're in charge, then get me to a safe place without needing to be on display all the time because I've got to be happier than I am now, and it's your job to make that a reality." Her face screamed a challenge. "That is if you're up to the task."

Monroe chuckled. "You know just when to play that card, don't you?"

"I've been known to have some level of intelligence." She said haughtily.

"You are smart and a smartass. You're also topping from the bottom in your own way. If I'm the decision-maker, then you let me decide without trying your emotional blackmail or challenges to my manhood." He shrugged, then grinned with an evil glint in his eye. "But if needed, I can fix your attitude, your mouthiness, and you're topping with a few rounds of my rubber paddle."

She grinned. "Get me what I want, and I could agree to a session."

"Oh, you're going to have a few sessions before it's all over, sweetheart. I'm just trying to decide if I do the first one now. Walking might be optional after I'm done with you for challenging me at every turn. Sitting will be out of the question. Both are things you'll need to do when we relocate. Besides, anticipation about just what I will do to you will keep you on edge for now."

Mallory hesitated. Monroe had a reputation with that rubber paddle and his techniques with women who poke the bear, as it were. Instead of heeding her usually more logical mind, she simply shrugged. "It's better to challenge authority than to be blindly swept away by it."

She knew she was headed to the proverbial woodshed, and she couldn't have been more excited. Mallory needed things to get popping to help her out of the doldrums. She just hoped it would be in a more secluded location than Sharlee's guest bedroom. She could handle some embarrassment, especially since she knew it was something everyone around here seemed perfectly fine with, but a complete session with Monroe for the first time should be private.

Humiliation was not her kink. They had discussed it, and it wasn't his either. He loved to spank, but it was a kink they both enjoyed. Monroe was clear that if she needed to use her safe-word or the caution word, and she didn't, there would be trouble. He played at taking her power in the bedroom, but he didn't honestly want to strip her of any independence and control in her daily life. Well, after this, hopefully brief, interlude. He said he liked his woman to be strong, and all his mannerisms declared that to be true.

Monroe was an attentive, overly observant, and incredible lover. He took care of her too well, better than any other man had ever done, and she craved another sexy spanking night with him to relieve the stress that was building to insurmountable proportions. She wiggled in his lap at the tingle in her belly. His control allowed her to let go, release the tension and stress, and just enjoy the benefits.

Spanking, wax play, and flogging gave her an endorphin high she couldn't deny was incredible. Monroe was a master edger, and she loved to hate that play. Mallory was never good at oral because no man seemed interested in reciprocating until now. She intended to get better because as much as he worked with her, he deserved the same. Monroe had perfected his technique so well Mallory reached her release in a way that kept her humming for a while afterward.

She waited for him to make the next move because he was right. She wanted to let him take care of everything, but she also needed to follow her instincts.

"Mal, sit here and make a shopping list. There are canned and frozen staples, but nothing fresh. I'm going to round up Jac on the phone and check on Sharlee to see if we have any results from the facial recognition and to get the keys from her."

He slid Mallory over to the spot on the bed next to him and got up. He kissed her unsuspecting lips, and she looked into his eyes. "Thank you."

His hand gently cupped her face in his rough hands. "You never have to thank me for being the man you need. You can, however, thank me for not coloring your ass in the way you so richly deserve while we were here. I'm a patient man."

MONROE'S BRAIN WAS racing. Mallory needed space from her kidnapping twenty-four-seven. He got it. He was feeling the experiment under glass sensation as well. His responses to the situation were being watched, his handling of the FBI, the police, the meltdowns. Everything seemed to be on display. He blew it off mainly because he got it. When you are surrounded by observant men and women, little escapes their attention. Professionally, it was helpful and desired. They had your back. You had theirs.

In a relationship, things weren't so cut and dried. Monroe's women were usually well-established, capable women who knew their worth. It was important in his lifestyle that the women be just that, self-assured. That strength of inner self allowed them to release their power to him so that he could return that gift to the woman pleasurably.

Mallory was his, and it was time he made decisions based on them as a unit, not as a work assignment. He gave the orders on this, not Jac. Monroe didn't interfere with Jac and Sharlee or any other couples except to tease and offer advice when requested. Now it was time he demanded the same of them.

"Jac," said Monroe when his partner and boss answered, "I need to take Mallory to one of the safe houses, and I'm thinking the one in the country."

"Agreed. The local news has just connected us to Mallory. Who are you taking with you? You usually know more about where everyone is and who is available."

"I think we could probably handle it alone. No one knows where we are, and the house is secured."

"Negative. We live by the buddy system. You're going to need someone there, so how about Garrett?"

"Garrett will not want to sit out there with nothing to do all day."

"Actually, he could use some quiet time to work through the new clients' dossiers we have. Besides, he needs a break, and he's refusing to take one. He says he's fine, but when Calli disappeared, he never recovered, not completely. He's been going full speed ever since. The man is a few years older than I am, and I'm taking breaks. Hell, I need them. So does Garrett."

"I'll call him as I gather things up."

Chapter 12

It didn't take long to settle into the self-contained safe house they named The Lodge, ten miles outside Reynaud and Associates' offices. It was in a wooded neighborhood with few homes, but all with good security. Kaden and Carter had set up the security for most of the select houses in the area, and when this house came on the market, Jac snatched it up and modified it. The group had found great success using it since then.

Mallory started working on a puzzle, catching up on her reading, watching cooking shows and then attempting to replicate the recipes. Monroe suggested she start more basic, like meatloaf. Mallory wanted to ignore him but looking up the first recipe she wanted to try and seeing the prep time as one hour, she decided simple was good, too. Besides, she made a world-class salad.

Monroe answered his phone right after breakfast the third morning they were at the Lodge.

"Arturo, how are things with the case? Have you found the accomplice yet?"

"The general consensus is that Romaine was playing games because they could find no evidence that there was an accomplice. They believe he did it alone. I think that if Mallory believes there is another person, we should operate under that assumption for now and proceed accordingly."

"Right. Have you talked to Jac, or do you want me to disseminate the information?"

"No, Jac was unavailable, so I called you. If you would pass it along, that would be helpful. Oh, and there won't be a trial for Mallory's kidnapping as Romaine has admitted to that. He's admitted to the other young woman and to the three bodies we've found so far. I hope that helps Mallory to get back to her life."

"It definitely helps. What about the last places Romaine has lived?"

"We've uncovered some of the first places he lived and have ruled them out after a rudimentary look because they were run-down apartments in concrete jungles. No one knows how long he lived at those places or when he left. According to one manager, and I quote, 'We don't give references and don't keep records.'"

Gutierrez seemed satisfied with that bit of information, but Mallory couldn't accept it.

Mallory explained her thinking to the men on the phone with them. "I can't help but think that it isn't likely that the man lived half of his adult life a regular guy and then one day began this almost ritualistic way of kidnapping and killing people? He might have worked up to it, but he has to have done things before now."

Kaden, who was on the line with Jac, agreed. "Good point. I'll start looking into that."

"Don't we think it has something to do with his desire to play at a kink club or something?" asked Kaden.

"Maybe not unless there was a precipitating event?" asked Garrett. "It's just a theory."

"Would that stand to reason, though? Enough psychologists agree that those in tune with themselves and who play are less inhibited by others' misinformation. They're good examples of self-actualization, therefore typically well-balanced, are less narcissistic, and more satisfied with life." asked Mallory.

"So, my thoughts are he wouldn't have been able to get past the screening criteria for a club and so possibly tried munches or parties where there isn't any real screening. Maybe he showed himself to be a loose cannon or something, and they banned him from local munches," said Monroe.

"But it would be nearly impossible to verify anything like that. It would have to have happened a while ago because I'm sure he's been doing it for much longer than anyone suspects. In a sick, perverted way, instead of being haphazard, he was too precise. It had become a way of life for him. The incidents were orderly. He was almost fanatical is an obsessive pattern, according to Mallory's account. Events had to happen in a precise way, such as the last victim must die before he or they could enjoy the next victim," added Jac. "Kaden will take that line of inquiry. Follow the pattern and see if other abductions fit it."

"I'm on it. Do we continue to work backward?"

"Affirmative. Otherwise, for now, we continue as we have done, doing our other jobs, keeping Mallory safe, and waiting on more from the FBI. Sharlee has been keeping Gutierrez informed as we go."

Mallory reasoned she had to ignore the persistent idea that another person did the crimes with Romaine and accept that it was no longer the focus of the FBI. They focused on finding bodies, systematically identifying them, getting them back to their families, and then on to the prosecution of Romaine.

Mallory forced herself to deal with the fact that life won't get better than this for now. The FBI would work on finding bodies for months, according to Gutierrez. Mallory decided to save her sanity. She would do best if she tried to go back to work. It had only been three weeks, but Mallory needed the distraction of focusing outside of herself and this damn craziness. After several days of telling Monroe it had to be this way, or she would live in limbo forever, he agreed to discuss it.

"It could take years to find all the women, if they do, and identify them, work their cases up and since he has already admitted to the three women found dead in the beginning, and the woman held captive for so long and then kidnapping me, he won't ever get out of prison."

Monroe tried to disagree, but how could he? It was the truth. "You're right about the timeframe, but I don't want to throw you into the world before you are ready. And what about the press?"

"I won't sacrifice who I am and my life or my happiness to this monster. He has taken too much from me already. I've been talking to Ivy's counselor over the last few days, and she said go for it when I was ready. If I find I'm not ready, then I wait longer and try again. I am going back to work. If that is something you can't deal with, then I'll go back to my place and live my life from there."

Mallory waited while Monroe pulled her towards his lap, but she diverted to sit next to him on the sofa. He kissed her cheek and held her hands in his.

"I want to keep you in tissue paper and only bring you out for special occasions. Better yet, right now, I'd love nothing better than to keep you tucked away from the world except our friends. Mallory thought that something would happen to you under my watch makes me want to say no."

"I'm scared too, but you said that one reason I attracted you was my independence. I'll take precautions, but let me try to be who I am."

Mallory could see by his demeanor that Monroe knew she was right, and it just about killed him. She hugged him. He stood to walk as he thought. It was his way of working things out. Mallory loved she knew that about him. She was learning about him.

"You are not sleeping without me again. Nor are we living separately. I refuse to go backward. And you aren't going anywhere without protection." His ferocious edicts were cute, really. Heartwarming. And unnecessary.

"Go ahead and give me all your complaints, all your logical reasoning why I shouldn't go back to work so we can get them all out of the way."

Monroe stopped his pacing. "I really want to spank your ass," came his gruff, frustrated response.

Mallory laughed merrily, all the stress rolling off her shoulders. "Maybe later, big guy. Look, I know you think that I will be unprotected because you won't be surrounding me every moment. I'm afraid of that too, but we must remember that nothing happened inside the Apothecary. I don't even know that Romaine ever entered the place. It all happened in the back of the parking lot. The store manager, Larry, said I am welcome to park next to the back door, so no one will see me come or go. I'll just be there in the back, filling and verifying prescriptions and the like, then I'll go home. I can leave at different times, so there isn't any consistency. Okay?"

"I hate that you already called to set things up," Monroe grumbled.

She walked up to the man she couldn't imagine living without and raised up on her tiptoes, palming the back of his neck to bring his lips closer so she could kiss him. "Of course I did. How could I discuss things with you if I didn't? I knew you would rather that I had the answers to your questions when you asked."

"I'd rather that you had spoken with me first." He stared into her pleading eyes, then lowered his head and nibbled her lips before sinking into her softness again.

Mallory obliged and kissed him back, settling into his warmth. She loved this man so much. Yes, she loved him. There was no way around the depth of her feelings, and she didn't want around them. She wanted to have the life she had dreamed of, and she'd be damned if she was going to let anyone stand in their way. She fell into his caress, allowing the emotion to wash over her.

He raised his head and spoke just millimeters from her mouth, his breath whispering over her. His tongue slid out to trace her lips. "You know, if you are well enough to go back to work, you are well enough to go deeper into play. I can pull out my rubber paddle and rosy up those bottom cheeks of yours."

Her eyes sought his. "How do you figure?"

"You want to go back to normal?"

His hands slid down her sides, to her back and on down to her ass and squeezed tight. Mallory squealed a little and went back up on her tiptoes in response. Her hand slid down over his shoulders.

"No, put them right back where they were." His voice was chastising. Out of instinct, she put them back around his neck as her panties received her gush of arousal. His grin was victorious. "Good girl. Now, if you would be that obedient about everything else, things would go so much easier."

Mallory dropped back down to stand flat on her feet. She attempted to take a step back but was blocked by Monroe's hold. Her huff of annoyance was loud. "I agree that I'm good with you taking the lead in the bedroom, but that's it. We are equal partners in all other areas and times, so don't good girl me to make it sound as though I need your approval."

His already deep voice dropped what sounded like a whole octave. "My agreement is important to you, just as your approval of what I do, is essential to me. Just because we play well in the bedroom and have chosen not to do that outside of it doesn't mean there aren't rules to live by that we both agreed to. What that means, my independent woman, is that you will respect me and do what I say, *wherever* I say it, if it is for your own good."

"I know we agreed that staying safe and healthy was primary, but I'm a pharmacist, and I think I have the basics of staying healthy down."

"True, but the keeping safe part is not always your first thought." He moved her strands of hair that escaped her clip to curl behind her ear.

"I weigh the pros and cons, and I take the path of least resistance that has more pros than cons."

"Then why have we not discussed your bodyguard?"

"My what? Oh, no. There will not be any of your team or anybody hanging around watching me." She backed away from Monroe, not allowing him to stop her while shaking her head vehemently. "I can and do say no to that."

"Hear me out. For the first week or two, let me get you a security guard. He would look like a customer, and we would let the manager in on who it is, so no one freaks out. He could look like the store security, which would help keep the store safe. Win-win."

"No, Monroe." She shook her head again and planted her hands on her hips.

"Yes, Mallory. You have him for two weeks, then switch, and someone will follow you to work and home and if you must leave for lunch for at least another week."

"Is that your only stipulation?"

He shook his head slightly. "Probably not."

"Then let's have it all. Then I'll tell you what I will accept and what I will not."

"Baby—"

"Monroe, I'm saying I'll compromise, but that's it."

"Woman, I'm getting my rubber paddle out. This is only about your safety."

"Fine, and if you don't sit down and work this out with me, I won't compromise, and I'll use it on you."

Monroe stood still and stared at Mallory. "That," he said with measured tones edged with humor, "won't ever happen, baby." She shivered. *No, it wouldn't.*

"And if you don't work this out with me, then your fun time won't ever happen until you do."

Mallory sat on the couch and crossed her arms and legs. Monroe got close enough that the rumble in his chest rippled hers. Her tummy tightened, and that telltale release of arousal was leaking onto her panties again. His eyes dilated and darkened. She knew her pupils were dilating as well. This man did it for her, and sometimes that was a damn annoyance.

"So, you are willing to give up my tongue on your clit, bringing you to the top of the mountain just so you can get your own way? Using sex as punishment or reward can backfire, sweetheart. If I don't get any, neither do you, and I know just how to heat your thermometer without breaking the glass. Do you want to see how well you can handle that?"

Her stifled moan was answer enough. "Please, let's just talk this out?"

"We will, and then you get a spanking."

"What? No way. There are no penalties for voicing my own opinion about my rights in this relationship."

"But you don't get to yell it. Ten. Nor do you get to use sex as a weapon. Ten more."

"With your hand."

"Okay, but if you do it again, I'm adding more with my paddle." His raised eyebrow punctuated his statement.

She sighed loudly. "Not fair, but I'll agree so I can go back to work."

Monroe had been playing, and it got her off sexually, but she needed him to see her point of view. When Monroe sighed and dropped down next to her, Mallory knew things were going to work out. She prayed she was making the right decision. She still had nightmares most nights and was afraid that going back to work after less than a month would worsen her nightmares. It was as though he read her mind.

"These are the concerns I have. You still have nightmares, and I'm worried this will make them worse. You don't know what your triggers are, so you don't know to avoid them. I have another big job coming up next week, and if you are freaking out at work, I need to know that you have someone there to take care of things. I won't be able to concentrate on my work if you don't have that."

Mallory pulled her legs up under her and leaned into the broad chest of the man she needed more than anyone. More than anything in her life, she wanted Monroe and who he was when he was with her.

"What if I can't go back?" she whispered, her fear loud in her words.

"Then we figure something else out, or we try another place. It might not be the job. It might be the place. Sweetheart, I have no idea how you're going to react to being back at work in the place where you were kidnapped. I don't think we can do more than guess until you do it. I hate to let you out of our total protection, but if we don't, we will never know. So, as much as I hate to say it, I'm okay with you trying to go back, but you must know that I will have you yanked out of there in two seconds if there is any sign either you or those around you can't cope with being there."

She spoke, her voice muffled in his chest. "I can deal with that."

"Can you deal with the fact that we have to stay at my place for a while? Sharlee and Kaden have scrubbed you from the internet, but that doesn't mean people didn't already check out where you live. I don't want to give them any opportunities to get to you."

"How long?"

She was comfortable in her townhome, but honestly, since all of this happened, and she learned what being the center of someone's world really felt like, she didn't want to go back to living alone. It was a bluff when she said she would go there because it was the last thing she wanted to do. Mallory needed a compromise, though. Giving up one's singleton life wasn't as easy as it had first sounded when she was looking for a partner.

"Do you mean how long will you need to live with me, or how long will you need to stay out of your place?"

"Both?"

Monroe gathered Mallory into his lap and helped her curl back in comfortably. "Baby, don't you know how much you mean to me? How special you are to me? I never want you to leave my side. Mallory, I'm falling in love with you. We can stay at your place or mine, but I'm leaning towards mine because we have better security there. And we aren't in the middle of everyone when we want to get a little loud."

"But what would I... wait—" Mallory sat up, jostling his jaw slightly. "Did you say you were falling in love with me?"

Monroe laughed. "Yes. I believe I have been half in love since the second time we talked on the phone, and you spoke about everything. You held nothing back. If I asked, you answered. And then you got yourself off for me on the phone. I was hooked."

"Great, now I'm embarrassed." Mallory tried to duck her head back down, but Monroe didn't allow that.

"No, I needed that. It surprised me you did the phone sex, but pleasantly. It was refreshing and honest. I knew you were for me when you trusted me, even in your hesitation. So, when it's clear of potential danger, I don't mind living with you in your place, but those are my concerns."

"We'll talk about it again later. I'm good at your house, I think. I've never seen it."

"No, I guess you haven't. We'll remedy that this weekend. I'll move us over there, but I have a two-day job that I need to finish first. I'll have to leave you at Jac and Sharlee's for the time I'm gone."

"Monroe, I—"

"No, that is non-negotiable. You already have 20 swats coming, so before you say or do something you will soon regret, the answer is yes, sir."

"Yes, sir."

"Good. Now, find something to keep you occupied while I have a meeting in the office, and then we will have dinner before the fun begins."

MONROE PLACED THE LAST dish in the dish drainer and tossed his towel on top. "Now it's time we close up and head to bed."

Garrett had finished dinner, and at Monroe's insistence, he'd gone to shower. Garrett slept in the front room on the broad sectional sofa instead of sleeping in a bedroom because they were at the other end of the hall and away from the door. The sofa was soft, and he swore it was more comfortable than his bed. Mallory didn't believe him, but she allowed the statement to go unchallenged.

Mallory discovered herself liking Garrett more and more. He was older than Monroe by a couple of years. He was certainly fit and had fast reflexes. Still, he rarely did the more energetic assignments, his words, not hers. Mentally and physically, he beat any thirty-year-old man hands down that wasn't already working for Jac. But he did bodyguard often like now.

When Garrett returned, Monroe did the nightly perimeter check. "Why do you pick the bodyguard jobs?" Mallory asked as she sat down near him on the sofa.

"I like the fact that using your head is often more advantageous than your brawn. I also like that you rarely sleep outside because I've paid my dues. This is a cushy job, and I like it." He shrugged. "Besides, since we have Josie doing the books, I only have to gather the day-to-day paperwork and take it to her. I run the budget, in theory, make acquisitions, but I need more to do than that."

"Monroe does the scheduling?"

"He does. He likes that kind of personnel crap. I feel like it's going to make my head explode."

"Don't you have a personnel person?"

"Nah, we hire, fire, make most personnel decisions between us. Mostly Monroe and Jac. Keeps things simple. Monroe has a way with people and can figure things out to help without stepping on toes."

Mallory looked for Monroe but didn't see him yet, so she returned to the conversation. "I'd have thought that was Kaden's forte."

"Kaden is the woman whisperer. Even Ivy says it's his gift, so we use Kaden to figure out what to do when the women go off-plan."

Mallory crossed her arms. "Meaning when we don't do what you want us to?"

"Sometimes. It is also when one woman has decided their way is better than the agreed plan. Something to note. We don't like rules ourselves, so we don't make them for entertainment. They are there for a reason. Don't forget, we are more experienced in the ways of survival and warfare than we will ever let any of you become.

"Whether you like it or not, you're part of our family now, Mallory. Get used to all these mouthy, opinionated, and protective brothers and their clannish women because you are now one of them."

"That's the only part that makes being with you bossy men worth it. The belonging, the connections. Otherwise, you'd be out."

Garrett laughed and kissed her forehead. "I think Monroe has a few more things that keep you tethered to him. "

Mallory wondered if Garrett spanked his women. She shook her head and wondered when she looked at the world through kinky lenses. She didn't think she did with others, but inside this team that made no bones about the fact that they worked hard, played hard, and loved passionately, it was a natural thought path.

That love included over-protective instincts and being all in when it came to giving their women what they wanted and needed. It also included that realm of play that each couple worked out for themselves.

For Mallory, she'd known some things flipped her sexual hot switch more than others. She knew things like loving, dominant men that were putty in their woman's hands but stood their ground when needed was on her list. Spanking had always excited her, and later, light bondage joined the playlist.

And when Monroe gave her everything, then took for himself, giving her fast and furious when she wanted and slow and easy when she didn't was something she had never experienced with another man. She had her fair share of experiences to compare with, and she could say with confidence, Monroe was a thoughtful lover.

Monroe was like that and more. He didn't want her to pleasure him unless he had pleasured her. He'd said it was because once he had gotten off, all he wanted was to snuggle with her, maybe talk a little, and go to sleep with her in his arms. She felt selfish to want that order of events too, but since he offered, she accepted. Mallory loved giving him pleasure, and at first, he was reticent to allow that, but she convinced him it was something she needed as well.

She watched as Monroe went past the window in his last walk-through of the property. Monroe covered every base before coming inside. Her man had one fine ass, and when he was working either here or at Jac and Sharlee's, he was intense, not letting anything get past him or go by the wayside. He was why Mallory felt the confidence to return to work, but she wouldn't tell him that just yet. Not when her victory was so hard-won and so recently gained.

Monroe and Garrett took turns doing the security checks. As Mallory waited for Monroe, she thought about Garrett. She knew nothing about his life, really. No one had ever mentioned a wife or girlfriend and no children. He was an attractive man in a *rough around the edges* kind of way, like Monroe, but he also had a bit of sophistication about him that was hard to miss. He was always neat and clean, his beard well-trimmed like Monroe's darker one.

Garrett reached for the remote. "You about to head upstairs?"

"Yes. I'm just waiting on Monroe to finish walking the grounds." Garrett nodded, and Mallory decided not to wonder any longer. "Garrett, do you have a wife or girlfriend that no one has mentioned? Am I going to have to buy them chocolates or something to make up for you being away from home so much lately?"

Garrett laughed. "Monroe is right. You're damn cute for a doctor. But to answer your question, no, no one is waiting for me at home."

Mallory was instantly contrite. She knew what it was like to want something, and have it brought up that you didn't have it like a love interest. She knew that feeling very well indeed.

"Oh. I'm sorry if that's a touchy subject. That was inconsiderate of me. I try not to step into other's personal space."

Garrett chuckled. "Honey, you are with the wrong group of friends and certainly the wrong man if you are going to worry about everyone's feelings all the time. We are sensitive to each other but always honest because trust demands it. That can hurt sometimes. So, no harm done, but I'm curious why you think it's touchy?"

Mallory shrugged. "Just the way you seemed a little sad when you said it."

"Monroe said you were intuitive. Yes, the last proper relationship has been a while. My last lady left without even a '*goodbye, it's been nice knowing you*' conversation."

"You loved her."

"I did indeed. Still do. Not sure if permanent relationships are for me."

Mallory reached over and laid her hand on his, sitting on his thigh. "I thought that too until I met Monroe. I was positive that my life was too busy to spare anytime in a committed relationship because they are hard work. I mean, I wanted it, started to look for someone, but didn't hold out much hope."

"Yeah, I'm having trouble seeing women in a different light after Callie."

"Callie, that's her name? Well, I guess that makes sense, but don't close yourself off like I did. If Monroe didn't plow through my barriers, I wouldn't be happy now. You'll lock eyes with the woman of your dreams, and nothing else will matter. Not your plans, your protective wall, what others say, nothing. I hope you find her soon."

Garrett patted Mallory's hand, still resting on his. "I don't know about that for me. I'm a tough old bird, set in my ways, but I'm damn glad Monroe found you."

"Hush, you aren't old, and promise me you will keep an open mind when it comes to finding a woman."

"I will promise to do the best I can. Now can the touchy-feely shit be over?"

She laughed. "Yes, I'll leave you alone, for now."

"Monroe said you were a brat. I'll tell him you need an extra few swats from me."

"You will not," she said as she stood up. "He needs no incentives. Speaking of which, what's taking him so long?"

"Good question. Go into the bedroom and lock the door," said Garrett, suddenly more alert as he stood and began long strides to the front door. He opened the heavy inner door and reached for the outer metal one when Monroe yanked it open.

"Everything as it should be?" asked Garrett.

"I don't know, but I think so. There was rustling in the underbrush at the eastern corner of the yard, and then the security camera came on near the sound. It was likely a bear or something, but I couldn't be sure without seeing it. All quiet now."

"Sounds good. I sent Mallory to the bedroom." Garrett turned around to see Mallory standing in the living room. "Which I see she didn't do."

"The door was open before I got there. You didn't say run."

Garrett shook his head. "Mallory, you need to remember what I said earlier about rules." He nodded in Monroe's direction. "Take your woman to bed. I'll stay up a while longer."

"Going now, but I'm keeping one ear to the ground. I'll relieve you at six unless you need me soon."

"Night," Mallory said before leading the way to the bedroom, knowing she was well protected. She hoped Garrett would find someone soon. He deserved to be happy.

Chapter 13

O nce she finished her shower, she stepped aside for Monroe to hop in. "I'll be out in a moment. I just need to do a quick suds and rinse. Do not put on clothes."

Instead of responding, Mallory made a production of stretching and bending, showing all her wares. Monroe knew what to do with women who teased their men. "I'll be fast, but until I do, I want you standing in the corner and think about why you are getting your ass peppered with twenty swats."

"With your hand."

"Mal, why am I going to spank you?"

"Because I love it?"

His eyebrow raised, and he had to work hard not to show his amusement. "Besides that. What did you do?"

She looked down at her feet and sighed. "I yelled at you, and then I tried to use sex as a weapon to make you do what I wanted. But to be honest, you didn't want to listen."

"Twenty swats, with my hand. And I listen to everything you say. We'll discuss this further when I come back. I want to send you to put your cute as hell nose in the corner, naughty girl because it's the only part of this that will be actual punishment. Think you can do that?"

Mallory didn't say another word, though she looked like she wanted to say plenty. She had declared the couple of times he'd used it recently; she didn't like it.

"I hate standing in a corner. It's a colossal waste of time. I'm a professional, for heaven's sake. Professionals don't stand in the corner."

He rubbed her arm as a physical connection. Although the bruises had finally healed, the memory still had her flinching if he reached toward her face while she looked at him. When she was held tight to him, she didn't react in that fearful way. The first time she jerked her head away, it was a sharp, physical pain in his chest. Then the anger took over, and he wanted to kill Romaine.

"Colossal, huh? Your professional hat comes off when you aren't at work. When you're with me, you're off duty and all mine. And what's mine finds her ass in trouble when she steps out of line. And you are hot as hell standing there, so I can ogle your sweet bottom as an additional benefit for me. Besides, you know it gets you off to be dominated."

"But not put on display."

His eyes were warm and kind as he watched her plead with her eyes. "Baby, you need to recenter after all the changes. That's why I use the corner, to give you some breathing space. You won't take it otherwise." His face grew stern as she opened her mouth to reply. He kissed her quickly. "And we both know it. I require you to do nothing but bring yourself back into focus."

Mallory was well aware that Monroe was privy to most of her secrets, so she didn't attempt to hide her arousal. In fact, the little minx had used it to her advantage. He'd given in on things he wouldn't have, like sitting outside on the steps that were not shaded from the sun. She'd done it for too long, and her face and shoulders burned.

"I'm disappointed in you, Mal. You know better. Never fear. I know how to make it feel better."

Yeah, he'd enjoyed that spanking. When Mallory showered and coated her skin in anti-inflammatory and aloe cream, he'd peppered her ass with his experienced hand and then brought out his paddle and landed two good swats. He'd transferred the burn.

Mallory was smart and didn't want any swats added, even though he had no doubt her panties were slick with her arousal at the anticipation of just that. She slowly made her way to the nearest empty corner. She didn't consciously want him to add an implement to the party but knew it would be his well-used leather belt if he did. His paddle was for real infractions. The safety kind. According to Mallory, the paddle was an implement she loved to hate, but the leather made her warm all over. He figured he'd switch to another belt for daily wear and keep the one he now used for swats to her begging butt when needed.

"Now," he said as he strode to the bathroom, "I expect you will have thought about the way things went down and what needs to be different. Or not. You know I enjoy looking at that fine ass. In fact, poke that set of cheeks out more. Yes, very fine indeed."

She wiggled at his sincere appreciation for her assets, and he liked that. He never wanted her to think he disapproved and was anything but eternally grateful that she had chosen him to introduce her around at the little gathering where they had met. From that moment on, his mind was on her.

Everything about her was vital to him. He walked into the bathroom, stripping as he went. He flipped on the shower and didn't wait until it warmed up but jumped in the initial icy stream and let it invigorate him before settling into the much hotter typical shower he took.

Monroe wondered how hot Mallory liked her showers? He knew she favored a long hot soak, but it was just another thing that he didn't know about her. He was trying to fill in the blanks as fast as he could, but it was going to take time. While he worked through them, he found himself frustrated he didn't know it all.

Professionally, he was calm, collected, patient. He deliberated things and acted on his conclusions with conviction. That was how his personal life had been as well until Mallory. Now he was reactive, less patient with those in his way, and at times his determination wavered.

She unraveled him, and he hated the lack of confidence in his logic, but he loved having her in his life. The guys said he would work it out. He hoped it happened soon, or he would be a basket case. He rinsed off and got out, grabbed a towel, and dried off as he walked into the bedroom. Time to get his woman warm and tingly before he took her to the stars.

Chapter 14

Mallory could hear Monroe as he returned from his shower. She had memorized his routine, so she could imagine him toweling off in a particular manner. He dried the back of his neck and hair in a quick, rough manner. Then he went over his shoulders, dried his arms from top to bottom, first the left one, then the right. Next, he moved to his back, butt, and belly. Finally, he bent down to get his legs and then the jewel box, carefully covering that area.

The rest of his toiletry was fascinating too, but he would have skipped it and tossed the towel near the bed as he did when he wanted to have sex. Mallory wondered if he did the same thing as she did, visualizing her habitual actions. It was so intimate to learn his habits and routines so well that she didn't need to see him perform them to know what he was doing.

She heard him open the drawer, but she couldn't quite tell what he was bringing out. Next, it was quiet. Too quiet. What was he up to? Her brain earnestly tried to devise what was happening. Monroe could be a sneaky one.

"Mallory," said the voice that meant so much to her, warmth, comfort, security, love... should she tell him? Would it push him away? It was too early. Was there a time minimum? What was the protocol? He whispered again, this time with a touch of amusement.

"Are you napping?"

"What? No. I almost sat down and did that but figured you wouldn't appreciate it."

"And the number of swats would have increased."

"Yep, that was the main reason. Can I please turn around now?"

"You may and then go on over to the bed. I'm going to get the naughty payment out of the way so we can get to the good stuff."

"If you wanted to, this could be good too?" Mallory hoped he wouldn't call her on topping because she really needed to get off.

"Oh, you're going to like this when it settles in."

He sat on the bed and patted his thigh. Mallory hated this part. When a spanking was spontaneous, there was no feeling of shame when you were pulled over, and the spanking began immediately. But that was actual punishment, and she didn't and probably wouldn't get that, no matter how much Monroe inferred it.

Once she was settled, Monroe massaged and kneaded her butt cheeks to bring the blood up. She knew it helped with bruising and all that, but at this moment, it was just more delay. She wiggled and jumped when Monroe answered with a stingy smack.

"Ow. I was just getting settled."

"Uh-huh. Don't add lying to your list. It will double your count."

"No, no. Sorry, sir. I really was just trying to get things going. I'm jumpy and was hoping that all this tonight would help calm me down."

"I know, sweetie. It's why I don't ping you for topping."

Damn, he could read her mind. "No, sir. I'm sorry, Monroe."

"Okay, tell you what. I've got this pretty gem tipped place holder I thought I'd use."

"Place-oh, not a plug." Another handprint of stinging flesh. "Sir. Please, I don't like them."

"Oh? I didn't see it on your limits as an absolute no. In fact," he pulled out the sheet he had in the nightstand drawer and went to the section about asses. "Yep, all are marked either yes, or willing to try. Your plug play experience is marked, some experience, willing to try."

"It was a mistake."

"So, are you safe wording on the plug experience? It really does enhance the spanking effects, and I think you will love it, but," he shrugged.

"I'm not safe wording, sir." He was right. He usually was, and she needed his expertise to bring on some amazing orgasms to take this awful stress away.

"Mallory, are you sure? I'll be gentle and will make sure you get what you need, but we can try it another night if you need to pass on this tonight."

"No, sir. I'm good."

"Positive?"

"Dammit, Monroe, I said it's fine, now get on with it." Two slaps landed on her ass. Then he waited. She smacked his calf out of irritated frustration.

He chuckled, and as a way of response, he flipped open the top of a bottle of lube, the sound familiar because she had used lube often enough on her own. She shivered as her bottom cheeks were spread, and cold lube, no, not cold, room temperature, drizzled down into her crack and massaged into her virgin entrance.

Yep, he was her first back there. When they first discussed limits, Mallory didn't tell Monroe because she didn't want him to know how much of a novice she had been because she really liked him. He was experienced, looking for someone equally experienced, or at least more knowledgeable than she was.

If she said anything now, he would be disappointed and maybe angry. She would have violated his trust. The trust that, in this type of relationship, was key to staying together. It put the dom in a dangerous situation if he thought one thing and played accordingly, only to find out that wasn't the case. Not only was it a safety issue, it was much more than that, but Mallory couldn't tell him now, so she prayed it was as good as he had said.

"Don't tighten, baby. Remember to try to relax. I'll be as gentle as I can." While he spoke, his finger invaded her dark place, and she screeched. He slapped her ass again. "Stop that. This is a finger; you know how this goes. Now no more yelling."

Mallory didn't answer, or she might let it slip what she couldn't tell him. Instead, she concentrated on the sensations she was feeling in her backside. An invading finger that wiggled and gave her an oddly exciting, funny feeling. Tingling engulfed her whole lower region began causing her to release arousal fluid, and she expected more and craved more.

When Monroe pulled his finger out, she moaned. His answering chuckle was followed by the sound of more lube, and before she had fully processed his next move, the plug was sliding in and out of her darkness. She moaned her appreciation for the sensation, the experience, even the fact that he questioned her reticence.

"This is so good."

Monroe didn't chuckle this time. She vaguely noticed he stilled for a moment and then continued to seat the plug firmly before landing a hard spank on her ass, followed by another. He continued to land his palm over and over on the full of her ass. Monroe never hit too high, and his aim was accurate. He landed several swats over the protruding bit of the plug. She grunted when she felt the sudden jolt.

"That's twenty, Mal, but you have another five."

"What? Why?" she asked breathlessly.

"You lied to me. You have never had a plug before. Never experienced butt play other than a few spankings done less than skillfully. Why?"

"I didn't want you to know I was so inexperienced. I mean, you wouldn't have given me the time of day if I had said I've had a beginner's class and about five or six rounds of play. Everything else I did was to meet Chas' needs. I met my own needs, inadequately, later after he had gone to sleep."

"What the hell are you talking about?"

"I wanted to be with you. I didn't want you to think I was too much trouble."

"By being inexperienced? Mallory, I would have known anyway. The way your eyes would light up when you saw a basic scene going on, or how you would flush and look down when someone would find their release. How you moved closer to me when we saw a sadist flogging his pain-seeking partner at the party. Baby, I already knew because you told me. But you put me in an untenable position, and you risked your safety because you lied to me."

"I'm sorry!"

"Yep, hold that thought."

He stood and laid Mallory on the edge of the bed. The tale-tell jingle of his belt buckle told Mallory how he intended to teach her this lesson. She could have safe-worded, but it wasn't the five swings of the belt; it was the reason for them. She violated the trust they were building. The tears started before the first leather landed on her already tenderized backside.

Monroe was silent as he swung the leather against her displayed backside. His silence was even worse than being angry. She had hurt him, disappointed him, and maybe this would cause him to withdraw from the relationship. He said he was in for the long haul, but she'd never lied to him. The second stripe landed, and she was balling. By the fifth swing of the belt, she was having trouble breathing between the sobs. The first twenty were tingly and ouchy, but the last five tore at her soul.

Monroe was rocking her and murmuring nonsensical words in her ear in his soothing, smooth tones, comforting her, stroking her arms. The tears kept coming, and soon she didn't even hear his words over the torrential waterfall.

Finally, Monroe must have decided it was enough purging because, as she slowed her crying by necessity to breathe, he spoke again. This time, she could understand him.

"Mal, listen, baby. Take some deep breaths and let them out." When her crying revved up again, his tone darkened. "No. That is enough. I know you needed the purge, and I'm all for that, but you're making yourself sick now, and that's too much. If you don't start breathing and slow the crying, you will vomit soon."

Mallory nodded her head. He was right. How was she going to face him? She prided herself on honesty, but she lied about something so fundamental in their relationship.

"Mallory, baby, it's part of the learning process we are in right now. We have to tease out the important bits of the lifestyle and our dynamics in it." Mallory nodded, so he continued in his whisky smooth voice. "I know you're worried about things, about my reactions, but don't guess what you think I would want if you don't have some good indication. Tell me, ask me, show me, whatever works, but don't make assumptions."

"You still want to be with me?" she asked in a stuttering, halting rhythm.

"There is nothing in this world that would stop me from loving you, wanting to be with you. If you are unfaithful to me, that will shake the foundation, but even then, I would want you even if I didn't stay with you."

"I would never cheat on you." Her hiccups were still strong.

"I don't believe you would, but my point is we will make mistakes, we will fix them or make up for them. I heard make-up sex is great, by the way." Mallory sniffed and giggled.

"But on the plug, I would have gone slower, explained what was going on, why I thought it was something you would enjoy. Instead, you robbed yourself of an orgasm that I know you would have reached because you were so responsive."

"I'm sorry," she whispered.

"I know, but you also took the enjoyment from me because I knew I didn't give you the first experience you should have had." He looked at Mallory and handed her another tissue. "If you start your waterfalls again, I will pull out the rubber paddle, and at least you will blubber for a better reason."

Mallory laughed when she heard his bluster that was all noise, no substance. She loved him, and the revelation blurted from her lips. "I love you."

The room was quiet. He sighed. "I know, sweetheart, I love you too. That's why we have to try hard to get this right. No more hiding your thoughts or feeling. No more covering up your experiences or making up ones that never happened. Open and honest is the motto for each day. And if you are ever in a situation, or I am, anything I say will be the truth. Good or bad, it will be honest, so you will never have to wonder. You do that as well, and I'll always know and can plan based on that knowledge." Mallory nodded. "Words, sweetheart, your Dom needs words, and so does your lover."

"I understand, and I'm sorry that I screwed everything up."

"Good, because there is a part B to this dishonesty."

"What?"

"You are taking the limits list that I have, and you will slowly go back through it again. You will be very specific and honest about what you have done, haven't experienced, and whether you would like it again, to try it, or couldn't consider it."

"But the rest are right."

His Dom's voice came out, and Mallory was a goner. He was right, and she knew he wouldn't back down on the requirement. She was familiar with this Monroe.

"Young lady, do you need some up close and personal time with the rubber paddle to help you see the benefits of doing as I say?"

Mallory tossed her head back before straightening again. "No, I get it."

"Good, tomorrow is a good day for you to start on that. I'll be gone on a job, and then I'll leave for a two-day gig. You will be at Jac and Sharlee's. Then we will pack up and go to my house."

"Okay."

He grinned at her easy compliance. "Good. But now, I need to love on my woman, so climb in the bed and lay spread eagle in the center."

"Mmm, I could get into that." She paused and looked back at Monroe before crawling to the center of the bed. He swatted her butt once. Looking back again, she said with an impish grin, "Sir."

Mallory noticed for the first time that the plug had disappeared. Where it went and when it had been removed, she'd didn't know, but she knew that there was some kind of transporting magic in that kind of backdoor play, and she would try it again soon. Maybe revisiting the limits list was a good idea. She had more insight now, and while blood play and other items were firmly in the "No, thank you" column, some things like booty play had moved up in her estimation. Monroe had done that. He introduced new things with a twist and a gentle hand.

Even when Mallory thought it was too much, she had agreed early on the first meeting when they had met to allow him to show her new things. In turn, he promised to stop if he saw or heard too much anxiety or if the scene wasn't going the way he had expected.

And she trusted him. Monroe said that was the key, and it did actually influence everything. But she knew it all came down to him. His protection of her in every way, his confident possession of her sexual desires and right now, he was the center of her mental health and any stability she possessed in every part of her life. So making herself totally vulnerable to him, spread eagle in the center of the bed, was not only natural but exciting.

The echoing sound and the shock of the sting in the shape of an impatient man's handprint brought Mallory out of her head.

"There you are. Where did you go?"

"Sorry. These days my mind often wanders without notice." She scrambled into place.

"You okay?" The honest concern in his tone was like a gentle breeze rejuvenating her mind and soothing her soul.

"I am. Am I in the right position?"

Monroe watched her for a few more seconds, and when he seemed to believe she was okay, not saying it just to please him, he nodded and leaned over her body on display. Tweaking her puckered nipples, he smiled that particular way that gave her shivers of worry and yummy trembles of anticipation.

"Good. I now revoke your talking privileges until I say you can speak again. Safeword excluded. Understood?"

Mallory nodded, and again he watched her for another moment before nodding in approval. He pulled up the sheepskin-lined leather handcuffs attached to the bed. He left her ankles free but being restrained was one thing she was sure would be a trigger. Blindfolded was another.

Her breath was becoming more shallow, and her heart rate had kicked up, its beat being felt and heard in multiple pulse spots on her exposed body. She was becoming overly warm, her skin showing a sheen of perspiration as he touched her. Her arousal was like a wildfire. She wiggled.

Mallory knew by now that Monroe would not allow her to stop his progression to her pink bits. Still, she instinctively wanted to, however mentally and physically, she was waiting for him to continue. Monroe didn't stop his progression. He spoke in the build-up of reaching her pink flesh, most likely red now.

"Mallory Sasse, I love every fucking thing about you. I love the little, tiny hairs so much like newborn down on the top of your ears, to the quiver in your soft belly."

His kisses and touches descended to Mallory's mons, where he ran his fingers down her landing strip before opening her pussy wide for his delight.

"This is so beautiful, baby. You are exquisite, and I can hardly believe you are offering yourself to me. You're a goddess and I, a mere peon."

He leaned down and took possession of her lips, wasting no time inserting his tongue to duel with hers. When Monroe lifted his head, leaving them both breathless, Mallory followed his lips, trying to reconnect. He shook his head in a way that said she knew better.

"You are a goddess, and I'm your peon, except in the bedroom. Here I am, the god to your goddess, and there are consequences for being naughty. Topping is naughty."

He rolled Mallory over and landed a couple of swats to her still warm bottom, and the whimper she gave him told him she not only felt it, but it was morphing her yearnings into full-fledged need.

His gentle touch slid over her warm skin lightly, his fingers tracing the very spots she was feeling her own pulse. His lips following his fingers. Her temple, her neck, the base of her throat, her breast. He continued after a few passes, massaging her breasts, and tweaking her nipples to the concave in her hips, gently kissing every place he touched.

Mallory's sex trickled with arousal in waves as her undulating core muscles contracted. She had no control. Monroe had it all. And she fucking loved it. His finger slid right onto her clit without hesitation. This man didn't need to hunt it down. She jerked when he touched her overly sensitive bundle of sexy nerves. His digit teased, traced, dipped in the pool of liquid passion, and played before coming back out, only to insert two fingers inside her. But they, too, were withdrawn as she tried to move her hips to keep him deeper inside for longer.

"Naughty girl."

He slapped her pussy, his fingers hitting her clit perfectly, and she lost her breath as the building climax peaked. She cried out and held her position, stiff and still until the first intensity crested, then she began bucking. He leaned over her thighs and slapped them to signal she should stop. She ultimately did. He flicked her now exposed clit, slamming her into another orgasm.

When she finally noticed her surroundings again, Monroe was angling her pelvis and plunged inside. Mallory, without thought, met the rhythm he created. She took her unbound legs and wrapped them around Monroe as he quickly worked his way to pounding as he pistoned in and smoothly slid out. Her heels dug into his flexing ass as he took her.

Mallory became lost in the repetitious tempo. "I'm about there, sweetheart. Get yourself off."

Without further instructions, Mallory did just that. She would not achieve it without help after the two hard ones she had already had. As she watched him throw his head back, she redoubled her efforts, and she was right there with him, enjoying the overwhelming pleasure of completion.

Leaning down to kiss her after disengaging Mallory's ankles from around his waist, he strode to the bathroom and brought back a washcloth to help with Mallory's clean-up. It was always so embarrassing to submit to his care of her lady bits because the frenzied passion was over, her libido satisfied, and the cleansing was very intimate during her cooldown. Awkward. But it was just what this man would do, gently take care of her needs while showing her, in his own way, that there was nothing she would hide from him, ever. She loved him for every little annoyingly exasperating thing he did to demonstrate she was his.

Chapter 15

"Where is Mallory?" demanded Sharlee. Monroe gave the phone an irritated male look totally lost on Sharlee but made Mallory giggle groggily. Monroe looked at the clock on his nightstand out of habit. He looked over at Mallory as she snuggled back under the cover and put her head back on his shoulder.

He whispered his gruff reply. "There had better be a reason you are using that tone with me at this time of the night, Charlotte, or my paddle will be coming out."

"Monroe, listen to me. Do. You. Have. Mallory?"

The purely dominant voice changed instantly to concern. "Yes, of course. She's right here. What the hell are you—" His tone darkened. "Talk."

"Oh, thank God. Another woman has been abducted. They recovered her body just an hour ago, but the woman looked like Mallory from the back and even from the side angle. Reporters are questioning if it is Mallory. I'm running the woman's photo through the data bank now, but I think it's time we put Mallory on the Keep Safe System Roster and possibly lock her down. We've overlooked something."

"Roger that. When do you want to do it?"

"Now. I don't know what's happening, but I'd lay odds it has something to do with Mallory getting away from the

184

kidnapper. There has to be an accomplice. Oh, and Monroe, something else since you're awake. The woman Mallory saved from the cellar has just died. About fifteen minutes ago."

"Damn."

Jac's voice came over the speaker. "Let's talk about added security measures and the new information tomorrow. O-eight hundred."

"Copy that. We'll be there."

JEANNE HAD MISCALCULATED, not paying attention to the signs that she wasn't grabbing the right person. She'd focused too much on capturing the woman that she hadn't noticed the differences. Hadn't noticed it wasn't that Sasse woman. Once she'd pulled out the I.D. to verify she had the right one, rage roared through her veins when she realized it was not the pharmacist. When Jeanne finished with her, there wouldn't be anything sassy about her. She'd be scattered to the four corners of the earth. But right now, she had another problem.

Her master had wanted that woman, that pharmacist. After all Jeanne had endured, after all she had done for her master, she dared to want another to keep. It was one thing to keep the other women for a while to get his rocks off. It had been a relief not to have to satisfy Master's baser needs, but she'd been with him, cleaning up after him, slaving for him for fourteen years. She deserved his loyalty.

Craig spoke of how perfect Mallory Sasse was and how he was going to keep her. When he acted like he had the queen of the world in the cellar, Jeanne had known it was going to be a problem. He'd never treated anyone else with the care he treated that pharmacist. That's when Jeanne knew she had to get rid of that woman. But the pharmacist had escaped and gotten Jeanne's master thrown in jail. Jeanne was going to make that woman pay for taking her master from her.

Then the FBI found the bodies. They could find more because there were more. Jeanne's life was over, and it was all because of that bitch pharmacist. She would have to tighten her strategy. The next one she grabbed would be Mallory. Once she was taken care of, Jeanne would go on and find her own playthings. She might even try that hulk of a man that seems to be the pharmacist's boyfriend. It would take some planning, and she could do it, but first, things first.

Chapter 16

M onroe was recounting his night with Garrett when Mallory stumbled into the kitchen, barely awake, looking like a beautiful wreck.

He hated that the news of the kidnapped and then murdered woman had reignited Mallory's nightmares for most of the night. Monroe had hoped she would fall back to sleep when he took the call so he could have waited until morning to tell her, but his luck hadn't held out. Mallory asked the moment he hung up. Monroe tried to deflect her questions, but she wouldn't have it. She demanded to be told, and he obliged.

Mallory finally went to sleep out of sheer exhaustion, only to wake up from dreams often. Monroe had dozed in between dreams. Finally, at five, he rolled out of bed and showered in the second bathroom. Garrett rolled out right behind him, and while Monroe was explaining the night's revelations, he watched Mallory enter the room, then stop walking as though she wasn't sure she knew where she was.

Garrett left to hit the shower while Monroe checked in with his girl. He watched her teeter her final, unsteady steps further into the kitchen, and his heart hurt for her. The fact that she walked directly into his arms should have given him a boost to his ego, but all it did was remind him that his woman wasn't safe, and he didn't even know who presented the threat.

"Hey, baby. How are you this morning?"

"I feel like hell, and my world is out of control. I can't sleep more than an hour or so without having another nightmare, and I'm a prisoner even though I'm no longer captive in that cellar."

"I bet it's scary as fuck, but we can take control. Let me tell you about Keep Safe. It's a program that Sharlee created with hardware help from Kaden. It allows us to be alerted if you are in trouble and then to find you."

"I'm still in danger, aren't I? Whoever killed that woman thought it was me, didn't they?"

"We believe it is a possibility."

Mallory burrowed deeper into his arms. "Possibility? Hell, it's a reality. Maybe I should just pick up stakes and move to a more remote area, so I don't have to worry every time I go outside for the rest of my life."

His chest rumbled from his reaction. "You are not leaving my sight or the team's, and I can absolutely guarantee you that my baby isn't going anywhere that I don't also go. Since I'm not moving and you aren't running away, we are going to take this head-on."

His commanding voice got his point across, and when Mallory shivered in response, he knew it had. He set her slightly away from him and spoke briskly, as though it was a typical morning in their everyday life. He fooled no one.

"Now, want coffee? How about breakfast?"

She'd turned him down and then took the coffee but later left the cup in the car untouched.

MONROE ESCORTED A MORE awake but still shaken Mallory through Jacquard and Associates' doors. She hadn't been to the offices before, and it definitely looked like nothing but business happened behind its entrance. There was a distinctly powerful feeling here, more than when the team conducted business at Jac and Sharlee's house.

The Feds got a little bit agency happy when they collaborated on designing and installing the security. They also had some input on the business floor layout. Downstairs was a different story, giving the teams a feeling of familiarity. Jac and the guys designed and put that area together, and Monroe much preferred it there. But today was business.

Instead of letting her dwell on the sterility of the reception area manned by someone she had never met, he rubbed her back and then settled his hand above the curve of her very luscious bottom. He steered her to Jac's office, where they were met by a friendly face and Becky's sunshine smile.

"Well, hello, you two," said Becky.

Becky gave incredible hugs that were completely sincere. Mallory turned to accept Becky's hug. No one turned her down if she offered them one, including Monroe. The women stepped apart, and Mallory spoke.

"I needed that. It's been a hard night. I know you must have heard about the mess last night."

"Jac told me. I'm so glad it wasn't you."

"Thanks, but that means Jac and the guys must figure out a safety net plan for me so I can go back to work."

"Mal, I'm not sure..." started Monroe.

"Ignore him," said Mallory, "he has already agreed. And I'm going to see Sharlee about this protection program she has."

"Yes. Keep Safe Security System and Device."

"That's the one," said Monroe. "I hate to rush away, but Sharlee sent me a text asking where we were. Tell Jac I'll be back in a couple of minutes, and later you ladies can have a visit while we work on this plan."

Mallory let out a huff of annoyance, but Becky readily agreed. "Sure. I'll make you fresh coffee when you get back, Mallory. Maybe we can have lunch. We'll see how it goes, alright?"

Mallory nodded and tried to give Becky a return smile, but it came out as a grimace.

"Let's go, Grumpy," said Monroe, as he shuffled her along the corridor until they got to the end of the hall and waited for Sharlee to open the door.

The metal door slid open, and the first glimpse of Sharlee's office blew Monroe away. He hadn't been in with the equipment set up. It looked like he'd walked into the space center control room. Mallory's mood shifted again, and she smiled in genuine enjoyment. The women seemed to connect so well. Jessie rose from the corner chair and sauntered over to the small group.

"Hi. I'm here to be the demonstrator since I've used it and obviously have so little importance with which to fill my life."

Mallory laughed. "I gotcha beat on that little market, chickadee."

"Yes," agreed Jessie. "You certainly do, but not for long."

"Can we get moving on this? I have things to do, and we're behind schedule." Sharlee was all business now that the greetings were over.

"You have a schedule?" Mallory asked with incredulity.

"Watch it, friend. I have another friend with a red rubber paddle, and I know he is heavy-handed, so just watch it."

How Sharlee kept a straight face when her eyes were sparkling so much, Monroe didn't know. "If you girls decide on lunch, use the lunchroom, not the restaurant down the street. Hear me? Oh, and don't forget Becky. And call Ivy."

With that, he dropped a toe-curling kiss on Mallory's unsuspecting lips that left them both gasping for oxygen before his long legs took him out of the room.

"Whew," said Jessie, "Our guys are so hot." Mallory agreed with her star-struck grin.

"Focus," Sharlee said. "This is where we begin."

After two hours of learning, Sharlee declared them ready to go live. "Now, the Keep Safe System is connected to your phone, you've practiced using the program, and I'm satisfied you can use it if you need it." Mallory thought the most challenging part was finding something to use as an activation combination. They decided on Zero@R. We have zero at our house, or something similar would work. It took a little while to figure out how she could do that naturally, but they figured it out. Jessie left an hour ago, after the demonstration part of the training.

By the time lunch rolled around, Mallory had finished talking about or experimenting with the *KSS* program. Her phone had been *KSSD*, and Mallory felt like punching anyone who suggested she practice more on the *KSSR*.

"You're right. I tend to go overboard on it, but I know it saved Jessie and would have done more to save Ivy if she had believed in it enough to learn the system better."

Ivy entered the room at the perfect moment to hear Sharlee's words. Mallory feared there would be a problem, but Ivy shrugged and plopped down in one of two chairs in the corner.

"I can't deny she might be right. I didn't think fast enough to make it work as well as it could, but also, I was knocked out, so," again, she shrugged.

"That's true. Anyway, we know it works and so if you find yourself in that kind of situation, activate the system. It can't hurt, and it could help. Now ladies, let's grab Becky and Jessie and find some food."

As the women walked into Jac's outer office, Becky was just hanging up the phone and closing up her desk.

Sharlee walked towards her husband's office door. "You ready, Becky?"

"More than. Jac's gone. He and the team went somewhere. Guess they have a few jobs to discuss and divvy up. But Monroe said to go to the cafeteria, and our lunch is ready for us. Jessie will meet us there."

"Oh, what are we eating?" asked Ivy.

Sharlee shook her head. "When the guys order, we get pizza or subs. When I order, we get healthy. Now, when Jessie orders, we get whatever she has a craving for. Becky orders what's quickest."

Mallory laughed and realized she hadn't done that as often as she used to. She would often laugh before she was kidnapped. Now she did it so much less that her brain made a silent comment when she did. Pathetic.

They walked into the lunchroom and found their food in a large box marked with Becky's name on it. The scent of Manuel's enchilada and fajita platters permeated the room, and Mallory smiled.

"Which one of the guys ordered this? I'm so very impressed with whichever one it is," said Jessie as she walked in, rubbing her belly.

"Better than sandwiches, for sure," said Sharlee.

Mallory smiled. "Monroe. He knows how much I love their food, and so I'm sure he ordered it."

Becky smiled. "You know, I always knew there was a different Monroe under all that macho, rubber paddle garbage. His no-nonsense cover is so blown."

Mallory's expression softened. "Really? He is intense sometimes, sure, but he's so loving and protective. He tries to do whatever he can to make things easier for me. Feeds me what I like, watches movies I want to see, lets me do the dishes before I go to bed, even though he would rather do them right after dinner. He is really the best kind of guy to be with."

Sharlee reached into the box and unloaded it. "It's because he's in love with you. He might love us like annoying younger sisters, but he is *in* love with you. Makes all the difference."

"It does," agreed Mallory.

Sharlee pulled out the meals and counted. "Who else is coming?"

"Me," answered Jessie as she strolled further into the room. "I finished with my audits about an hour ago, and Monroe sent me a text to come down for lunch. I could smell Manuel's food halfway down the hall. He always orders extra for me because I'm pregnant. I'm starved. What do we have?"

"Enchiladas and fajitas," said Ivy.

Jessie picked up a fork and a paper plate. "Yum, are we sharing?"

Mallory nodded. "Of course." She stopped as she thought about how she had answered for everyone. She felt so part of this group that she hadn't considered that not everyone was into sharing. "Unless I spoke out of turn?"

"Nope. I'm going to have a little of everything," answered Sharlee. The women sat down and dished up.

"This is so good," was mumbled over, "I have to go there for dinner." And so the conversation went. There was talking, laughing, and teasing, interwoven with a little serious conversation. The hour was up in a flash. Becky's cell phone alarm went off, and so did Sharlee's, signaling the end to lunch.

"I'll finish up here, ladies. You all go back to work," Mallory said as all four women left to return to their offices.

Even Ivy had a project she was working on. It was nice that Jac allowed her to combine her home business with her Jacquard and Associates business in her office. Jac didn't care so long as it didn't involve bringing in any clients to his business.

Becky now worked in Jac's outer office instead of the business reception area. It was safer for her. They had hired a previous service member to man the desk. While Mallory didn't know what it looked like before, she was sure it must have made Becky more exposed if Carter's demands were any sign. He sure loved Becky, and by the way she glowed when he was in the room or anyone spoke about him, Becky was in love with him.

There was so much violence in these men's and women's previous lives that Mallory couldn't understand why they wanted to find a civilian job that did the same thing. Garrett had said it was what they knew, but Mallory didn't believe that was the reason they stayed.

Jac was a hard taskmaster. He allowed others to do the work they hired them to do, but Sharlee had said it wasn't always that way. Jac was very hands-on. Very intense anytime they took on the high-profile jobs, which he hated. When they had a VIP to protect or extract from some sticky situation, Jac was all in. Now, he chose the team best suited for a job, and he directed when needed.

Garrett was the operations guy on the ground and in the office. Monroe was their strategist for all jobs at home, using his skill in personnel matters and the field. His talent was even more valuable on the ground when working with Carter's well-known trait was his fast-processing time. He and Monroe worked well in tandem. Monroe, like the other team members, was observant, something Mallory could attest to.

His excellent memory didn't always bode well for Mallory, but she usually benefited from his ability to remember what she liked and disliked. He didn't seem to forget when she recently blew up at him because of the stress that she didn't tell him about. He made her purge all the worries the last time and then sent her to soak in the tub. It was Heavenly. Then he edged her for what seemed like hours but was more like twenty or thirty minutes. While she still thought she shouldn't burden others with her problems, she was learning that Monroe wasn't just anyone.

She pulled out her tablet and checked her email while she waited for Monroe. There was a message from the Apothecary. Opening with trepidation, she wondered if they would terminate her employment because she had been gone too long. True, she had both paid and sick leave that she had used, but that was gone, and they needed to hire a temp pharmacist, which was very difficult to do. As she read the email, she relaxed. It was the paperwork to come back to work. Mallory smiled and checked on other mail. She needed to get the final agreement from Monroe, and then she thought she might be ready to try.

Looking at the list of emails, as she began deleting the trash, she saw one message from the district attorney. Until now, they had allowed the communication to go through Agent Gutierrez, but evidently, that didn't work anymore.

Ms. Sasse,

We have tried to reach you this morning but have been unsuccessful. I hope you are well. I need to speak to you. Please call at your earliest convenience.

Kurt Rogers,

District Attorney

Mallory picked up her phone and started to call but remembered her phone didn't work well inside the office due to the interconnected alarms, cameras, electronics, and computers everywhere. That was likely why they couldn't get hold of her. Forgetting she was to stay inside, she stepped out to the front sidewalk to call.

"Ms. Sasse. Thank you for calling me."

"Yes, I apologize. I'm at Jacquard and Associates offices, and my cell doesn't work well in here."

"Understood. Could we make an appointment to discuss the case?"

"Sure, but it will have to be when Monroe is available to be there, too. I don't think he is going to allow me to go anywhere alone. In fact, you can count on it. You can come to me. I'll be at Jacquard Reynaud's home for a few days."

"I rarely do that, Ms. Sasse."

His hesitancy to meet her where she felt safe was odd, she thought.

"Well, I suppose you will have to wait, then. How about Monday of next week?"

"What? No, that won't work."

Mallory could feel her heart rate rise and her skin breaking out in perspiration. She wasn't sure why her reactions were so intense, but they were, and if she had learned anything from Monroe, it was to listen to those deep, visceral feelings, even if you have no idea why they're there.

"Let me call you back."

Mallory hung up before he could respond and hurried back inside, but before she did, she had the uneasy feeling someone was watching her. Her belly cramped, and she felt icy tendrils of fear slide down her spine. It almost felt as though she were in danger. The hairs on the back of her neck even stood up. Her nerves and imagination pushed her to slip into Becky's office, and immediately she had a slightly less heebie-jeebie vibe.

"Hey, any sign of when the guys are going to be done?"

"No, sorry. It could be a while. Here, let me get some coffee going; plus, I know where the pastries and donuts are hidden."

"You mean the guys haven't found and eaten them?" Mallory tried to match her mood to Becky's, but it was no use.

"I know how to hide things," said Becky with a conspiratorial grin. "Besides, I put out little treats to put them off the scent. Come on."

Settling back on the comfy sofa in Becky's office with a big cup of creamy sweet coffee and a bag of donuts somehow made Mallory feel better. Monroe might have something to say about her choice of foods today, but he was taking a long time, so what was a girl to do? Besides, she needed fortification to tell him about the phone call and the apprehension she felt when it was all over.

MONROE, GARRETT, CARTER, Levi, Mark, and Jac turned into the office while the rest of the teams continued to other parts of the building. Monroe made a beeline towards Mallory and lifted his eyebrow when he saw the donuts in front of her.

"Don't say anything. I've had a stressful day."

"Is that so? Well, we're leaving, and you can tell me all about it while you pack your clothes for Jac's place tomorrow."

"What? I thought you weren't going yet."

"Sorry, but we have altered things in the plan because of the client's changes, so we have to adjust accordingly. It's a simple bodyguarding job but still needs some finesse." He pulled the plate with two remaining donuts away from her and put it on Becky's desk.

When he turned to respond to Levi, Mallory took a big bite out of a cherry-filled donut and then stood to walk out. She'd only eaten two before he had arrived, but she had saved the filled one because she liked it, and Mallory would not let him take away her treat. She needed the sugar support.

Monroe finished his conversation and turned to lead Mallory out. She ducked under his outstretched arm and walked ahead, chewing her beloved pastry. A solitary swat landed on her ass, making her jump. She wasn't like this usually, but sometimes a girl had to break the rules. She loved that Monroe could take a little bratting.

She felt the warmth from the mighty smack across her butt, and she grinned, then giggled, feeling airy and light from his attention. When they stepped outside, the same graveyard shiver raced through her body. The dread returned, and she looked around to see if anyone was watching her. There was no one in sight.

"Mal, what's wrong?"

She hesitated too long. "Nothing."

"Honesty, remember?"

Damn, he had to pull out that card. He was going to be so hard to get anything past. And right now, it didn't annoy her. She was grateful.

"I was out here earlier, and it felt like I was being watched. I felt it deep in my belly. And that dread, like something horrible, is going to happen. Like I'm being observed maliciously. I can't shake the fear." Monroe was instantly on alert and pushed her back inside.

"Get Garrett. Tell them, Code Gray." His demand, heavily infused with urgency, caused her to hesitate for a moment in time. Mallory felt frozen. "Mallory, now!"

That snapped her out of limbo. She rushed inside, telling the reception that she needed Garrett immediately. The enormous man at the front desk pressed a button, and Mallory could hear lots of movement, more noise than one man would make, from the hallway. Jac, Garrett, and some man she had only seen in passing raced through the hall and burst outside.

For the first time since hearing the decision, she understood why Jac decided no one manned the front desk unless they were well trained. Man or woman wasn't the point. It was the level of training. Evidently, this man passed the test. He put her in the office behind his desk.

"Don't leave until we come and get you." And the door closed behind him.

Mallory's thoughts went completely wild. Was someone outside? Did Monroe see a person out there? Did the guys catch him? Her lack of knowing what was going on was killing her, but she didn't dare open the door because her imagination and fear stood firmly in the way.

Before her kidnapping, she was reasonably fearless. She wasn't unsafe or a risk-taker, but few things made her afraid. After the kidnapping, her imagination had grown exponentially, and the possibilities of danger lurked everywhere she turned.

Ten minutes later, Becky entered the little room Mallory was in, instantly relieving her chaotic thoughts.

"Becky, thank goodness. I'm not sure I could have handled the waiting alone for much longer."

Becky hugged Mallory and sat in the cushioned chair beside her. "Are you okay?"

"Yes, I'm not hurt or anything. But, what's going on?"

Becky shook her head. "Not sure exactly. What I do know is half a dozen of the guys are scouring the bushes, and Sharlee is scanning the footage from today."

"I don't understand. I just told Monroe that I had the creepy feeling that someone was watching me, and I had it earlier when I stepped outside."

"When did you step outside?"

"Before I showed up in your office after lunch. I went out to talk to the Prosecutor, and I felt the same eerie vibe when I was out there. It was so bad that I hurried to your office. At first, I thought it was the attorney because he was hard to deal with but maybe not."

"Why didn't you say anything? Keeping things like that from the guys makes them crazy."

"How could I say anything when they were at their conference?"

"You need to learn that where our men are concerned, nothing is more paramount than our safety and wellbeing. They would have checked things out then. Afterward, if they found nothing, they would have had the camera video reviewed. If there is anything that I've learned from Carter and

Jac, it's that we need to pay attention to our gut instinct and what it's telling us and inform the guys when things feel off."

The door opened suddenly, and Mallory screeched. Becky put her hand over Mallory's while Mallory's palm went to her throat as though genuinely fearful. Monroe swore under his breath and grabbed her up, holding her tight to him.

"Are you okay? I'm sorry about that. I must have scared you, but we needed to check the area fast and then comb for any debris left that would have told us if anyone was watching close enough to leave a sign." He kissed Mallory before ushering her out of the small reception office.

"I'm okay. I don't know if I was really being watched. It was just a strong sense that someone was out there."

"Well, your inner perceptions were right on track. We found a couple of empty water bottles, gum wrappers, a store sandwich wrapper, and a deep indentation where someone had sat for quite a while."

Mallory squinted her eyes. "Why would they do that?"

"That's what we're trying to figure out."

"But wouldn't your cameras show someone there?"

Monroe scanned the lobby. "Not necessarily at the angle they were at. They were just off of the property and behind some bushes that belong to the next business. We will have to extend our camera's reach in the corner. We should have been better prepared."

Jac came around the corner. "We were. Someone has moved the angel of the camera aimed at that spot."

"What? Wouldn't we notice the change in angle?" asked Carter?

"Maybe, maybe not. If whoever did it worked at night, at just the right time, like when a headlight hit it, or if it were pitch outside, it would be hard to pick up in a simple scan review."

"Monroe, you and Garrett get Mallory home. Pack her up and bring her to my house first thing in the morning, so there aren't any more surprises." Jac turned to Mallory with what Sharlee referred to as his serious face and said, "Good listening to your gut. Monroe is rubbing off on you."

"Excuse me? Maybe I'm rubbing off on him," she answered.

"Oh, you are," smiled Jac. "You most definitely are."

Chapter 17

Monroe needed to keep his head on straight and his shit together. He quickly glanced over at his girl and wondered how long it would be before they eliminated the threat to her. It was apparent that there was someone else out there, a copycat or accomplice. It didn't matter because both were just as dangerous, just as lethal. And whoever it was, had connected Jacquard and Associates to Mallory. And that set off all kinds of warning bells.

Monroe stopped at a light and turned to look at Mallory, interweaving his fingers with hers. "Now, tell me all about what was going on the first time you were outside earlier today."

When she would pull her hand away, he tightened his hold. "Nothing really. We finished lunch and everyone had work to do, so I was sitting in the break room when I got a call from the district attorney, Mr. Rogers."

"You didn't tell me he'd called."

"I didn't have the chance before you were yelling at me to get Garrett. What is Code Gray, anyway?"

"Don't change the subject."

"Not changing the subject," Mallory said while trying to carefully disengage her fingers from his. He held fast and sighed.

"Code Gray is suspicious activity. Code Red is fire, Code Black is we've got trouble—go in *dark*. Code Pink is we have a naughty woman trying to get out of explaining herself."

"What? Oh, cute. The call with Mr. Rogers was hard to hear so, I had to go outside to get good reception."

"Okay, but what did he want?"

"To talk to me about another interview, but something didn't sound right. He wanted me to come to him. I said he could come to me next week, but Mr. Rogers vetoed that idea. I said I would have to call him back and rushed back inside. That's why I was in Becky's office because it spooked me."

"And she gave you donuts," replied Monroe wryly.

"Right, that didn't hurt anything. It helped to calm me down. That and coffee, and company."

"Okay, we have to work this out. I'm going to be gone the weekend, and so I need to know you are going to stay right where I put you."

"Don't be ridiculous. Of course, I'm going to stay at Jac's. Look, Monroe, I didn't intend on leaving from the offices, but I couldn't imagine it would have caused so much concern."

"Sorry, you're right. I'm just so pissed that we didn't realize someone was outside our doors. Our last office was in a high rise, and no one could get to us without being allowed on our floor. The elevator skipped our floor unless we unlocked it."

"You don't know they were there to watch anyone, really. You're just hyper-sensitive to my possible vulnerability."

"Damn right I am. I'm not about to let you risk harm just because you're not as concerned with your welfare as I am. And come to think of it, why is that?"

"Because you are worried enough for both of us, and I trust you to keep me safe. It's when you aren't around that I can get spooked, like earlier today. Besides, I'm tired of being a victim already. I'm not like those who play it up. I don't want it at all."

"Yeah, sorry about that, and you should have known, but I'm telling you now that you break into a meeting if there is any possible menace to your protection and safety. Got me? You are more important than anything in my life. Anything."

"Okay. Thank you." There was a pause, then Mallory asked, "When do you leave?"

"Tomorrow morning. I have to check my gear, and you have to pack for your slumber party at Sharlee's." Monroe softened his intensity, and his face relaxed. He kissed her joined hand. "The ladies are coming over tomorrow night and staying the weekend with you since we are all going to be gone."

"Jac is going to wish he'd gone too," said Mallory with a laugh.

Monroe laughed. "No doubt."

MONROE AND GARRETT dropped Mallory off the next morning before heading out. Mallory, watching them drive off, knowing she wouldn't be able to contact either of them, gave her the worst kind of empty feeling. She had grown to love Monroe and build a strong fondness for Garrett. Mallory hoped for a love interest for Garrett again. He needed it. She stood in the doorway and watched long after their car topped the far hill and was on its way to their next assignment.

Monroe had told her she was safe and promised he would be cautious as always. He had stopped reassuring her with any facts when she stopped hearing them. Instead, Garrett drove, and Monroe sat in the back, holding Mallory in his arms. She wouldn't admit it, but Mallory had shed a few tears, and it took some herculean effort to stop them before they became their own sprinkler system.

Leaning against his impressive body, smelling his shower gel that always had that hint of pine, she relaxed and try to pretend Monroe was going to work. It worked until she had to get out of the vehicle that the reason she was at Jac's again came crashing back. Monroe was skilled, field experienced, and was the team's tactical strategist, so, along with Carter, Garrett, Levi, Kaden, and Mark, they were unbeatable, or so they all said. It was an easy gig, they said. No worries, they said.

That knowledge didn't comfort her erratic thoughts enough nor slow her quickly beating heart. It didn't calm her imagination nor stop the frantic, chaotic thoughts of her misreading Monroe's intentions toward her. Yes, he said he was committed, and yes, he had shown it, but watching him leave made her irrational brain crazy.

An arm wrapped around her shoulders, and she could smell Becky's coconut, lime, and lily perfume from a soft, womanly body and Mallory tried harder to relax as Becky brought her in for a hug.

"I remember the first time Carter had made his intentions known and then left. I conjured up all kinds of hairbrained scenarios, but you know what? They aren't true. They weren't then, and they aren't now."

Mallory side-hugged Becky back and stepped away. "That obvious, huh?"

"No more than when Sharlee did it, or Ivy, or Jessie. Ivy moped and went riding, Sharlee spent her time trying to triangulate their position, and Jessie drank Pepsi and kept checking her phone. That girl nearly vibrated with the amount of caffeine she put away. But this weekend, you aren't going to do any of that."

"Because I likely can't find them on the computer. Monroe told me he would not call me while working, but possibly in the evenings when he wasn't on watchdog duty. I can't ride a horse well, and I only drink Dr. Pepper."

"And because we won't let you, smarty pants. I bet you get Monroe's paddle often, girl," declared Sharlee, walking into the room.

"Not often enough. Monroe says I like it too much." Mallory shrugged when she saw Becky and then Sharlee stare at her in disbelief. "What can I tell you? A girl likes what a girl likes."

Jessie walked in the room with her Pepsi, "And evidently, this girl likes Monroe's paddle."

Becky, obviously the more matronly of the group, groaned and shook her head, but she couldn't hide her grin. "Monroe was looking for a woman like you. I'm glad he found you."

"We found each other."

"Yes, you did. Now, can we have brunch yet?" Jessie asked, rubbing her enlarging belly.

Sharlee smiled in understanding camaraderie. "We're waiting on Ivy. She's driving herself."

At just that moment, a sporty black car that looked like it cost a fortune pulled into the circle and parked hurriedly. The women watched their last participant rush up the steps and didn't bother knocking.

"What's the matter, Ivy?"

Gone was the playfulness of the group. The Jacquard and Associates women all became more alert and intent on listening to Ivy. Mallory noted their ability to turn on the intensity from playfulness without a pause. She had seen the guys do it but was impressed their women could do it as well.

"Not sure, but there are some people who tried to get in behind me, and the guard stopped them. He closed the gate on them and—"

Jac rounded the corner and spoke with all the authority his military training and experience had taught him, now wielding his CEO status. There was never any doubt on his part that the women would comply with his commands when he interrupted Ivy.

"Charlotte, get me more eyes on the front gate. I've called in a few more security guards, and Finley is locking Storm down. The rest of you go into the den, and if you hear anything that might give you concern, you get into the safe room."

Jac followed Sharlee, who had taken off at his first words. Mallory didn't know what was happening, but she already wished Monroe hadn't gone this weekend.

Ivy resumed her tale. "Like I said, there were two cars behind me, and when I got in, they were trying to ram the first gate. I did what I was told to do, and that was to cross over the entrance and then stop, so security could slide the gate closed before the group behind me could push their way in. Then I slipped in the second gate, and the others were outside the first."

"Who could they be?" asked Jessie.

"Reporters," answered Sharlee as she entered the room. "They're gone now, but it seems whoever was watching outside the offices yesterday saw Mallory. Whether it was Mallory they had been looking for or any number of other reasons, they have come here with reinforcements."

Jessie frowned. "They aren't reputable papers, surely."

Consternation crossed Becky's face. "We aren't doing any direct government jobs right now, not that they would know that, so not sure what they want."

Ivy spoke up. "It is probably Mallory. Ever since the news broke identifying her, they have been hounding the complex where she lives and The Apothecary. The manager of your complex has said in several reports that you aren't returning. Is that true?"

"No, but maybe that is what the district attorney wanted to talk about." Mallory waved her hand, "All of this mess. It shouldn't surprise me, but it does. I'm so sorry. I could go back to the safe—"

A booming male voice spoke into the room. "You are going nowhere, young lady. Is that understood? Don't make me improvise on Monroe's rubber paddle."

Mallory came up short. Curbing the automatic urge to answer with the word "sir" and not trusting her voice, she nodded.

Jac seemed to realize how harsh he sounded and softened his tone. Squatting in front of Mallory as she sat on a sofa, Jac grimaced. Mallory stiffened. He placed his hands on her knees.

"Sorry, Mallory. I didn't mean to frighten you. I can keep a better eye on you if you stay here until Monroe and Garrett return. Reporters aren't harmful. They are just hugely annoying. I prefer to keep their antics on the other side of my privacy gate."

"But if they're not a danger..."

The tips of his fingers tapped her on the thigh. "They aren't, but someone else might be. They will just bring the copycat or the accomplice to you. Reporters seem to forget that they act as a beacon when they are on the hunt for their story."

"Okay," she said as she exhaled a sigh. "I didn't really want to go, anyway." Her relieved smile caused Jac to bark a short laugh.

"I needed that bit of humor. So no going anywhere outside the house?"

"No, I won't."

He patted her thigh and stood. "Good. I have some work to do, so if you ladies will excuse me, I'll get back to it."

Murmurs of response rumbled quietly, and as soon as he left the room, they all started chattering at once. All but Mallory. Her face was feverish from the directed attention that Dom of Sharlee's had given her. Whether they played or not wasn't Mallory's business, but Jac was wasting his talents if they didn't. She could think of nothing but *"yes, sir"* when he was talking to her.

Mallory thought about what he'd said. She didn't want anyone to know where she was, but it seemed her story had been plastered everywhere. So much so that Monroe had finally forbidden her to watch another news show. She had protested but found she didn't want to watch them any longer and skipping them lowered her anxiety... a lot. She got radio news reports, though, and that was enough.

"Brunch ladies," called Sharlee as she ushered her companions into the dining room.

"WHEN DID YOU AND MONROE finally do the deed?" asked Ivy, who had the least effective filter of them all.

"I don't think you can ask that," said Jessie in hushed tones.

"Yes, I can. I just did." Ivy turned back to Mallory.

Soon they were off subject to a more socially acceptable conversation, and Mallory didn't have to find a way to dodge the question, but there were many more awkward ones shot at her by all the ladies. Even Finley joined in the fun after Storm was asleep. Finley was a different kind of woman, open to a point, but it was obvious the woman had secrets.

"Monroe is so serious," said Ivy. "It's intimidating."

"Not as serious as my Mark," said Jessie.

Ivy grinned in, "No one is as serious as your Mark."

Everyone laughed, and Mallory assured them that Monroe might have rules he was adamant about, but he wasn't serious when he was with her.

"He cracks jokes?" asked a confused Sharlee.

"No, but he isn't serious. He is normal... you know, he pays attention to me. I guess his intensity shifts to me when he's home."

"I get that," said Becky.

"Monroe was always trying to keep us in line with that rubber paddle until you came along. We knew he'd be Daddy material," said Jessie. "Thank you."

Mallory cocked her head. "He sure is bossy and has enough rules, but I don't know about the Daddy bit."

Was he the kind people meant when a man was demanding and hot as hell but would protect his woman with his life? Yes, he was the spank your ass then talk, kind of guy. Not a daddy dom, but a Daddy.

Not completely satisfied she had found a niche to put her man in, Mallory instinctively understood that he didn't fit that mold entirely. He didn't discipline out of sternness, although he sure was when he did. Monroe loved the play. Lucky for them both, she did as well. They didn't do much role play, but sexy played nearly every time they got in bed. Not all-out sex, but teases raised the heat through sensuality.

The others nodded sagely. "He is definitely a daddy," declared Ivy.

"Yep," said Becky. "I think Carter is as well, but he is more of the nurturing kind."

"Anyone can see it when he's with you," agreed Finley. "That wouldn't be for me, but I can see it works for you two."

"What about your men? Are they Daddy material?" asked Mallory.

And the conversation took off in a different direction, moving the spotlight from her and her relationship with Monroe to other, less uncomfortable areas of her life. Unfortunately, the group came around to her emotional situation many times throughout the weekend. While it made her wiggle in her proverbial chair to talk out her feelings and the way her life had taken unexpected turns, it was also a way to tease loose the knotted tangle of emotions she had been avoiding.

Avoidance was never her typical response to roadblocks, but it seemed relevant in all but her most personal, emotional side. There was avoidance all over in that department. The adage she had lived her life on, *you have to put in the work to get what you wanted out of life*, was proving true yet again. So she gritted her teeth and talked about what she wanted out of her relationship with a man, what she'd been missing, and how Monroe filled those needs. And he did. The women thought so, and more importantly, Mallory thought so.

Jessie settled back into the corner of the sofa and pulled up her legs. "So, when I was deciding if Mark was the man for me, I balked at his machismo in the beginning. I mean, what I thought was machismo, but I learned that Mark was actually trying to hold in his overwhelming need to wrap me in cotton and put me in a safe room forever. He had an overwhelming fear that what we had would vanish if he didn't lock it down."

Everyone murmured in understanding. Did Monroe feel that way? Is that why he was gritting his teeth more and starting and stopping sentences more often? Did he find his desire to protect what he considered his, causing him angst? Sleepless nights? Inattentive days? Because until she moved into his bed, that's what she'd felt. Did she still think that? Maybe.

"See, I think all our guys have this tremendous need to find cotton wool to wrap their possessions, us, but they don't because it isn't practical," said Ivy. "Or acceptable."

Becky nodded. "In more than just the facetious way. I think that Carter tries to figure out how to do things that meet all my needs, and I've fallen into that mind trap until recently. I've wondered if all his needs are being fulfilled and if I could do something to better meet his desires and try to make sure we are also going in a direction we mutually want to go."

Sharlee agreed. "Yes, and not just in a sexual gratification way or what do you want for breakfast. In more of a reach for your goals, kind of way. You know? I allow Jac to lead the way too often in my favor without making sure it's what he wants."

Mallory sat up straighter. "But how do you know? I mean, you have been with your guys a while. Monroe and I met less than two months ago. I don't know him the way you know your men. What signs do you look for to know he might not be getting his own fulfillment?"

Jessie, who had been picking at her shirt while the others were speaking, suddenly looked up. "Mark has things I know he likes. Things like certain foods, and I eat them even if I'm not crazy about them myself but not allergic to them. I try to steer things his way, but he usually short-circuits my efforts.

What I ended up doing was telling him how much it meant to me to be able to reciprocate. It has helped us grow closer."

"Relationships are hard work," said Ivy. "But it feels so good when you get through. And if you get a little angry sex in there," she smiled, "it's a win-win."

Just thinking about angry sex lit Mallory's fire and melted her core. She hadn't ever had that with Monroe, but she had experienced a little irritation sex, but angry sex with Monroe would be explosive.

Sharlee added, "So much better than frustration sex because there is a desperation in that. The sex is still good, but it's needy, not passionate."

Finley had remained quiet in the relationship conversations. Mallory had the feeling she was measuring what they were saying to how she felt with possibly Ryker? Maybe Levi? Or was there someone else?

By the time the weekend was over, Mallory was panting for so many reasons to see Monroe. She tried to forget that they would have to drive through the gate with reporters camped out. Not many, she hoped. Especially since Romaine was going for his second bail hearing. She was more than ready for Monroe to get home and take over her protection detail.

The ladies were great, but a weekend was almost too much. Mallory's cheeks were sore by the time she began packing her things to go home. She wanted to go to Monroe's home. What would he have chosen for his house? Looking back, she hadn't realized that no subject was off-limits with the women amongst themselves. Her face stayed hot with embarrassment, laugher, or tiredness most of the weekend, but she felt like she was part of a posse now. "Her friends" was an actual reference in her life now, and it was an incredible feeling.

Playing with little Storm was heartwarming, and her maternal instincts pushed forward. She thought the desire for children had diminished after the kidnapping, but it hadn't. If anything, she was afraid that if she didn't take what she wanted out of life, it wouldn't happen. Mallory resolved to have that happily ever after she had once dreamed of daily. Becky seemed to have the baby itch, too, if that longing look in her eye was accurately interpreted. Maybe they would be the next in the group to start a family.

Breakfast over, the return to work marked the beginning of a new week. As Mallory watched Becky, Sharlee, and Jessie get ready for work, she resolved she would return as well. She loved her profession and wanted to get back there as soon as possible. Damn her reservations. Ivy had nothing to do until later that morning, but she left with the others because she said she needed to "put on" her face. Jac stayed home with Mallory, waiting for Monroe and Garrett.

"I can just go in with you, and Monroe can grab me from there," said Mallory as she dropped her pack in the entryway.

"No, it's much further for the guys to go, given the direction they are coming from, so we'll just stay here. Coffee?"

Chapter 18

Monroe was as antsy as a little kid going to the circus. He anticipated seeing Mallory but was also frustrated because they would deal with the question of a copycat or an accomplice. And the bigger question was, where were they? He and Mallory needed to resolve this. After Monroe and Garrett had discussed things with the guys as they waited for the plane to get off the ground, he knew they were all in agreement. Get this done, answer the questions, move on. Things had been hanging on for entirely too long.

Monroe wouldn't give anything for his family of friends. They were the best, and he knew it. Just have them agree to back him up, join with him to finish this mess was more than Monroe would have ever expected from regular business associates. He never doubted they would agree with him, but later, openly discussing his love for Mallory was immensely freeing.

Carter leaned over to get Monroe's attention as they sat in the waiting area for their plane to board. "Okay, are you saying you have no doubts about Mallory? I mean, aren't you worried you cement this connection in trauma?"

Monroe leaned forward and ran his hand through his hair and then used those same fingers to comb it back into place. "No, because we've shared scenes together several times, gone to another private party, and played there a bit, then we spent almost two weeks on the phone for hours before her abduction. We were going on a final, regular date before making the relationship public."

"Aren't you worried you've moved too fast?" asked Levi. "I mean, I'm not interested in making any commitment for a while and honestly, I've watched the stress you guys go through. I'm pretty happy just supporting you. I'm not into going through that myself."

Kaden stood when their boarding group was called and slapped Levi on the back. "Yeah, I remember those days of being free, unencumbered, and still hadn't met Ivy. Believe me, when you find the one for you, those walls come crashing down so fast, you have to dive out of the way to avoid being crushed."

Mark was naturally contemplative and not prone to lengthy discussions. Still, he looked at Levi and spoke with his typical seriousness, allowing his heartfelt sincerity to come through loud and clear.

"When you find the woman that is for you, your soul mate, the one person in the world that completes you, there is no settling for anyone else. You will move heaven and earth to keep her with you and then to make her happy. And when that time comes, when you find her, we will be right there to support you. It will happen whether you're ready for it or not, but it's the best thing that can ever happen to you."

Mark leaned back and resumed his silence. The rest followed suit. Sitting next to him, Monroe noticed Garrett was quiet until Mark spoke.

Under his breath, he said, "And sometimes it can destroy you."

Monroe renewed his determination to finish this mess so his girl could be safe again because it was past the time they find Garrett's woman. Whether Callie wanted to be found was irrelevant. They needed to throw that door open or find closure. This open, seeping wound wasn't healthy.

JAC CLOSED THE DIGITAL file on the weekend security job and nodded to Sharlee, who sat down beside Kaden on a sofa.

"We have a new focus this week. I know we have been running information in the background, but considering what happened Thursday afternoon at the office, we need to step up our planning and end this game. We all need to get back to business as usual, and Mallory needs to heal."

Sharlee looked at the team. "I have a handful of good leads, but Jac hasn't thought we should pursue the ones that aren't sure things, and I have to agree. We don't even know if there is another person. The copycat kidnapping could have been a one-off."

Jac nodded as he sat in a chair, turning to face the team. "Right. We aren't the FBI and have limited resources. We have to be smart about what we go after. Unless it's something that will help us, we turn over whatever we get to the FBI and move on until we find evidence that will help us find the answer to our primary question."

Monroe said, "Okay, so first, Mallory wants to go back to work. I don't know how she can, but I also don't know how to stop her. Inactivity is driving her as crazy as the fear that someone will approach her uninvited."

Kaden smiled. "Rubber paddle not working for you?"

Monroe answered, his smile strained. "She loves it too much."

Levi whistled. "She was made for you, man."

Another pinched smile. "Agreed. Any ideas how I give her what she wants without going mad myself?"

Garrett spoke up. "Yep. I've been her bodyguard when you can't be with her. I think we have built a rapport that would allow her to agree to me continuing in that capacity for now. Besides, as stoic as she appears to be, not letting things get to her, she is a mess, not knowing if she is truly safe or not. I'll pick her up and take her home. Or, if she needs to drive for some reason, I can follow her then hang out in the store keeping an eye out."

Mark spoke up. "She going to be okay with that, Monroe? Rapport or not, her employer would have to agree, and Mallory would have to be comfortable with it."

"She'll be comfortable with it if she wants to go to work," said Monroe.

Sharlee crossed her arms. "That is cute on paper, but women don't like to be told what to do without input. I say we bring Mallory in to finish this discussion. Let's ask *her* if she is going to be cool with this set-up."

The grumbling around the room showed reluctant consensus. Jac motioned with his head for Sharlee to get Mallory.

"While Charlotte goes to get Mallory," said Jac, "I need a relief schedule for Garrett."

"What kind of relief are we talking about? How long are her hours?" asked Levi.

"We can bring lunch, or I can order it in. That isn't an issue. It's that I'll need to take a bathroom break at some point and stretch my legs. I guess Mallory could lock herself in her office when I'm taking a break, but I don't like that as much."

Jac nodded. "Agreed. Levi will relieve you from eleven to one. That way, you will have a break without compromising our operation."

"I can relieve Garrett," said Monroe.

Jac shook his head. "No can do. You might have been seen with Mallory. And I need you and Carter to run down Charlotte and Kaden's leads. Mark has a job this week. That leaves Levi."

"Except Fridays. I have a regular assignment on that day."

"Right, well, Monroe, do your thing and send me the schedule."

"Roger that."

The men were talking amongst themselves as they waited. It seemed like a long time to wait, but just as Monroe was standing to go in search of Mallory and Sharlee, the door opened. Sharlee swung a plastic sandwich bag that held assorted business cards.

"The reporters left these at the security desk. They're from all the people who wanted an interview, preferably with Mallory, but it sounds as though they would take anyone with information."

Monroe opened his arms for Mallory, and she sat next to him, allowing him to weave his fingers with hers. She leaned on his shoulder. Monroe's gut had been jumpy all weekend, but he knew Mal was safe. It was the only thing that allowed him to concentrate on the assignment of some rich buggers in a merger.

The business executive had security, and his wife, a little thing about Mallory's own age, had none. Garrett took her as his responsibility because even though the CEO didn't seem concerned about his wife, the team was more inclined to protect her first. With Garrett on the job, the rest could concentrate on their client, knowing eyes were on his wife. If anything happened, Garrett would cover her.

Monroe leaned down and kissed Mallory's temple as he watched Sharlee toss the baggie on the table in front of Jac, who dumped the cards out on the table. Unwilling to touch any of the cards, he used a pen to line up the nine cards in a grid pattern. After perusing the cards quickly, Jac called out the names on each card and their affiliate newspaper or local channel. After reading six cards, he tensed.

"Charlotte, get your tweezers."

She rummaged in the container that Ivy had previously used to hide her evidence when her life was in shambles and pulled out a long pair of scientific tweezers. Monroe's body tightened, muscles clenching again. His body was achy often these days. He kissed the top of Mallory's head before getting up and, in three long strides, was standing next to Jac as he placed the card back into the resealable bag and laid it on the scanner.

Once scanned, Sharlee threw the images up on the screen and what lay in front of them all was a business card of sorts. It was made of a heavy parchment paper, something Monroe remembered making in school as a kid for a project.

On one side, there was a hand-drawn hourglass with neatly printed letters that read:

Braylon and Associates

The Timekeepers

And on the other side was an hourglass that was almost out of sand, and it read:

The time for celebrating is almost here

Mallory squinted as though trying to tease the message out. She started to tremble, and Garrett swore before nodding at Monroe, who wrapped his arms around Mallery. Monroe answered the swear with his own curse as he resumed his seat on the middle sofa and pulled her into his lap. Mallory curled into his arms. He rubbed her arms, and someone shoved a crystal glass with a finger of whiskey in his hand. Mallory pushed it away.

Monroe's voice was full of confused anger. He spoke to the room. "I don't know what is going on yet, but I think we need to stay in the safe house for a little while longer." He leaned down to Mallory. "We need you to stay hidden for another week. Then, when you're ready, we'll start you going to work to see if you can do it. I'll explain the plan as we go back to the safe house. But I promise you, if there is any concern, you are out of there. Got it?"

Mallory shook her head in disbelief. "I just need to figure out what it means. Celebrate? Who will be celebrating, and why? I have no clue if this person is friend or foe."

Jac leaned forward in his chair and rested his forearms on his thighs. "Good point. Honestly, right now, we don't even know if there is any significance to this at all. It could be something of great importance or none at all. A prank. But whatever the implication, we are not leaving you alone. Anywhere. We won't expose you to anything that could be harmful if it is in our power to control."

"I know that. I do, but all these thoughts run through my head. Who is this person, this accomplice? Do they exist? I'm tired of being a victim, but this scares me because I don't really know what any of this means."

Jac stared at Mallory. "Mallory, when you go to work, if you go, there is going to be some fencing around you. I won't budge on that, so don't try to change my mind. You aren't going anywhere that someone on the team won't be with you. You are part of us now, and we take care of our own."

"Meaning what exactly?"

"Garrett is going to stay as your bodyguard. Levi will relieve him for a few hours midday. More or less depending on what else Garrett has on his plate that day, but you will be his priority."

Mallory looked at Monroe, and he watched her lip thin in a stubborn line and her body stiffen. He knew what that meant and leaned down to whisper before her rebellion surfaced more. "It's this or nothing, my girl. I don't want you to go back at all, but I'm trying to understand how you might see things. I promise you; it all goes away if you refuse this offer."

She hissed back, "I'm an adult."

"Who is dangerously close to getting her ass kissed vehemently by my paddle. I'm compromising here, but you are my hip buddy if you choose not to take the precautions. I told you that when you turned over the hard decisions to me, I took that responsibility very seriously. This is my call, not yours. I will decide when you are ready to handle the stress and strain of holding the reins again. You agreed."

"But that was before," she snapped hotly.

"Before what? Before the kidnapping? Before the arrest, the copycat, the subsequent murder of someone else or the death of the other captive? Was it before they found more bodies? How many shit things have to happen? How many horrors do you have to experience before you believe me when I say enough? How fucking long before you believe I would die trying to keep you safe? Before you trust me to do the right thing?" He waited a few seconds. "Well?"

Mallory looked like she would cry, and it killed Monroe, but tough love was called for here. He knew she understood the problem, but maybe it hadn't sunk into her foundational beliefs.

"Okay, fine." She said tightly. Her voice rose with her level of anger as she struggled to remove herself from Monroe's lap. He strengthened his grip, unsure who she was angry at, but he figured she was angry with the world. "I'll take a fucking bodyguard with me when I decide to go back," she hissed. "But it won't be because you told me to."

There was that instant she processed with dismay what she'd said, and Monroe saw Mallory's face when she realized how childish her last words had sounded. Then, as though the charged emotion of the moment and the conflicting ups and downs of her levels of fear since the kidnapping was suddenly too much for her, her face crumbled. The silence in the room was deafening. And then she burst into tears.

Monroe stood to go. The intensity of the flood was overpowering everything else. Time to leave and get his baby home. Monroe smiled tenderly and kissed her. He was still irritated, but he swallowed it down. Mallory was the one he had to pay attention to, not himself. She tried to kiss him hard, and he returned it but cut things off short. Mallory whimpered her need. The emotional deluge of anger, embarrassment, and fear of the unknown that she had been battling for weeks created the need to get his physical reassurance. He could give her that.

"I know, sweetheart. I know. Let's get you home," he whispered into her hair but didn't expect her to hear him. He gave the nod, then tilted his head at Garrett, who jumped up and followed the two out.

THE RIDE SEEMED ONLY a few moments to Mallory. She found herself in the back seat of the SUV, thinking of nothing but getting skin to skin with Monroe. The smoke glass between the front and back seat was in place before Monroe spoke.

"My way, my speed. No noise, no movements to meet me. This is going to be down and dirty."

He pulled her clothes around to expose the parts he needed, and with little foreplay, Monroe entered her slick entrance. It was hot as hell as Monroe took from her what he needed and gave her what she needed. Hot, heavy, intense sex brought her to climax without the edging, the foreplay, the concern that she got off first. Monroe followed her almost immediately.

"Get yourself around, baby, because we have just entered the gate to the house." If Monroe hadn't held her tightly to himself, she was sure she'd have fallen over.

"We'll take a nap before we start dinner," said Monroe. "After I check the perimeter."

Garrett, the good man that he was, said nothing.

OVER THE NEXT WEEK, Sharlee kept feeding the FBI possible leads but was frustrated because she wasn't getting anything but a confirmation of what she had sent them. Monroe and Garrett turned away from the safe house, and Mallory went back and forth on the bodyguard agreement.

When Monroe was gone, she didn't mind the thought of one, but when he was with her, she voiced her opinion on how stupid an idea it was. How impractical it would be and how uncomfortable it would make everyone. The team knew none of those things were true, but for now, until the rubber met the road, there was no use arguing the unchangeable fact that if she went back to work, she'd do so with a bodyguard.

It was Garrett who ultimately got through to her. His friend was right when he said he seemed to have a rapport with her that others on the team did not, and Monroe was not above exploiting that. Monroe was glad they'd connected. Since losing Callie, Garrett held back from the other couples more than he did with Mallory. Monroe would be jealous, but Garrett was Monroe's best friend, and it meant a lot to him that Garrett had taken the time to get to know and like Mallory.

It was official. There were no more things happening concerning the case, so Mallory decided to go back to work. To say that declaration was met with anything but enthusiasm, would not have been the truth. But to say Mallory seemed to understand the hesitancy wouldn't have been entirely accurate, either.

"I think you are all used to drama happening, and you can't let go of the fact that someone is out there looking for me. There isn't anyone. We over-reacted to things we found. No DNA on anything outside the offices. No women are being abducted. Nothing."

"Don't forget, he tried to stick to women that seemed to have no one in their lives that would have noticed them gone for a while. Not like you. He overestimated your lack of engagement. And you underestimate my amount of engagement."

Monroe's Dom had been coming out more often, causing some heated conversations. Mallory had picked her battles, which helped the level of harmony. Monroe sat back and supported her by holding her hand and rubbing her neck as Jac went over the work plan, but he did not enter the discussion. No one was rude, and everything was civil, so while it irritated Mallory, she was doing as she had said, determined to put this behind her. She was a victim no longer in her mind, and Monroe was hard-pressed not to shout *thank fuck*.

"I can't live my life as though I'm made of ancient porcelain, nor can I show fear. Therefore, I've decided I'm through living my life in anticipation of the other shoe dropping. I won't torture myself like that. I appreciate your willingness to help me, but I can do this on my own. Thanks, Jac, but no thanks."

Monroe almost laughed at Jac's disbelief. The man who could convince a blind beggar to give up his walking stick was being thwarted by Monroe's woman. He watched with amusement as Mallory stood her ground, causing Jac to flex his hands and run the palms over his khaki-clothed thighs. He would not enter the fray because Monroe had already paddled her, pleaded, and had angry sex. While that was hot as hell, he preferred to keep more control when fucking her brains out.

Garrett came around and squatted in front of Mallory, and Monroe immediately knew he'd get through. The earnestness in his face and the no-nonsense tone he spoke with assured Monroe that she would capitulate.

"Mallory, listen to me, sweetheart. I know you're tired of all this crap, and I get you want to take control, but there is taking over the right way, and then there's throwing away your command of the situation because of over-zealousness. You want to continue to manage the way your life goes, and that starts by easing back into your former life." He grinned, "But this time, you have handsome, brawny brothers and cute kick-ass sisters to come alongside you. You aren't alone because we have your six."

She was melting. "Where were all these friends when I needed someone to protect my fourth point of contact yesterday?"

Garrett laughed. "Sorry, that is the one area that has stipulations attached. Ass protection is a situational issue."

"You bet it is," mumbled Monroe, who was gratified to get not only a grin from Garrett but a giggle from Mallory. The tension released.

"So, are you going to risk your hard-earned position, or are you going to let me bolster you along with my presence? Not forever, but a little while."

"I hate that you make so much sense. Fine, you can go with me."

Garrett kissed Mallory's cheek and stood, his tone one of authority. "So this is how it's going to go."

Mallory rolled her eyes but appeared to listen to his rules. When everything was set, Monroe kissed Mallory and gave Garrett a chin lift. All good. Now for the actual test. Would Mallory's return to work draw out the copycat or the accomplice if one exists? Hopefully, they would find out. Monroe cringed at the thought of putting Mallory in even a whisper of danger, and therefore he made sure she knew what the outcome could be when they were alone.

He sat next to her at the dining table after they put dinner in the oven. "Mal, I get you want to go back to work, make life more normal again. But I also need you to know that some unintended consequences may come from that."

She patted his hand, then left hers on his. He turned palm to palm and wove his fingers in hers. "If you mean more nightmares, I realize that. I hope that I can prove to my conscious mind that there aren't any problems, and my subconscious will believe it and let go of the trauma."

"I hope that works. A full night's sleep will work wonders for you. But that isn't what I mean, baby."

Her eyebrows showed her consternation. "Then what?"

He rubbed her hands with his as they sat entwined on the tabletop. Looking into her eyes, he gentled his tone. "What might happen is that there really is an accomplice or a copycat who finds out you're back to work, and they try to grab you from there."

Mallory was quiet, but Monroe didn't want to push her to respond. Better she chewed on that a few moments before he asked her for thoughts.

"What should I do?"

Monroe kissed her hand, holding his lips there for a moment. "I think, if you know the risks and know that we will be there all the time you are, then you should go and possibly help us flush him out."

"Or her."

He nodded his agreement. "Or her, however, it's doubtful to be a woman given the violence of the acts."

"Probably, but don't discount the things a woman is capable of doing."

"So, I shouldn't underestimate what you can do?" said Monroe, wiggling his brows suggestively. "How long do we have before dinner is ready?"

"I think we can squeeze out about twenty minutes." She answered with a sassy raising of her own brows and a salacious grin. "What did you have in mind?"

In response, Monroe stood, his lips hijacking hers as he pulled her cotton pants down. His lips didn't leave hers as she wrenched the pants further down, and he grabbed for her shirt, reaching underneath to expertly release bouncy, firm breasts from their captive garment.

"Monroe," she entreated with desperation in her tone as he dragged his lips from hers to remove her shirt and his. "What about Garrett?"

Mallory had unbuckled his belt, and he dropped his pants, his glorious manhood standing at full attention. "Front or back," he rasped as he ran his finger through the cleft of her feminine valley to test for readiness. He pulled a breast in his mouth and sucked.

"What? I don't know what... oh my God, that's good."

The pop that sounded when he released her breast brought another moan from Mallory. "Back it is."

Wasting no time, he flipped her over the back of the upholstered dining room chair and made a quick calculation. Not quick enough for Mallory, who began pushing her ass in his direction.

"The wrong angle for ass play, so quit teasing, naughty woman." He slapped her bottom crisply and felt the slickness on her thighs when he parted them to make room for entry.

She rotated her hips and tried to grind her clit against the upholstery. Monroe slapped her bottom several times, and she became more frantic. "Please. Hurry."

Monroe needed no more encouragement. He slid his staff in fast and hard, going deep. "So good," she mumbled.

"I won't last," he said between pumping inside her. "You had better get yourself off the best you can without any direct clit action. If you don't," he continued, more breathless with every thrust, "You won't get to next time."

The wet sound of their flesh slapping together as he continued to piston into her incited more gyrating from Mallory. Another slap, another whimper, another gush, and Monroe knew he was losing his control.

"Mallory, now," he warned. "It's now or never, baby. I can't hold out much longer."

Monroe leaned down to kiss her neck, running his tongue along the salty perspiring skin, and then he bit between her neck and shoulder, lightly slapping her sopping lower lips, and heard her scream her release. He grunted as the fire raced through his body as though it would scald him, find release in her greedy and grasping heat. He kept pumping until there was nothing left.

They were both hot, heaving, slippery, sticky messes. Monroe checked the time on the stove as he pulled back from his lover. Mallory didn't move. Catching his breath, Monroe turned the oven off and scooped his woman into his arms, headed for the shower.

Chapter 19

After two weeks of Mallory going to work, the team thought they might be able to let her drive herself with someone following her, and someone stayed with her. After another two weeks without incident, Monroe agreed to allow her to try it unaccompanied during the day; however, he wouldn't budge on traveling to and from work. Too many things happened in cars.

"Mal, this is it. I'm not debating on the travel. You're using your own vehicle, which I still think is a bad idea, but you won't go or come home without escort, and if you want to lunch out, you need a teammate with you, and that is not one of their women only. You get me?"

She lolled her head back as if she were hard-pressed to concede to his demands but ultimately said, "Yes, I get you."

Monroe threatened to take the paddle out and not in a fun, sexy way, either. She had learned the difference soon after she met him. She never misread that cue again.

"How long are we going to worry that someone is out there? It has been months."

Monroe pulled her close and kissed the top of her head as he hugged her. "I know, baby. Let me work through this. They are still finding bodies, and with every discovery, I fight the overwhelming urge to grab you and hide you away."

"I know. But I'll never get past this if I can't go to work alone."

Mallory was tired of being followed, tired of being afraid. She hoped that soon there would be no reasonable excuse they could give to dog her every step. Only then would she be free of the babysitting brigade.

Mallory mumbled while her face was tight against his chest. "To think people pay for this kind of attention. Maybe I could tease this person out into the open, and then we could nail his ass and go on."

"You had better be kidding, or that paddle, my cuffs, and an assortment of delightful toys will be brought out to use consecutively and simultaneously," was his gruff answer.

"So not the fun kind, huh?"

Monroe chuckled good-naturedly. "No, not the fun kind for you. I'd enjoy playing with you in any capacity, baby."

Mallory pulled back from his arms and made eye contact. "Okay, fine. But please figure out whether this guy did it alone because I don't know how long I can handle this. I feel like it is my new mantra."

"Understood, my love. Now, could I interest you in..."

Whenever she thought she was at her wit's end, she reminded herself that if it weren't for their over-protective nature, she would never have attempted to go to work at the same place. She would have left town long ago. Monroe didn't lose his cool or his commitment to her, and that was important. She could hold off for a while longer.

Mallory climbed into his lap. "I love you."

"I loved you first." He kissed her deeply,

"Did you really?" She unbuttoned his shirt with fumbling fingers. His hand stayed hers.

"Still hungry? Let's eat in the bedroom."

Mallory moaned her answer. Monroe stood with her still in his arms, and when they entered the bedroom, he brought her to the bathroom door.

"Get done what you need to do, then come out, naked."

"Is this how it's always going to be?"

"Nope. When you're round with my baby, I'll have to be more careful." He slapped her butt. "Now get going, woman or I'll take you right now."

Her throaty, aroused laugh followed her into the bathroom, and Monroe smiled as he crossed the room to grab his bag.

But as they played tug of war with Mallory's independence during the day and were playful and relaxed during the evenings, the nights brought terrors no one had control over. The forest retreat was very secluded, and Garrett really liked it out there, but after being in the seclusion for only a few weeks, the nighttime dreams became daytime nerves. Mallory saw a shadow around every corner. Her dreams were staying with her after she woke. Sometimes it was hard to remember she had been sleeping.

That afternoon, just before she went home, there was a scare. She checked that all her scripts for the day were filled. She always did a spot check to make sure there were no mistakes. Hanging her coat up on the coat rack, she turned back towards her office when Garrett yelled across the room the word "Gray."

That one word sent panic racing through her blood, sending her into lockdown in her office while he figured out what was going on. There was a man in the Apothecary trying to see Mallory personally. It was Garrett's job to decide what it was all about. It turned out he was a journalist, but the damage had been done.

She was at the end of an emotionally trying work week, and Mallory could do nothing but cry while Monroe snuggled with her, holding her for several hours until she had fallen asleep.

Mallory had a screaming nightmare that night that she could remember vividly. The unidentified person coming after her was more than one. It was a man and a woman, and they caught her, taking her from the bedroom while Garrett was showering. She had taken hours to drop back off asleep.

She showered with Monroe the following day, just in case, but she was wearing down from the lack of sleep and the irrational worry that was all too present in her life. She'd gone to the team's physician, and he gave her a low dose of anti-anxiety medication, and it helped, but only minimally.

"Mallory is right. Sometimes the cure is worse than the disease. In this case, the eggshells she has been walking on trying not to upset the balance are causing more harm than not doing it. Nothing has happened, and we haven't identified one person out of place that would make me think she is in danger. Did we get this wrong?"

Garrett sat back in his armchair and crossed one leg over the other. "Well, there was that reporter and what about the note on that homemade business card?"

Monroe grunted. "I think it was a prank. A sick prank, but one, nonetheless. It has to be because that was weeks ago."

"We had to be sure, but I think we're probably okay. Should we put it to the team?"

Monroe rubbed the back of his neck. "I could call Jac and get his opinion, but I think we try it starting Monday. I'll be available, so you don't need to hang out. We should move home this weekend, too."

"I knew the cushy job would eventually end." The men chuckled and then got serious again, going onto other work business.

Conversation done, Garrett stood to leave when out of the kitchen came Mallory with a frying pan in her hand, ready to clobber a supposed intruder.

"Whoa, honey. That could hurt someone. What are you doing?" asked Garrett as he disarmed her.

"I thought you had broken in, and they were coming to take me. I might have hurt someone if you hadn't said something."

Monroe had scooped her up in his arms and brought her to the sofa. "I'm sorry, baby. We were trying to be quiet," he said as he kissed her temple and tightened his hold on her.

Mallory was trembling. "I see shadows and the boogie man everywhere. I can't stay here any longer. It gives me anxiety all by itself. I'm not a wilderness kinda gal, I guess. Please, I need to go home, Monroe."

"Garrett, grab your things. I'm taking Mal home."

"Are you sure—"

"My home." They moved out that very evening.

On Monday, Monroe escorted Mallory to work, but he left her to handle the day as she had before the kidnapping. After he had checked to make sure she was clear on finding him and the rest of the team if needed, Monroe, still uneasy, made a beeline for the offices and his team. Time to end this shit.

Chapter 20

Sharlee was working on so many projects that she had been rubbing the markings on the keyboard off, or so Jac said. When he wasn't on assignment outside the office, Kaden had also spent long hours searching for more places where Romaine might have buried other bodies. The team gathered in the conference room to decide what they were going to do. The connections weren't as easy as once thought.

"He's playing us," said Carter. "He enjoys the attention, and now he's just stringing us along. There aren't any more women. The FBI hasn't found one in weeks."

Jac was pacing. "The problem is, they are still finding bodies. That being the case, it's hard to say he's lying when he says we haven't found all his stashes. Yes, it's been weeks, but they have several other places to look."

Mark leaned his forearms on the highly polished mahogany conference table. "Maybe we should stop helping the Feds by giving them places to look. I mean, they wouldn't have found any bodies after the first place if we hadn't kept digging."

Sharlee shook her head. "Those poor women deserve to be found and buried where their family can find them. It's important to finish this."

Jac stopped his pacing. "I agree, but that being said, Sharlee and Mallory can't keep this up for much longer. Sharlee needs to stop feeding the Feds information, and Mallory needs to move on."

Levi sat quietly in the back corner but nodded. Carter seemed distracted, too. Monroe knew his team and Carter was strategizing, and Levi was soaking in all the conversation because he was the one who often volunteered for the tough stuff when it came to assignments. The guys didn't let him take all the heat, but he would have if left alone. Monroe hoped he'd find a girlfriend, which would take the desire to be superman out of him. It sure did, Monroe.

Sharlee pulled up her computer screen. "They have recovered twelve bodies so far, and that monster still shook his head at the question, have we found them all?"

Jac added his frustration. "I had a conversation with the FBI this morning. It wasn't Romaine. It was some other yoyo. Romaine's supervisor, I think. They told me they are working in an orderly, chronological fashion and appreciated that Sharlee found the last place he lived, but they would work their way to it."

"That's a fucked-up way to look at it," mumbled Kaden. He spoke louder. "I mean, if we say it's more likely to be a spot that they would find the next ones on their list, shouldn't they listen to us? We've found the last four sites by following the clues and sheer determination."

Mark tossed his cell on the table. "Gutierrez listened to us and found the first bodies. He understood that you always work backward from your problem to find the solution quicker. What changed?"

Garrett leaned back in his chair and snorted. "What's changed is that this is a high-profile case, and the supervisor is looking for a feather in his cap, so he has taken over the investigation. The Feds have been known to sacrifice their young if it gets them higher up the food chain."

Monroe, true to his tactical thinking, spoke up. "We take it on ourselves. I'd add Arturo in if he wanted in, for his federal jurisdiction, but if not, then we go it alone."

Levi whipped his chair around and faced the entire group from the end of the table. "That's if we go through the front door. I say we go through the back door."

"Fuck yeah. I haven't been able to go dark in a while, and my skills are getting rusty," said Carter.

Monroe realized that Sharlee and Kaden had found a place where bodies could have been buried more recently. Off the grid, on a supposed empty property, they'd found the former addresses of Romaine, and while there would be the temptation to try them first, what if he had only been doing it for twenty years? That would mean most of the sites they had would yield them nothing. It was better to start from where they had found Mallory and go backward.

"And if there is an accomplice or a copycat, we are more likely to find them in more recent times rather than later," said Monroe.

Jac nodded. "The Feds think that there is no accomplice, and the copycat was a one-off."

"What do you think?" asked Mark.

"My gut tells me they're wrong." Jac held his hand up as the room got restless. "But, I don't have proof. If anything, the proof of silence would tell us they are right."

Carter glanced around the table. "So, what's the plan?"

Sharlee grinned. "I'm glad you asked."

They sat around the table, formulating a game plan. Monroe texted Mallory to see if she was free.

"HEY, BABY. ARE YOU getting ready to have lunch?"

Mallory sighed. "I'm taking a late lunch because the other pharmacist needs to go to a school luncheon with her son."

"That might be you in a handful of years." Monroe's voice had become rougher, eliciting salacious thoughts of being bound to his bed and at his loving mercy. It also brought to mind the simple fact that Monroe wanted to have babies with her. He had been open about his feelings, but Mallory didn't feel like she could commit until this mess was over.

"Oh, you think so, huh?" she teased back, wishing they were sure of the future, and she could take it further.

"I know so. I also know that you won't need to take off to do those things."

"And just how am I going to go to school events in the daytime without taking time off?"

"By having your own pharmacy."

"Having my own... how did you know?"

"That it was something you had thought about? Sweetheart, I told you that I might miss some things, but I'd always be listening and watching your cues. I can't read your mind, but I can read your face, your body language, and now I'm so much better at interpreting things with you."

"And you interpreted that to mean I'd want to have my own pharmacy?"

"Yep. You left lots of clues. You have been researching cost, business classes, even real estate. That could only mean a pharmacy in your line of work. I guess it could be a drugstore, but I don't see you running one. No, a pharmacy is more in your wheelhouse."

"I have to get back to work, but we'll be talking about this later, Mister."

"Is that the way you speak to your Dom?"

She laughed. "No, but it is the way I talk to my boyfriend. Look, I should go."

"Mal, wait. Can you stay in for lunch? I don't have anyone there to trail you. We have a job to do this afternoon, but I'll get someone on the team to come by to check on you. Let me order you something."

"I'm fine. No one needs to check on me. I'll leave around five today because I left at four yesterday."

"Good girl. Don't go off plan, and I'll see you then."

"Sounds good."

It felt so good to be able to talk to Monroe about her dreams and her ideas. He didn't shoot them down or explain why her pharmacy idea was faulty. He took her desires at face value, and Mallory was sure that she would have his support if she went that route. Having a life with him would be incredible, including having his children. The fact that she could think about the future meant maybe her therapist was right. She was moving on, slower than Mallory would have liked, but still. If she could make that happen, she would want it. She smiled so broadly her belly tingled. Mallory kept that glow that Monroe always gave her just when she needed it and went back to work.

MONROE AND CARTER HEAD out to the site that Sharlee and Kaden are sure is a place that Romaine was using just prior to focusing his sights on his mother's home. Evidently, if the information is correct and Monroe knows it is, Romaine lived with his mother but maintained a separate property listed in his brother's name.

Sharlee pointed at what was presumably her screen while she talked to them over a secure chat line. "Looks like Romaine had a brother that was some years older than him. He died in a car accident four years ago, and from the Google Maps view, it looked occupied three years ago."

"I thought Romaine lived at his mother's house then," said Carter.

She nodded. "Right, but like I said, someone was at least using this property three years ago. Sorry, there are no aerial views that I can locate. It's a bit out of the way but still on the main road, so that is how I got any photo."

"Did you check ownership and utilities?"

"Don't insult me. Of course, I did. All still in Romaine's brother's name."

"Right, so send us the coordinates, and we'll check it out," said Monroe. "Sharlee, can you have Garrett swing by the pharmacy and check on Mallory?"

"I can. Let me know what you guys find."

"Will do."

They had been driving for a little while. "Are you sure you put in the right coordinates?"

"Yep, but feel free to check yourself. Becky said you tend to micro-manage."

"She did, did she? Well, measure twice, cut once."

"Speaking of Becky, are you ever going to put a ring on that woman's finger?"

Carter shrugged. "I have tried. I swear, but she simply doesn't want to make a mistake."

"Meaning she isn't sure about you?"

"No, meaning she isn't sure if she's ready to commit. I'm not pushing her." He shook his head for effect.

"You might work on that insecurity with her. I mean, you have been dating for what? Over two years?"

Carter sighed. "Yeah, I'm working on that with her. But if she isn't ready, I'm not pushing her. When it's right, it's right. I want marriage, but not sure I'm ready for kids. She wants kids. Not sure she can commit if I'm not ready for the whole enchilada."

"Sorry, man." Monroe nodded to the right. "Hey, is that where we're going, up ahead?"

"I'd say so. Stop before we get to it. This road is fairly deserted. We should do a little recon before we go marching into the property. I'll get my gear, and let's see what we can discover," said Carter.

As Monroe secured the vehicle, he was glad he left Garrett in town. He would get his paperwork done and check on Mallory. Something just felt off today. He'd call her when they were back on the road. But it was the middle of the afternoon, so there shouldn't be any problems.

Garrett was just monitoring Mallory if she left the building for lunch and going home. They figured she was safe if she was leaving the house, but anyone could lurk in the shadows when she got off. Forcing his mind from Mallory, secure in the knowledge that Garrett was close to Mallory in case she needed help and to make sure she got home safely, Monroe concentrated on what he was there to do. Find evidence and the answers they were looking for.

As Carter and Monroe approached the small house on the property, it was obvious it wasn't vacant. Monroe knew they could have rented it out to someone, but he didn't believe that was the case. He figured someone that knew Romaine, someone that might have been willing to carry on in his footsteps, lived the house in.

"Sharlee, get Jac online. Your supposition that this property is still being used is correct. We'll check it out. We need to know who is here now and what their relationship is with Romaine. The signal is dicey here. Text may work better. It's silent and gets through even if the signal is weak."

"Roger that. Say safe."

"PUNCH IN YOUR CODE and leave a message."

Mallory tried one more time and got the same message, so she punched in the code Monroe had created for her after the first night they met and waited for the tone.

"Hi, it's me. I wanted to tell you I think I'm going home a little early, so I should be home by five. Can you let me know you got this? If I don't hear from you, I'll assume you are still busy and will just go home by myself. In fact, let's count on that. I love you."

Monroe must be pretty busy not to answer, or likely he was out of range. She told him she was leaving around five today because she had left at four the day before, but something was off. Her gut was unsettled, and there was a sense of dread. Maybe she would leave between four and five. The decision eased her some, but not completely.

She knew everyone was working on finding out if there were any more clues to the accomplice or copycat, and today should determine that. If not today, then in the coming days. They hoped. And Mallory had to put her trust in that happening. The strain was getting to both of them, and they needed to end it.

The anticipation she felt thinking she could finally identify the faceless ghost that presented in her nightmares more often than not was sickening and exhilarating. A typical reaction, according to the therapist that Ivy had recommended. Mallory spoke to her once a week whether or not she thought she needed to, and just that conversation with someone unrelated to the events eased her.

Mallory contemplated calling Garrett or someone else to tell them the change of plans, but she decided she wouldn't. She didn't feel unease about going home. It was about staying later. No need to disturb others because she knew to the core of her being that as long as there were missing women that fit the profile, and so long as Romaine kept saying to the Feds, "keep looking," they would continue to scour every clue to locate every woman. She needed to block that out and create a new normal. No, she would get herself home tonight.

Mallory looked at the clock, 4:35, time to go home. Her belly was jumpy again, and she felt an enormous urgency she hadn't experienced to this degree since the kidnapping. She closed out her office work and locked everything up. Flipping off the computer, she waited until it had shut down and then she grabbed her purse and headed out the door. Locking her office, she said goodnight to the others and put her hand on the pharmacy door.

As she exited and took the few steps toward the outer door, the customer bell sounded, grabbing her attention. The person who entered was wearing a ski mask, and Mallory froze in place. She could see the intruder, but a partition hid Mallory. When he presented a gun, she knew what she had to do. Getting help would be better than being there, and honestly, she wasn't sure she could deal with the fear.

Hoping she was making the right decision, she keyed in "0@R" into her cell and turned the ring tone off while praying she had enough battery for what she would need before shoving the phone in her front pocket and slipping out of the door.

THIS SPACE WAS CRAMPED, and if the bitch didn't come out of the building soon, she would have to go get her, which would mess up the plan. She had promised the homeless man he could stay at master's brother's home if he pretended to rob the store, but it was taking too long. She could hear her master say very clearly, "Impatience will be punished. Stay the course, and I'll reward you."

She would earn that reward.

Chapter 21

Monroe and Carter entered Jacquard and Associates at 4:20 p.m. Monroe had just enough time to debrief Jac and get to the Apothecary to follow Mallory home. Carter sat next to him in front of Jac's desk and began talking.

"Seems like a woman is living there alone." Carter described the living room to those gathered. "It appears most of the living was taking place in the main room. We found no clothing that would typically belong to a male, but items like newspaper clippings were in a stack. She or they taped those with photos of Mallory to the wall behind the articles, all with stick pins in her face."

Monroe scratched his head. "No computer, no landline, no television. Since the woman wasn't there, it was hard to know if she had a cell phone. She does have a vehicle because it is leaking a little oil and the tracks are fresh. She seems to sleep on an old sofa. There was minimal food in the fridge and garbage in the can, and very little else looked to be disturbed except the bathroom, minimally. But a woman wouldn't be able to do what was done to that last victim."

Sharlee walked in, followed by Kaden. "Why not? And you look like shit, by the way."

"Brat. You obviously need a round with my rubber paddle, but I'm too tired to do that, so I'll leave Jac to be the attitude adjuster."

"Charlotte, we do not appreciate your bluntness today."

Sharlee gave a little sound of outrage before changing it to sympathy for Monroe, giving his shoulders a short massage. "Okay, again, I ask, why not? I promise you; women can be as cold and calculating as men. Besides, it fits."

Jac leaned forward. "Explain."

"Mallory has always maintained Romaine spoke of a wife. And let's face it, if you're married to a monster of this magnitude, then you are assisting or turning a blind eye."

Kaden sat on the edge of the desk. "This is the first proof that she was right about the partner, but not about the wife part. There are no marriage records anywhere, so unless they married in a foreign country, which didn't happen because Romaine has no passport, then no wife. Maybe they have a Master/slave relationship, and he has her living in his brother's old place."

Monroe called Mallory while the others debated the likelihood of a woman murdering the latest victim and the call went to voicemail. Monroe heard a ping come through on his phone and hit the message. It was probably from Garrett. He punched in his code and heard Mallory's voice telling him she had changed her plans. Checking the time, he knew he had missed her, but Garrett would have known the change as well and gone to follow her home.

Monroe called Garrett, and when he didn't pick up, he tried Mallory. Same thing.

Jac called Gutierrez. "I'm not lead on this investigation any longer, Jac."

"Understood, but I needed to tell you this information because every time I steer information to your jackass superior, he blows me off after taking down the info. I'd say, if you want a little credit for the work you've done, this is the place to check out. It's up to you, but it's a good lead."

Arturo hesitated for a few seconds. "Okay, you haven't sent us on any wild goose chases yet, so your intel is solid. Give me what you have."

Jac informed Arturo that since this place is as likely a spot to dump bodies as the home Romaine was in, he should jump on it. "Someone lives there but very simply, and their imprint is minimal."

"Okay, send me the coordinates, and I'll get out there in the morning." Jac was good at drawing a line when they didn't need to overstep the boundaries and when it needed to happen.

"Arturo said to leave it with them. I'm inclined to do that."

Leave it with the Feds. What was becoming Jac's mantra was past nerve-wracking, and the others understood Monroe's desperation. When Sharlee, Ivy, Jessie and even Becky had their safety in jeopardy, the men had the same feeling as their own women. Monroe remembered the anguish that Garrett had gone through when he went looking for Callie and hadn't found her for a time, only to immediately lose her again.

As Monroe felt he had enough proof to tighten his security around Mallory, he dialed Garrett. Since he'd checked on Mallory earlier in the afternoon, he would have known she was taking off sooner than first thought.

Garrett still didn't answer. Sharlee broke through the debate. "Shit, there is a robbery in progress at the Apothecary, and the thief is still inside. Law enforcement is on their way."

There is a ping on Sharlee's phone and then one on Jac's computer. Then Monroe's phone.

"Mallory has initiated the Safe and Secure program. She was likely inside. The phone is still sending, but I can't understand what is being said. I need my computer." Sharlee hurried out of the room.

Jac called out to the room. "Where the hell is Garrett?"

Carter sent out the call to get to the Apothecary, and Kaden sent out a ping to track Garrett's phone. "Garrett is already there."

"Good, now let's get moving and end this shit so I can get Mallory out of there. Who the fuck would rob a pharmacy in broad, fucking daylight?"

"An idiot, so it should be easier to take him down knowing he doesn't plan well," answered Carter.

Jac and Kaden stopped Monroe before he walked out. He shoved past them before they could close ranks. Levi strode in and quickly assessed the scene, then stood in the doorway.

"If you want to keep that pretty boy face, you had better get the hell out of my way." Monroe was not joking.

Levi just stood his ground with a slow smile on his face. Monroe had vetted him and knew the man was skilled, but Monroe's fear for Mallory overrode his good sense, and he rammed Levi. After several attempts to get Monroe to see sense, the four surrounded him and escorted him to Carter's SUV.

"You aren't fucking driving, so shut up and get in, or you won't go at all. I'll have you held here," said Jac to Monroe.

Carter jumped in the driver's seat and tossed his blue light in the window, flipping the switch to activate it. Then he hit the gas pedal.

"Where'd you get that?" asked Levi.

"Souvenir from my glory days as CID. We have to get the camera feed and find out what happened."

"Here," said Kaden as he held up Jac's laptop that he'd snagged as they left the office. "Sharlee sent the feed."

They watched the best they could as the robber came into the Apothecary. One of the inside cameras was live streaming, and they could see each person in the pharmacy, and it looked like the intruder was asking about something. Everyone shook their head no. They scanned the group and didn't see Mallory.

Monroe reached for the laptop. "Let me see that."

Kaden released his hold, and Monroe then proceeded to scan the group carefully. "She's not there."

Kaden nodded. "We said that."

"No, I mean she isn't there as in her jacket is gone. She's already left."

"That's great. I mean, Sharlee should be tracking her," said Carter. "So now, where do I go."

Kaden spoke excitedly. "I'm getting Sharlee's same signal. I still have Garrett at the Apothecary. But the tracker says Mallory is going in the opposite direction of your house."

"Okay, we're here," said Jac. "We'll find Garrett, assess the situation, and beat feet to wherever they triangulate Mallory. Garrett probably thinks Mallory is still inside."

They turn down the alleyway in time to see an ambulance arrive. Three doors open before the car comes to a complete stop, and four men pour out of the vehicle, headed for Garrett's truck.

MALLORY'S HEAD HURT. She lay on the uncomfortable floor of something and tried not to throw up. As she slowly cleared a small hole in the fog that filled her head, she realized she was in a car, her car. It was difficult to think, painful in fact, but she willed herself to listen.

Her mind slowly focused. All she could remember was she had walked outside the pharmacy intent on getting away quickly when she saw Garrett's truck in his regular waiting spot. Hmm, he didn't get the memo, I guess. Oh, well, she had to get out of there before the robber discovered the only pharmacist on duty left. Garrett would have to keep up because she didn't have time for pleasantries today.

She told Bluetooth to dial 911 and pulled out into traffic with the plan to stop a safe distance away and wait for the police. She was glad she had already activated her Keep Safe Program code and mentally verified the phone was still in her front pocket because of the weight pushing on her thigh. Cold steel made contact with her head. She had a flashback to the first time that had happened.

"Climb in, Mallory." The words that signaled her nightmare experience were seared into her memory.

"Pull over," said the voice she was sure she'd heard before. There was a quality that she recognized.

"911, what is your emergency?" asked the dispatch worker over Bluetooth.

"I said pull over." Her head jerked back hard. "Disconnect the call." Which she did with trembling hands.

Mallory hoped the woman wouldn't realize that the car's wireless device wasn't self-contained. It would need a phone to initiate the call through to the emergency dispatch. She pulled over, and as soon as she had put the car in park, the woman demanded she go to the backseat. At least she wasn't in the trunk again.

"Hurry up, I don't have all day."

Then the woman laughed in a manner that made Mallory's belly turn cold. It was more of a cackle, a maniacal sound. The woman was unbalanced. She was talking as though someone was with her. Her precise way of wiping every place she touched, her movements meticulous and subdued, belied the violence she was engaged in.

Mallory hesitated as she stood in the space that created a "V" inside the opened back door. Evidently, that was the wrong thing to do. Blinding pain stabbed through her head and pierced her eyes. She grappled with the urge to just go to sleep, just close her eyes, and the pain would disappear, she told herself. The pain had overcome her, and Mallory did as her body demanded. She allowed the pain to drag her into unconsciousness.

Now, as her thinking came online again, Mallory realized her head was hot and swollen, throbbing in time with her pounding heart. She never could shake the information that Romaine had never married and did not have a wife or common-law wife. If she'd heard a voice or saw someone she thought had something to do with this shit fest, she would have pursued her theory. She would have gone towards danger because she was determined to end this and live her life.

But now, she didn't feel so brave. Mallory felt physically ill, and she wanted Monroe. That thought reminded her of the phone in her pocket. They should have located her by now, and Mallory knew Garrett wasn't behind her when she'd stopped on the side of the road because he would have stopped the woman from forcing her in the backseat. He wouldn't have let the kidnapper clobber Mallory unless he was hurt and unable to follow them. Let him still be alive, she prayed.

Mallory wanted to touch the throbbing, tender spot hit with what was likely the butt of a cold, steel pistol, but she didn't dare alert the other woman of her consciousness. The woman was mumbling to herself, and Mallory listened. It was hard to discern what she was saying, but she heard enough to make her blood run cold.

"I'm smart enough to do this. She's the reason you're in jail. No, I won't. She has to pay. I heard you won't ever come home to me, and she has to pay even if you wanted her more than me." Then she screamed, "Stop!" and pounded the steering wheel.

The woman was utterly mad. That would either make this easier or harder. Mallery remained still and tried to feel the phone in her front pocket. Yes, it was there. She could only pray that the fall hadn't broken it, and it was still transmitting, or at least it still had power left.

Monroe would be manic with worry, and his fear for her safety might push him to do something foolish. Her anxiety rose, concerned for Monroe and his judgment. But once the vehicle turned onto a road that sounded as though it were little more than a gravel and dirt trail, Mallory became dead still, her brain running over scenarios and means of escape. Was the woman working on her own, or were there others? Listening but trying to move very little, Mallory was miserable and terrified. All she wanted was Monroe's arms wrapped around her, telling her it was all a bad dream.

GARRETT WAS ARGUING with the ambulance and two officers when the group arrived. Mark pulled up right at that instant, and Garrett gestured for him to come closer. Jac and the others headed in Garrett's direction. Sharlee tapped into Jac's Bluetooth speaker in his ear and Kaden's laptop. Carter shoved the SUV into park and threw open his own door. The sight of four menacing men and two more coming from two different directions was enough for the younger cop to partially draw his gun from the holster.

"Stay where you are," ordered the police officer.

"Put that away. These are my teammates. My business associates." The cop did re-holster his weapon, but he kept his hand on the handle.

"What the hell happened to you?" asked Mark, who ignored the cautious police officer.

"Dammit. I'm going to be all right. They already gave me a GABA, something antagonizer to mitigate the effects."

The EMT interjected. "GABA receptor antagonist. It will, as Mr. Sullivan said, mitigate the effects, but it won't take away some of the side effects like a headache."

"I'll have a fucking headache for a while, but I will, whether I sit in the hospital waiting until they officially tell me I'm going to have a headache, or I can sit here and wait for my client. Why the hell are all of you here?"

"She isn't there," said Mark as he approached. "Look, her car is gone."

"No, she's inside, and her car is right... hell! Where did she go? What's happened to her?"

Jac answered as his group approached. "There's a robbery going on inside. Mallory got out before he came in or simultaneously, but she activated her Keep Safe program, and we've seen that something happened just as she was pulling out into traffic. The camera's range ended there. I'm sure whoever has her thought they were out of range already. Now, let them fix you up while you give me your sitrep."

Monroe pushed in between the men. "We need to track Mallory, not sit here rehashing what has already happened. We can do that after I have Mal back safely."

"We are still triangulating and have no idea until we get a read on her. We have no choice but to wait, Monroe, but as soon as we know, we will be on it." Kaden said. Monroe paced beside Garrett's SUV.

Jac ignored Monroe as he paced and swore but made eye contact with Carter, who gave an almost imperceivable nod in response. "Garrett, what happened to you?"

"Not sure, exactly. I was waiting for Mallory when I heard a ruckus over by the dumpster. I checked the immediate area around me and saw nothing, but I continued to hear some rattling, so I got out of the car and walked over to see what was going on. When I got there, it had stopped, and there was nothing out of place, so I headed back to the car and right after I got into the seat, someone jabbed me with something in my shoulder off my neck. I think I must have moved because if it had gotten into my vein, I would not be conscious now."

The EMT said, "It seems to be some tranquilizer, and we will get the report in a few days of exactly what kind, but they did not measure it for a man of Mr. Sullivan's size, so it was short-lived."

Monroe reappeared in front of the EMT and said grimly, "More likely the dose for a much smaller woman."

The EMT nodded. "It's possible."

Jac touched his ear and activated his Bluetooth as he walked away a few steps and then held his hand up. "We have a signal and a direction. We're following it for as long as we are able. Let's hit it. Monroe, Carter, and Levi are with me. Garrett and Kaden, you're with Mark. Let's go get our girl."

"We'll need a statement," said one officer.

Jac reached into his wallet and handed them his business card. "As soon as we have our team member back, we'll call you, but this is our company. I'm sure your boss knows us."

"We'll need to check the vehicle for evidence."

Garrett waved to them. "Perfect. Take it home, and I'll grab it when I come in to give my statement tomorrow. Sound good? Call me tomorrow when you're done with my car, and I'll come in and give my statement."

Garrett took the ignition key off his chain and tossed it to the closest officer before following Kaden to Mark's car. Without another word, the team got into their separate vehicles and left the scene.

Chapter 22

Mallory heard the woman talking to someone who wasn't there. "Master, I've gotten her back for you. There isn't anything left to do but kill her and bury her on the property before I move on... But I thought that's what you wanted... She's pathetic. She was too easy to knock out. There wasn't any fun in it, and it looks like she won't ever regain consciousness before I kill her. Maybe I should wait... Yes, Master, I'll stick to the plan. I didn't have to put on a wig this time. But what about that man? The one who was waiting on Miss Pharmacy... I understand. I didn't leave enough evidence that they could find me. Remember, Master, they think I'm dead."

The chaotic conversation continued, but Mallory had a plan now. Monroe and Garrett had been teaching her some defensive moves, and Ivy had shared some of her skills with Mallory, but not enough to really help yet. She tried to focus on the moves she could remember.

Everything seemed to fly out of her memory except the one combination of moves that Monroe had made her practice repeatedly. He had given her an alternative ending move for a woman. It would have to do.

The car came to a slow rolling stop. Mallory tried to control her breathing like Monroe had been teaching her for play, but this had real stakes, and they were high. The highest. All thoughts were temporarily suspended when the abductor opened the front door, and Mallory heard the crunching of feet on the dirt and gravel pathway. The pinging from the car's notification system warned that the woman left the front door open, but her kidnapper ignored the irritating sound. Mallory forced herself to do the same.

The back door opened at her feet, and Mallory prayed she didn't move until she had full use of her arms and legs. She made herself as limp as possible, knowing it would make her nearly impossible to remove from the floor of the car. She hoped it would give Monroe and the team more time to find her. After trying to pull Mallory out of the vehicle and getting little success, her captor began talking angrily with her "master," whom Mallory assumed was Romaine, who was sitting in prison.

She was ranting and railing at a tree that appeared to be the symbol of Romaine to her, or maybe she thought it really was him, but she was a woman gone mad. Mallory eased out of the vehicle when the woman yelled at the tree again and then supplicate to it.

Mallory slipped around the car and was going to slide into the driver's seat when her abductor noticed her. Mallory reached for the keys and flipped on the ignition, firing up the car, but the back door was still open. Her attacker was about to climb through the back. Panicking, Mallory turned off the car, grabbed the keys, and ran. Never mind waiting to use her skills. If she could run, she would run. Thankfully, she'd changed her shoes in the office before she had left. Heels were never a running shoe.

Going as fast as she could, Mallory pulled her forgotten phone from her front pocket and tried to use it, but there was no signal. Praying that would not impede Sharlee and the guys from finding her, she continued to run, hearing the woman follow her, but the distance was becoming further and further away. Obviously, the other woman had not been required to do PT as Mallory had since aligning herself with Monroe. Mallory was never more thankful for the enforced drudgery than now.

Jac's exercise routine and Monroe's version of exercise had helped her regain her previous fitness, and in some ways, she had exceeded it. A stitch in her side had Mallory gasping for air and pressing hard into her flesh to alleviate her pain. Walking was going to have to be enough for right now until the pain subsided. Mallory listened for the woman but couldn't hear her. There were forest sounds, but nothing to pinpoint it as the other woman.

Mallory had zigzagged when she ran, so she hoped she'd confused the other woman enough to not find her before the guys did. But now, Mallory found herself hopelessly lost. She didn't dare go back the way she had come, even if she was lucky enough to stumble in the right direction because somewhere behind her was a lunatic looking to harm her.

At one point, it appeared her attacker would stop, but she swore, argued with her imaginary friend, and then spun off as though she were angry. She said something more about her house and the grounds, about other women and digging. She was obviously upset that whatever her plan had been was now foiled. So how much of her plan needed the house?

It seemed like Mallory had been gone a long time, but, according to her phone, only a couple of hours had passed since the crazy lady had kidnapped her. Even if Monroe and the guys showed up, she wouldn't hear them at this great distance, and they wouldn't know where to find her. The light was fading fast. Within thirty minutes or less, it would be gone. She needed to find someplace to shelter if she had to spend the night in the woods.

She had just left the forest because the isolation and the sounds of nature frightened her at night. The exertion, the fear, and the still fairly strong remnants of the crack on the head added to her feelings of defeat. No, they would find her. Monroe would find her.

Hurry Monroe!

CARTER SPOKE GRIMLY. "We're nearly to Stanton. That's where Romaine's house is. The one we went to check out today. Mallory's kidnapper is or was living there."

"So," said Mark, "Why wouldn't she go there unless the Feds have actually listened to us and started digging?"

They checked out the Romaine house, and sure enough, Feds were everywhere. Jac turned to Monroe and said, "We don't invite them in to help until we come up dry. We have better equipment and tracking than they do, so this will be the better route."

"Agreed."

Carter's face took on that determined look that Becky swore meant, "Everyone, get out of my face and let me do the thing."

The rest of his team joined Carter in his single-minded determination as they continued in the signal's direction. It had since stopped moving and sat on an unmapped road or area. Something was happening, and that had Carter driving as quickly as he could, given the area and terrain. Mark followed.

"What the fuck happened here?" asked Monroe as they approached an area that was now billowing smoke. His tone left no one to guess how desperate he was becoming. His anguish made each man cringe. "That's Mallory's car!" he yelled as the vehicle slowed down and the flames shot from the now blackened hunk of metal that was once a car. "No, no, no!"

Before his teammates could stop him, the door flung open, and Monroe leaped from the still rolling SUV, followed by all those not driving from both vehicles. Swarming around the heated metal, the back door was still open, allowing Garrett to look inside.

"Back seat—clear."

Within seconds came the second confirmation. "Front—clear."

What they had left was the trunk. Carter brought over his fire extinguisher and handed it off to Mark, who doused the flames at the back of the vehicle as much as he could. The tank would blow any moment as the flames crept back.

Carter pulled out his tool that was a mini jaws-of-life only, not hydraulic powered. It was Carter-powered. After a few seconds of set-up, he pulled the trunk hood back from the frame, and the trunk was accessible and pushed open. Smoke and heat greeted the men as they peered inside. One quick shifting of the blanket and melting plastic emergency kit showed no person.

"Thank God," said Garrett.

Monroe slammed his fist on the roof of the charred car. "Fuck. Now what? Kaden, where is the signal now?"

Jac brought his hand up to move everyone away from the fire. "Throw more chemicals on it, and before we leave, I'll call the fire department. No need to add to the drama by having a forest fire. At the distance we are from the town, we'll be gone by the time they arrive."

"We hope," said Levi.

The men gathered info and made their plan. Kaden and Mark moved the vehicles off and out of the way. They would watch the scene and the cars and monitor the communications from Sharlee in case Jac's headset lost signal.

The rest took off toward the last communicated signal.

MALLORY WOKE UP IN fear without immediately understanding why. As her brain unconsciously looked for the danger, her thoughts become cohesive, and she took in her surroundings, causing her breath to pick up and her autonomic response system to take over her breathing. She lost her bearings in the woods with a madwoman who held her responsible for taking away her security. As erroneous as that unstable perception was, it was a dangerous way of thinking. One that placed Mallory in fear for her life.

Taking a deep breath and holding it, using the box-breathing method Monroe had taught her in the early days when he taught her to control her reactions to the touches of pain he gave her when they played. It had enhanced her enjoyment. Later, when her nightmares merged with her daytime realities, he made her use the same method, giving her some semblance of control.

Now Mallory felt better just doing something that she and Monroe had done. And it did what it was meant to do, give her a sense of control. She would find a way out of here herself because it was obvious her phone didn't do the job or Monroe would be here already.

Mallory didn't know why the woman didn't shoot her when she had the chance, but what Mallory figured out was this was not the time to allow her fear to cripple her. Mallory started back in the direction she thought was the right one. Her phone display showed the time to be coming up on eight, and the darkness of evening had fallen in the woods, with true dark soon to follow. She needed to pick her way out of here and fast.

Try to locate landmarks you passed, she told herself, even though she knew there were few that she'd actually passed that had registered in her terrorized brain. She still worried that she would unwittingly run into the reason for her predicament today. The gunshot off to her right froze her in her fright. *Run*!

Scrambling over rocks and underbrush, enduring the brambles and bushes scraping across her skin, she barely acknowledged the blood running from her arms and face. She kept running until stopping to catch her breath. She heard something or someone tearing through the forest in her direction. It must have been something large because it didn't seem to worry about being heard or discovered. *Hide*!

Crawling under the overhang of rock with brush surrounding her, Mallory ignored the insects and other critters likely living in her makeshift hiding spot. She pulled the surrounding vegetation in after her. All the while, she prayed the team wouldn't find her stung by a hive of bees or the branches surrounding her containing poison oak or ivy.

Then it suddenly went silent. Willing herself to return to the 4x4 pattern, Mallory had barely gotten to the last step when the noise was upon her. She knew the object hadn't passed her, but it was as though it were floating over her or around her, but no longer stomping through the woods toward her.

There was a rustle of the branches in front of her as they slowly disappeared from the front of Mallory's hiding spot. When the covering was gone, Mallory tried to back into the solid rock behind her. When she saw a hand, she screamed with all her might.

"Mallory! Mallory, baby, it's me. It's Monroe."

Chapter 23

"**S**he exhibits behaviors such as has been identified as Stockholm Syndrome on Steroids," said the criminal psychiatrist after interviewing Jeanne Saginaw.

Mallory wasn't sure she could ever forget that look of pure hatred and rampant violence that Ms. Saginaw, the first kidnapped victim of Craig Romaine, showed her when she saw Mallory on the other side of the vehicle.

"The patient's inability, at this time, to separate her daily life and indeed her own desires from her kidnapper's is evident in many of her mannerisms. She speaks to her Master, yet she condemns him because he chose the last victim, the one he wanted most, and it was the end of their life together. It was by this victim, Ms. Sasse's, actions that Ms. Saginaw has lost all of her stability, including the source of her ongoing misery."

"Will Ms. Saginaw, in your expert opinion, have a chance to return to her previous life?"

"To ask that question is to make this situation too trivial. There is no indication that Ms. Saginaw cannot return to some semblance of her former life, certainly, but do I believe it will happen? It is unlikely."

"Do you believe she acted of her own volition to terrorize and kidnap intending to commit murder?"

"At this time, your honor, I am not comfortable making that statement. Did she do it? Yes, she readily admits that. Did she know what she was doing? Probably. Based on her life experiences and the state of her unbalanced mentality, did she feel that it was the only course of action she could take? Yes. It was the only course of action that was expected of her? Yes. Is she a danger to herself and others? Absolutely."

"What are your recommendations, Dr. Cooley, as to the disposition of this defendant?"

"For the foreseeable future, I believe she is criminally insane, and only time will tell if she recovers enough to be considered safe, but I don't believe we can hold her responsible for her choices from the day Craig Romaine kidnapped her as a teenager, over fourteen years ago."

"Thank you, Dr. Cooley. You may step down," said the judge. "Court is adjourned until tomorrow morning, where I will render my decision." The gavel slammed down once, signaling it was time to go.

Monroe and Garrett ushered Mallory out the side door and into the waiting SUV driven by Carter. They shuffled her into the car, and Carter drove off quickly. Due to the smoked windows, it was impossible to see inside, and it allowed the group to leave before the reporters expected them out the front entrance.

"Is that it then?" asked Mallory.

"Yes. You aren't required in court tomorrow. Your testimony finished your part of this mess. It's over." Monroe rubbed her neck and pulled her in as close as the seat belt would allow.

"I can't say I'm sad that I won't have to repeat that horrible story again." Mallory snuggled in close. His shirt that she was all but sharing muffled her voice. "I can't believe that because of being rejected at a club, wonderful insight on their part, by the way, it started the ball rolling on so many deaths."

Monroe responded thoughtfully. "The mind is something so complicated that one seemingly insignificant event can trigger a person to be taken so out of their reality that a new reality is created. That's what happened here. Romaine thought himself to be misjudged, and when he lost his girlfriend, that seemed to be wrapped up in his anger and all twisted together. We have dead tortured women and one woman who is just as demented as he is."

Carter glanced in the rearview mirror before going back to watching the road. "I'm done with this whole thing. I need to get back to normal. Well, after we have our debriefing later this afternoon. Think you are up to some lunch and one last review of things, Mallory?"

"No, but I'll do it because you guys saved me."

Garrett shook his head. "Sharlee's program did, in reality, but I think we all worked it well."

"I'm not going back to work at the Apothecary," Mallory said to no one in particular.

"Thank fuck. I didn't know how to tell you that you weren't going back. I already had your personal items removed."

Mallory sat up straight. "You did what? Without talking to me? I might have wanted to go back, and it is my decision, anyway."

"It is your decision, and you made it. It was just the one that I would have demanded, so we are on the same page. That's a good thing, Mal." He leaned in to kiss her, and she turned her head.

"It isn't the same thing. It was my decision, and I should have made it. I would probably have asked you to go get my things for me, so I didn't have to return there, but it's within my control if I say it. I don't tell you to stop doing PT every morning because you wake me up when you get up and then change your schedule to evening. You might have thought to do that but would not have appreciated me doing it for you."

"But baby, it's the same thing in the end."

"But it isn't the same road to get there."

"And that matters?"

"Of course it matters."

Monroe pulled her back to lie on his chest, and he kissed her hair. "I'm sorry. I guess I thought I was taking care of you and was glad you didn't protest."

"You were taking care of me, and I appreciate it, but it matters how we get to a decision. You have to ask me first."

"Duly noted. I apologize."

"Thank you."

"It'll take another thirty minutes to get to Sharlee and Jac's, so let's just breathe."

"Mmm, free air."

"THANK YOU, MALLORY," said Jac. "I think we have what we need for the records, and we will field any problems from now on with the Feds and the police. You can start to pretend it never happened if that is what you want to do."

"Like that could ever happen," remarked Sharlee. Mallory had to smile at the smack Sharlee got for her trouble. She made an outraged sound but winked at Mallory, causing her to smile even wider.

"Right," said Jac as he clapped his hands together. "Where's our whiskey?"

"Right here. I bought this on the best of recommendations, and no, you can't ask where," said Sharlee. She got up to bring back a bottle of deep gold liquid. "A bottle of twelve-year GlenDronach Allardice Scotch."

"It sounds intriguing," said Jessie. Mark gave Jessie a lifted brow, and she shook her head. "No sir, apple juice for me."

"Like I would serve a preggo. Please, you all must suffer as I did," said Sharlee. "No matter how excellent the booze is, you must watch."

They passed around paper cups, and Monroe offered one to Mallory. "I don't know if I can hold my liquor. I hardly ever drink more than a glass of wine."

Ivy nudged Mallory. "That's because we haven't had a night out on the town. Just wait until you do. It will change your mind about indulging because we have bodyguards while we do it. I can't tell you how delish it is to have our hunks of manhood sitting in the corner, taking turns being our bodyguards, and having to fend off the local vermin for them and us. It's free entertainment."

The men grumbled good-naturedly.

"You won't be drinking for quite some time, Jessica," said Mark.

"You're right, I won't, but because it's my choice, not yours."

"Do you care to discuss this?" Mark's rich tones darkened.

"Have you learned a new skill because your ability to discuss things you have already made up your mind about has not been your best quality?" Jessie's flippant answer had Mark's expression go dark, very dark. Mallory shivered.

Mallory looked at Monroe, who returned her look of concern with a smile. He leaned down to speak in her ear. "Those two do this when a big case ends. They will go home, and one or both will be in a mood. They do what they do to relieve their stress, and then they're done and back cuddling."

"Oh. Well, what about Carter and Becky?"

Monroe looked over toward his teammate and watched as Becky stood up and stomped off, tears streaming. "Carter must have denied Becky something."

"Why do you assume that?" said Mallory indignantly.

He shrugged. "That's just how it usually is."

"Right like earlier today, it was my fault because I didn't fall at your feet in thanksgiving for you to take over part of my life."

"Mal, we talked about this," he said as Mallory stood up, intent on helping Becky with an ear or supportive hand.

"Becky is the most thoughtful person I know. Carter should be ashamed," said Mallory. As she turned to walk away, Monroe swatted her ass hard.

"What the hell?" yelped Mallory.

Monroe smiled, but his voice belied his expression. "When you come back, you had better be bringing me my paddle, woman."

She smiled back. "It's at home. I'll go get it. You wait here."

Another swat landed on her butt. "Brat. I'll take care of you when we get home tonight."

"I'm counting on it." Mallory tossed her head back and smiled, wiggled her eyebrows, and turned to shimmy her butt. Monroe burst out laughing. She couldn't wait.

FOLLOWING BEHIND BECKY, who had seemed to disappear, she found Sharlee heading into the room that was set up as a lounge just in time to hear Becky ask if she could stay at Sharlee's.

"Just until I get myself an apartment," clarified Becky.

"Of course, you don't have to ask, but I'm curious as to why?"

"You've been living with Jac too long, girl. You sound like your husband."

"Sorry, occupational and marital hazard. Now, what is going on?"

Sharlee sat in a chair across from Becky on the sofa. Ivy was lounging in the chair next to Sharlee's. Jessie was sitting on Becky's left, and Becky patted the seat to her right. "Sit here, Mallory."

Once her closest friends had settled around her, Becky began. After about fifteen minutes of sympathy and ideas on fixing the fact that Carter was pushing Becky to get married but didn't want to commit to kids yet, they sat quietly.

"I need another drink," said Ivy.

"You do not," said Jessie.

Sharlee shook her head. "Besides, Jac wouldn't allow it. His home, his rules."

"You two need to settle on a date and work the rest out later," said Mallory.

"But what if he never wants children?" asked a distraught Becky.

"Negotiate," said Mallory. "Like a contract."

"But, um, we aren't like you and Monroe. I mean, we don't..." she shrugged at a loss how to put what she wanted to say.

"You don't play, you mean?" asked Mallory.

"Yes, right. That." Becky's face was intensely red.

"That's okay. I bet most business moguls don't either, but they definitely write and negotiate contracts."

Ivy sat up. "I'd like to hear about the contract you and Monroe have," she smiled, but it was obvious she was serious.

Jessie frowned at Ivy. "TMI. It's their business."

"You want to know, too," said Ivy.

"Well, sure, but I wouldn't ask."

Sharlee made a noise deep in her throat, and it sounded just like her husband. Everyone looked at her. "Stay on topic here. Now I think Mallory has a good idea. Go ahead, Mallory."

"Right, so the premise is that Becky doesn't want marriage without children and is afraid that Carter won't ever want children, so if she marries him, then he gets what he wants, and she doesn't."

They all nodded, and Becky agreed. "Right."

"So, based on the basic foundation of I love you, and you love me, and you both want to marry, those are the agreeable items. Now, we need to discuss trust because that is what the problem is here. You don't trust Carter to follow through, and he doesn't trust you to not force the issue before he is ready."

They continued talking for another fifteen minutes. "I'm still staying here until I get this worked out and signed," said Becky. "Can you come over to help me put it together, Mallory?"

"Sure, since I don't have a job right now."

Sharlee's phone rang. "Hello? Who... Callie? Oh my God, where are you? Why are you whispering? We'll come and get you immediately. We can. I promise it will be okay. You can stay here. No, I'm so glad you called. We miss you."

"Mal, we need to go. I've..."

He stopped mid-sentence when he heard Sharlee was on the phone. "Please don't hang up. Callie? Callie?"

Sharlee rushed from the room and headed to her computer, pushing past Jac, who stood with a grim expression.

"Can we not get one fucking weekend of quiet?" He held up a business card that looked like that crazy Saginaw woman's. Monroe grabbed it and read.

"Has the party started yet?"

The End

About the Author
Alyssa Bailey

USA TODAY AND #1 BESTSELLING Author of Diverse Romance that is realistic and sensual with a touch of suspense. A dyed in the wool Texan living in Alaska for half her life, Alyssa now divides her time between the beauty of Southeast Alaska and the piney woods of East Texas. She enjoys taking from her own experiences to create series in fictitious worlds sure to tease the reader's palate and invite them to sink into exciting adventures.

Alyssa enjoys writing consensual power exchanges between intelligent, sassy women who are not afraid to make a stand and loving men confident enough to give his woman space but masterful enough to keep her safe despite her choices. There is *always* a happily ever after.

Visit me online and sign up for my Newsletter:
http://alyssabailey.com[1]
Join my Facebook Group for fun and prizes:
https://www.facebook.com/alyssabailey.romance

Other[2] books in the Safe and Secure Series
Saving Sharlee: Safe and Secure Book 1

She has always been safe in her secret world, but once she is exposed, will she ever be safe again?

Sharlee Armstrong is happy spending her professional life in seclusion as Vapor, a highly sought out independent information broker. Though she has plenty of high paying clients, the offer from Reynaud & Associates piques her curiosity. During the interview, her libido is also piqued when she meets Jacquard Reynaud—gorgeous, sexy, and dominant.

The job, not just the boss, intrigues her and she accepts the offer. But things spiral out of control, and she finds her reputation, livelihood, and life in jeopardy. Jac and the rest of the alpha males on her new team demand she keep a low profile, but she has other ideas.

The minute she steps foot into his office, and life, Jac knows he has to have Sharlee, but first he must keep her safe—not just from some unknown threat, but from Sharlee herself. He loves her sass but worries that she'll find herself in real trouble if he cannot keep her under control. So, despite her protests, he takes her in hand. For her own good.

Will she ever learn to let Jac protect her? Can she let Jac and the rest of the team into her previously quiet, mostly solitary life?

Saving Jessie Book 2
With lives in the balance, what could she do but comply with their demands?

---

2. https://www.facebook.com/alyssabailey.romance

Accountant Jessica Roe kept her head down and always followed the rules. When she discovered possible illegal activity with her employer, she left that job and joined Reynaud and Associates. Life was good, her brother hadn't asked for money in months and she was now dating Mark Jensen. Within one week: her brother needed money, her old employer was trying to blackmail her, and she was nearly raped and killed. Not only is her savings at risk, but her relationship with Mark, her job with Reynaud and Associates, her friends, and her life.

Mark Jensen worked hard and played harder, preferring one-night stands to anything long term, until he hooked up with the company accountant. Jessie is a sassy, sweet, rule follower with a deep-seated loneliness about her that is unlike any woman he's dated. She has stolen his heart. Just when Mark had finally convinced Jessie to move in with him, her brother has more than money problems to lay at his sister's door. Suddenly, Jessie is over her head and making all the wrong decisions while trying to protect her new friends, brother, and lover.

When Jessie's past and present puts her in the middle of international illegal trade, it will take the whole team to keep her safe while they figure out the details and bring this operation to a crashing halt.

Saving Ivy Book 3

Passions burn hot when Kaden rescues Ivy from kidnappers, but she leaves without a word when her fears overcome her. Amid new chaos, Ivy reappears with the mob on her tail and nowhere to run but to Kaden. Will she beg for his protection? Will his wounded pride demand it of her?

It has been a year since sexy as sin, heiress Ivy Linton made the mistake of leaving Kaden's protection and his bed. She was confused about what she wanted out of life, so when Ivy found herself falling hard for Kaden, she panicked, leaving the only man she had ever felt secure. When she finds herself the center of attention of a man she worries is up to his neck in shady dealings, she needs to get away fast. After running to Kaden, Ivy finds that someone wants her dead, and the one man she trusts may not be able to keep her safe after all.

Kaden ignored his instincts and was too gentle the first time Ivy was with him, but he won't make that mistake again. And this time, there are strings attached. To keep her safe, she must agree to his rules and follow his commands, or there will be consequences. Going against organized crime is worth keeping Ivy with him safe and secure, but the price he demands is high, and he wants the first payment upfront.

AUTHOR NOTE: THIS ADULT romance contains mystery, suspense, second chances, power exchange, and sensual scenes.

Other Romance Books by Alyssa Bailey

Lords and Little Ladies: Georgian Historical, spicy

Lord Thayer's Choice

Lord Ashton's Decision

The Black Laird Requires

Lord Kendrick's Obligation

Darling Duchesses: Regency, Daddy Dom, Spicy

The Devil Duke's Little Distraction (May 2021)

Chase Abbey Series: Regency, Spicy, Suspense

Lord Barrington's Minx

Becoming Lady Barrington

Lady Caroline's Defiance

His Improper Lady

Safe and Secure Series: Contemporary, suspense, spicy

Saving Sharlee

Saving Jessie

Saving Ivy

Saving Mallory

Saving Becky (2022)

Saving Finley (TBD)

Saving Callie (TBD)

The O'Connor Series: Contemporary, Rancher, Saga, Spicy

Liam & Jocelyn's Story

Her Sweet Complication

Liam's Lessons

Loving Liam

Ciarán and Katherine's Story

His Gentle Persuasion

Rancher's Creed

Katie Consents
Quinlan and Cheyenne's Story
Quinlan's Quest
Accepting His Way
Her Balancing Act
Kelli and Parker's Story
Meeting Her Needs
Kissing Kelli
Keeping Kelli
Cián and Molly's Story
In Pursuit of Molly
Freeing Molly
Forever Molly
Clearwater Ranch Trilogy -Contemporary, Spicy
Piper's Plan
Camille's Second Chance
Josie's Refuge
Lone Wind Series: Contemporary, spicy Native American
Reclaiming Clover
Taming Texanna -American Historical, Native American, Spicy
Cowboy Welcome- Contemporary, Spicy
In the Spirit of Christmas -Contemporary, Sweet
Guardians of Refuge (Contemporary, Military, Spicy)
SEAL of Refuge
The Strategy of Love
The Tactics of Love

ANTHOLOGIES (HEAT VARIES)
Sweet Town Love
Historical Heroes
Hero to Obey (limited time)
Cowboy for a Cause (limited time)

MULTI-AUTHOR BOX SETS (Heat Level Various)
Love, Christmas 2 Movies You Love
Love, Christmas 2 Recipes
FREE Book Bites 11
Christmas Shorts
Irresistible Heroes
Tempting Protectors
Sexy and Seductive
Sweet and Sassy Summertime Vol. 2
Dear Santa: A Christmas Wish
Sweet and Sassy New Beginnings

Don't miss out!

Visit the website below and you can sign up to receive emails whenever Alyssa Bailey publishes a new book. There's no charge and no obligation.

https://books2read.com/r/B-A-MXIL-DFNRB

BOOKS 2 READ

Connecting independent readers to independent writers.

Did you love *Saving Mallory*? Then you should read *Saving Ivy* by Alyssa Bailey!

First, she stole his heart and left him bleeding. Then she stole from the Mob. Now he is the only one who can save her from herself. Will his price be too steep for Ivy to pay?

Kaden was perfect for super-rich, too spoiled Ivy Linton. When Kaden rescued Ivy and then took her home, it was soon obvious to all that they were falling in love. Soon, however, the realities of the dangerous nature of his job frightened her. Her own crazy life was already scary enough, so Ivy left one evening without a word.

She struggled to overcome the nightmares, the loneliness, and the loss of the only man she had ever loved. Now, a year later, the old worries were gone, but new troubles have emerged. Her mother is married to a mob boss, his second in command wants her, and she witnessed him commit murder. So, what should she do? Steal important information for life insurance and run like hell to the only safe person she knows.

Ivy was surrounded by trouble, but that's what he was trained to deal with in the military and now with Reynaud and Associates, of which he was one. So when Ivy left without a word a year ago, he was crushed but let her go, expecting her to return soon. She didn't... until now.

Amid the chaos of a bombing, his girl shows up full of secrets and the Mob on her tail, but she can still rock his world with a look. He was too gentle the first time but now the stakes are higher and the potential loss too great. Kaden must take control and eliminate the threat if he is going to keep her safe. And this time, he would make sure she stayed.

Read more at alyssabailey.com.

www.ingramcontent.com/pod-product-compliance
Lightning Source LLC
Chambersburg PA
CBHW070636260626
47161CB00007B/2721